Chitose Is in the Ramune Bottle

3

Hiromu

Illustration by raemz

Dressing Up

"Don't stare so much. It's... embarrassing."

Adventure

c o n t e n t s

Kazuki Mizushino

se
Is in the
Ramune
Bottle

3

Hiromu

Illustration by
raemz

YEN
ON
New York

Chitose Is in the Ramune Bottle 3

Hiromu

Translation by Evie Lund
Cover art by raemz

CHITOSE-KUN WA RAMUNEBIN NO NAKA Vol. 3
by Hiromu
© 2019 Hiromu
Illustration by raemz
All rights reserved.
Original Japanese edition published by SHOGAKUKAN.
English translation rights in the United States of America, Canada, the United Kingdom, Ireland, Australia and New Zealand arranged with SHOGAKUKAN through Tuttle-Mori Agency, Inc.

English translation © 2023 by Yen Press, LLC

Yen On
150 West 30th Street, 19th Floor
New York, NY 10001

Visit us at yenpress.com
facebook.com/yenpress
twitter.com/yenpress
yenpress.tumblr.com
instagram.com/yenpress

First Yen On Edition: February 2023
Edited by Yen On Editorial: Anna Powers
Designed by Yen Press Design: Andy Swist

Library of Congress Cataloging-in-Publication Data
Names: Hiromu, author. | raemz, illustrator. | Lund, Evie, translator.
Title: Chitose is in the ramune bottle / Hiromu ; illustration by raemz ; translation by Evie Lund.
Other titles: Chitose-kun wa ramune bin no naka. English
Description: First Yen On edition. | New York, NY : Yen On, 2022
Identifiers: LCCN 2021057712 | ISBN 9781975339050 (v. 1 ; trade paperback) |
    ISBN 9781975339067 (v. 2 ; trade paperback) | ISBN 9781975339074 (v. 3 ; trade paperback)
Subjects: CYAC: High schools—Fiction. | Schools—Fiction. | Friendship—Fiction. |
    LCGFT: Light novels.
Classification: LCC PZ7.1.H574 Ch 2022 | DDC [Fic]—dc23
LC record available at https://lccn.loc.gov/2021057712

ISBNs: 978-1-9753-3907-4 (paperback)
        978-1-9753-4576-1 (ebook)

10 9 8 7 6 5 4 3 2 1

LSC-C

Printed in the United States of America

Chitose Is in the Ramune Bottle

Hiromu

Illustration by
raemz

3

Hiromu

Hails from Fukui, resides in Tokyo. In the first volume, I told you that I would explain the meaning behind the Fukui term *skrishing* in another volume. Well, the answer is that it means "TV static." You use it like, "When I turned on the TV, it was totally skrishin'," but these days you rarely ever see snow static on TV. So high school kids these days don't know what the original meaning of skrishing was... When I realized that, I also realized I couldn't realistically put it into this series. (Lost opportunities...)

raemz

Born in California, USA.
Works mainly on social-network games and game illustrations. I've been looking for a pet-friendly apartment recently.

On the way home, I was looking at the moon.

So huge, so beautiful, so bright, so gentle. It looked like you could just reach out and touch it, but it was so, so far away.

Has the moon always been the moon, ever since it was born, I wonder. The thought came to me all of a sudden.

Must be a tough job. I mean, all that business of going invisible in the dark, then coming out to smile as a crescent moon, then finally returning to its full, round form.

It has to show up and shine tomorrow, even if it's feeling down. I wonder if it ever wishes it could just stay full for good, after all the work it has to do to get there.

It's not like it's shining all on its own, I recall a schoolteacher saying once. It's just reflecting the light from the sun.

If that's really true, that would mean the moon has to change its shape every day even if it doesn't want to. And all the while people are looking up and offering their unsolicited opinions: "Oh, it's the full moon," "It's a crescent moon," "No moon in the sky tonight; feels kind of sad."

—Does the moon dream of the sun, I wonder? It gets to shine bright and strong all by itself, beholden to no one, bringing energy to humans, animals, and plants alike.

That's pretty cool and all, but I think I prefer the moon.

Its presence eases my anxieties, lighting my way home as I walk in the dark.

It has to contend with someone else's light and bear all kinds of expectations; people even pray to it. And all the while, it watches over us, acting like it doesn't have a care in the world.

That's what I want to be.

As the thought ran through my mind, I squeezed my left hand, which was warmer than usual.

I know I can't become the moon, floating high in the sky.

That's one thing that was set in stone from the start.

So I'm content with performing a convincing impression instead.

Convincing enough that I could stand beside it and not embarrass myself too much.

—Hey. Could I become something like the moon to you?

The rain was like an old piece of stained glass.

The classroom windows shimmered with unending streams of rainwater, and the desolate sports field was obscured with a soft, almost transparent veil. It was the start of June, and the coming of the rainy season was palpable (and much earlier than usual). The skies were gray and heavy, pressing down relentlessly upon the entire town.

While it was dark enough to make you think that night had fallen early outside, the classroom was unnaturally bright thanks to the fluorescent lighting. It was as if only this piece of reality had been cut off from the rest of the world.

Lost in thought, I opened the window a crack. The air that came rushing in smelled of wet asphalt and earth, reminding me gently that the inside and the outside worlds were still connected. Visions of green rice fields and summery paths swelled in the corner of my memories for a moment, before subsiding once more.

I always used to think that I hated rainy days. But not anymore.

The rain beat out a steady staccato rhythm against a tin roof somewhere. I listened idly, feeling strangely uplifted, like a young girl jumping in a puddle wearing bright-red boots or like a dapper gentlemen closing his umbrella against the downpour and singing a nice little ditty.

"...tose? Chitose, hello? Earth to Chitose!!!"

"Ouch!"

I was just enjoying the moment when someone flicked my forehead hard enough to make a little *tukk* sound. Hmm, I wonder if *tukk* is the right sound effect to use for a forehead flick.

"What are you spacing out for, hmm?"

Beside me, Haru Aomi was regarding me with mild exasperation.

"Listen here. A proper lady is supposed to give the sexy man a gentle kiss after she observes him staring off into the distance."

"You want a kiss, huh? A big smackeroo?"

"I'm sorry. Please don't."

"Hmm? Are we still spacing out? You need another flick?"

"No. That one was like being hit with a rock hammer."

It was Monday, and we'd just finished seventh period. But even though class would normally be over for the day, no one was heading off to do school cleaning duty or homeroom. Instead, we were all still here, waiting in the classroom.

Today, we had a special eighth period. We would be receiving advice on our future options from some of the third-year students in the year above us.

As the best college preparatory school in Fukui Prefecture, Fuji High was blessed with these sorts of opportunities.

We were still only in June of our second year, but some students would start studying for college entrance exams already around this time. It was, of course, way too early to be taking the exams for any of our first-choice colleges, but hearing from the third-years about how they decided on their future options, or how they were deciding on them—that would give many of us some valuable food for thought.

"Look, Kura's here. Get it together, Mr. Class President," Haru said.

I looked up at the teacher's lectern and Kuranosuke Iwanami, the homeroom teacher for Year Two, Class Five. He was only mostly upright, and his hair was sticking up all over the place as he lazily opened his mouth.

"Uh, so as you know, today we're having a special session with the third-years to discuss your future options. That said, no need to take it all too seriously. Remember, these are your fellow students, so feel free to ask 'em anything that's on your mind."

He stepped away from the lectern, leather-soled sandals slapping against the floor, and sat down on a folding chair by the window.

"All right, guys," he called toward the door. "Come on in."

"Yes, sir!"

I heard a familiar voice, like a clear ringing bell, and then about ten upperclassmen all came into the room.

Walking at the head of the line was... Wait, seriously?

I got to my feet by reflex, bashing my knees against the drawer under my desk.

It was Asuka Nishino heading the line.

Seriously? No one told me.

Asuka was smiling confidently, impossible not to notice in the familiar old classroom setting.

Her short hair, which had a mysterious sense of movement to it, the little teardrop mole under her left eye, her skirt, which was neither too long nor too short, her white legs under it—everything appeared in sharp focus, to an almost artificial degree. And yet she was smiling like a friendly stray cat. The contrast between that smile and the rest of her appearance only served to highlight the otherworldliness of her looks.

That's how she appeared to me anyway, with all my feelings about her.

The boys in the class were getting their first look at Asuka up close, and they all wore matching slack-jawed expressions. Meanwhile, the girls were all watching her, too, somehow spellbound.

We had heard that several third-year students would be

coming, but I had never imagined that one of them would be Asuka. I bet she kept it from me on purpose to give me a surprise.

Usually, we only spoke outside of school, so I was suddenly embarrassed, like a guy inviting his crush into his bedroom for the first time. I looked away, without thinking about it.

…And then I made eye contact with Kura, who was smirking knowingly at me. *Want me to pummel you into eraser dust, Teach?*

I let out a little sigh, then looked back toward the lectern again, where Asuka was watching me from the middle of the group of third-years. Her smile said "Gotcha!" as she gave me a pleased little wave.

You know exactly what position you're putting me in here, don't you?

Heh. I grinned wryly, waving back at her, and just as I expected, I started getting all these looks like "What's going on here?" and "Geez, you again, huh?" and…

Um, Miss Yuuko Hiiragi, Miss Yua Uchida, Miss Yuzuki Nanase, could you stop trying to test whether looks can kill? My back and head are stinging from those daggers.

I turned to look behind me and met Yuuko's head-on glare. Yua had met Asuka several times walking to and from school with me, and Yuzuki had encountered her just last month, too. But I had never actually spoken to Asuka in front of Yuuko, and I would definitely be getting the third degree about this later.

I turned to my side, looking for assistance, and found Haru staring straight at me. There was a pause, and then she grinned.

Her response got my hackles up, just a little.

Well, I could give as good as I got. "What's up, feeling jealous?"

"Yep, majorly. Totally jelly."

"And peanut butter, right?"

"Who's she? Not one of your past girlfriends, I hope?"

"Don't talk like you're one of my current girlfriends."

Our usual dumb banter calmed me down some, and now I could pick up on the conversation between Asuka and the guy standing beside her. He looked like one of the jock types. He was taller than me, and pretty well-built. His short, neat hairstyle made for a clean-cut look, and his well-shaped eyes and nose told me at one glance that, yep, this guy's popular with the ladies.

"Friend of yours, Asuka?"

"Yeah, he's a lowerclassman acquaintance of mine."

I bristled a little at his casual use of her name, Asuka.

The two were in the same grade, so just as I called Yuuko and Yua by their first names, it made sense for him to call Asuka by hers. And yet it made me feel like maybe I was reaching somewhat by also calling her Asuka.

The guy grinned wryly and continued, as if he hadn't been after an actual answer at all.

"They're second-years. So how d'you know him?"

"I told you. We're acquaintances."

"Oh yeah?"

Was there a deeper meaning to her words? Or did she really mean it, that I was just an acquaintance? He probably took it as the latter. Well, it's not like I know myself whether there's any deeper meaning behind it.

The guy looked at me, the corners of his mouth turning up slightly.

Aha, this guy totally has a crush on Asuka. He's already sized me up; I can see it on his face. Now he's transmitting a mental message to me, and it says, "I know you rate her, too, but Asuka's already got a man, and that's me, so you'd better give up now, kid."

Watch who you're messing with. I'm Fuji High's premier man-slut, I'll have you know. Go get a hundred hate posts on the underground gossip site, and then we'll talk.

...My eyes fixated on Asuka's and the upperclassman's every move, and I realized I was getting more fired up than normal.

That guy got to spend a lot more time with Asuka than I did, and they probably had all these shared, daily experiences together. If she was a textbook, he'd be the notes scrawled in the margins.

I just had to sit here and swallow these completely obvious facts, but they weren't going down too easy. I felt like a little kid, bawling on his hands and knees after falling over in front of the toy shop. I was painfully aware of how pathetic I was.

—Honestly, I always feel completely out of step when I'm in front of her.

With a casual air, Asuka's classmate gave her a little push forward in her lower back.

I knew he was just signaling her to take the lead here, but if I only had a few seconds to ask him one question, it would be this one: You want your ashes scattered at sea or in the mountains, dude?

I was still in my thoughts when Asuka took a step forward, moving out of reach of the guy's hand.

"All right. You there, can you start the proceedings for your class?"

What? Wait. I don't need to actually cremate the guy.

I could always bury him out on the sports field with only his head aboveground and then force-feed him Habutae Mochi, a Fukui sweet delicacy, morning and night. He'll get sick of eating it within a day and wave the white flag, if it doesn't stick in his throat and choke him first.

"Hey. You over there."

Or perhaps this:

I could lock him up in a secret room and refuse to let him leave until he perfectly shucks 104 Seiko crab legs, a Fukui seafood delicacy. Those legs are pretty skinny, so it's a tough job, and he'll mentally break before he gets halfway through.

"Hey, you, the narcissist who always acts so cool and totally has a thing for me."

Who are you referring to? Couldn't be me.

It took the rest of the class giggling before I realized that Asuka was talking to me. *All right, my bad for being slow on the response, but could you please not make statements that'll require serious damage control on my part after this?*

"Erm, all rise."

Everyone got to their feet with a clatter.

"Bow...and be seated."

After I went through the formalities, Asuka nodded with satisfaction and then cleared her throat to speak.

"It's nice to meet you all. I'm Asuka Nishino from Year Three."

Echoes popped up across the classroom, variations on "Nice to meet you."

Kaito Asano's voice rang out more perkily than the rest. You rogue, you always set me at ease.

Then Asuka continued, not to be out-perked.

"All right then, so how shall we do this?"

I observed her with a mind that was slightly calmer now. It was clear that Asuka had Kura and her classmates' blessing to take point here.

The guy from before picked up where she left off.

"It's tough to get around to everyone in a big group, so can I ask y'all to split off into groups of about four or five? Then two or three of us will each pair up and come chat with you in your groups."

Asuka sneaked a quick look at me.

Knowing about everything that went down with Kenta Yamazaki and with Atomu Uemura, Asuka had to be wondering whether this plan would be all right with us. I gave her a light smile and a nod. Kenta was a bona fide member of Team Chitose now, and no doubt Atomu would buddy up in a group with Nazuna Ayase.

Our class was said to be filled with popular cliques, but right now, there wasn't much tension or animosity in the air.

Over the past two months, everyone seemed to have found their social niche, and there weren't any students who looked like they might be in danger of being left out in the cold when the groups were formed. No real need to worry.

Asuka nodded slightly. "All right, let's go with that, then. Give me a shout once you've formed your groups and let me know how many you are."

As I anticipated, everyone grouped off without any fuss and then, one by one, let Asuka know.

Tallying up the numbers, Asuka directed everyone toward an area of the classroom to sit in, and they all dragged their desks and chairs into little huddles.

I made sure that everyone besides Team Chitose had finalized their groups, just in case, before I announced our designated group's number last of all.

"There's eight of us here."

"All right. Take the remaining space for y'all."

Easier said than done, I thought.

Seeing Asuka in the midst of those third-year students, nonchalantly giving crisp orders... It was like seeing a new side of her, which gave me a ticklish sort of feeling. The other visiting students seemed comfortable following her lead, so it seemed that was their usual dynamic.

The Asuka I knew was always a lone wolf.

Standing alone and confident—independent, shall we say. I figured that at school she radiated that same kind of untouchable aura. And yet she was really smart. I guessed she'd be able to chat easily with others without any awkwardness, so maybe it made perfect sense that the rest of the class seemed to revolve around her. I mean, it's obvious when you think about how smart she is.

—And yet.

I felt somehow lonely, as if I had lost something.

I had no right to be disillusioned after pushing my expectations on her, something I warned her about only recently. I could feel my own words coming back to bite me.

But at the same time, it was somehow reassuring to know that Asuka was just a regular high school girl after all.

Pushing aside those worthless thoughts, I straightened my tie, which had come slightly askew. As I was making my way over to join my buddies, I heard Asuka call out to me from behind.

"Oh, by the way, I'll be calling dibs on your group."

"Seriously?"

"Yeah. I wanna talk to these friends I'm always hearing so much about."

"That's opening up a whole can of worms, you know?"

"For you, maybe. For me, however…"

"All right, all right, I get it."

Asuka could be a real demon when she wanted to be.

*

The chairs and desks scraped across the floor into a formation where we were facing each other. On one side sat Kazuki, Kaito, Kenta, and me, and then on the opposite side we had Yuuko, Yuzuki, Haru, and Yua.

Opposite me, Yuuko had apparently been waiting for the chance to speak.

"Sooo?"

Eyes darting about, I tried to act vague.

"S-so I wonder what kind of talk we're going to hear today?"

Yuuko put her hands together and laid them against her cheek, tipping her head to one side with a bit of dramatic flair and smiling.

"Indeed, what kind of talk will we hear, I wonder? From the

fine Nishino, the lovely lady who has been exchanging such meaningful looks with our own Saku?"

"W-well, I think if you ask the girl, she'll have lots to tell you."

"*The girl*, is it? I bet she's told you lots and lots as well, hasn't she, Saku, hmm? ♪"

Yeah, she wasn't about to let this slide. Yuuko was applying pressure.

Then Yuzuki interjected, giggling softly. "What's that, Yuuko? You haven't met her before now?"

"Are you saying you have, Yuzuki?"

"I met her just the other day, you know? She said she and Chitose are just regular friends."

"Really? I see, I see!" Yuuko looked relieved, breathing out slowly.

Thanks for the lifesaver, Yuzuki... Except she wasn't done.

"But then," she said, "Nishino also said something like, 'He really should develop a stronger sense of danger, or she might end up taking him away.'"

"All right, now I'm pissed. Pissed at Nishino for saying something like that so casually, and also pissed at *you* for being on the receiving end of that comment, Yuzuki."

I couldn't take this anymore, and I cleared my throat. "Hold on, Nanase. I don't remember her saying anything like that."

"You don't? You must not have been picking up on the subtext," Nanase answered flippantly.

Yuuko looked like she was about to burst. I turned away from both of them and toward Yua for help. My SOS must have reached her, because she cleared her throat, with a "Lord help me" sort of look.

"I've met her several times on the walk to and from school. Saku even introduced me to her. I didn't get the impression from their conversations that they were anything more than casual friends from different grades."

I love you, Yua.

But she wasn't done. "However," she said, "whenever Saku spots her, his face lights up like a little kid. And it's like I'm completely invisible to him, while he goes dashing over to her with his tail wagging."

Was that how she'd seen it, all this time? *That cuts deep, Yua. How can you fling an ax at my head with such an innocent expression on your face?*

I opened my mouth to speak, not sure what was even going on, when...

"Sorry, guys! I guess we kept you waiting, huh?" Asuka was approaching, hugging a foldable chair to her chest.

Her classmate was by her side. The two of them sat down beside Yuuko and me in the spot that would be reserved for the birthday kid if this was a party.

They were close enough to brush shoulders, which also annoyed me. But I resolved to act normal and hopefully avoid any more cross-examinations.

"All right then, so once again, I'm Asuka Nishino, a third-year student. And this is..."

"Toru Okuno. Asuka and I have been in the same class since second year, and—well, as you can see—she's surprisingly scatterbrained. So I'm here to pick up the slack."

Careful, Okuno. That's a dangerous spot to sit in. My left hand has a demon trapped within it, you see. It tends to lash out and choke anyone who gets too close.

And why was he blabbering on about stuff that had nothing to do with our future career choices? Was it for my benefit?

He was clearly trying to get the upper hand on me, but at the same time, it was also clear there wasn't much between him and Asuka worth noting. Still, I wasn't impressed, and I refused to return his smile. I didn't want to get into the ring with him, so I pretended not to even notice the way he was searching for my reaction.

Kaito cheerily raised his hand just then, clearly oblivious to the tension bubbling under the surface between Okuno and me.

"I have a question! Are you two dating?"

Okuno fielded that question. "Uh, I'm not sure how to answer that... Ha-ha."

His bashful smile was like that of a pro athlete, calculated to give the impression to onlookers that indeed, they were dating, or at least on their way there.

But Asuka spoke up and said, "Nope, we're not."

What a smooth denial.

Okuno looked rueful, while Kaito seemed jubilant. I kept an eye on them both as I spotted Asuka giving me a soft wink.

"Nor am I dating this guy here, got it?"

It was a very spunky, Asuka-esque response, and it cut right through any tension or assumptions. It was clearly meant not only for Okuno's benefit, but for the benefit of everyone here.

I felt my heart sink a little, like a kid who gets too into the game they're playing and accidentally smashes a priceless vase.

Asuka clapped her hands together and began her speech.

"All right, shall we get this session started, then? I think Kura probably already said as much, but feel free to ask any questions you have. No need to hold back. Around this time last year, I had no idea what I was going to do with myself, either. Incidentally, has everyone here started thinking about it already, even just vaguely?"

After everyone exchanged searching glances, Kaito offered his response.

"I haven't really considered the specifics. I guess I'm fine going wherever, as long as I can play basketball seriously. A sports scholarship would be nice, but probably a little difficult given the level of our high school."

Kaito was a gifted player to be sure, but Fuji High wasn't really known for its strong basketball team. Getting into college based on sports prowess alone didn't seem all that realistic an option.

Asuka giggled with amusement, as if his answer fit perfectly with the way I'd described his character to her.

"Then, Asano, you should start thinking of your options based on which college basketball team you'd like to play for, huh?"

Kaito seemed momentarily surprised that Asuka knew his name, but a moment later he seemed to shrug it off and grinned happily at her.

Haru was next to speak.

"I think it's pretty much the same for me as it is for Kaito. My parents are always saying that they want me to go to a national public college, but I have no idea which one I should shoot for in particular," she explained nonchalantly.

Asuka responded with an impish grin.

"If it's a national public college you're thinking about, then I presume you're studying hard already; isn't that right, Aomi?"

"How come you know about my academic performance, Nishino? *Chitose!*"

"I…I didn't mention the actual test scores."

"How could you possibly know my private, personal test scores?!"

"I couldn't help it. All I had to do was look over when I heard the groaning, and there they were in plain view."

"Ack…"

Asuka watched our exchange, spluttering with laughter and genuine amusement.

Once she managed to calm down, the talk continued.

"Let's see… Nanase, what about you?"

Put on the spot, Nanase put her hand to her mouth and thought for a moment before speaking.

"Hmm, I've been playing a little with the idea of leaving Fukui.

I could go to Ishikawa, Kyoto, Aichi, Osaka… Even Tokyo isn't out of the question, I guess."

"I see, so you're thinking of a college in a different prefecture. I kinda guessed you'd go in that direction, Nanase."

I'm sure it's the same everywhere else, too, but when Fukui high schoolers are thinking about college, there are only two main options: either leaving the prefecture or staying in it.

When you're considering leaving the prefecture, the popular options for Fuji High students are Ishikawa, the next prefecture over, or one of the big-name colleges in the Kansai region. It's definitely "the city" compared to Fukui, but it's still close enough that you can come home anytime you want. That's probably why, I think.

On the other hand, I feel like there aren't as many people who decide to head straight to Tokyo from the jump. Probably because it feels too far away from Fukui, and the distance makes for kind of a high mental hurdle to get over as well.

We were all thinking about it when Kazuki Mizushino joined the conversation, bouncing off what Nanase said.

"I'm thinking about a private college in Tokyo. There's bound to be a lot of pretty girls there, and I plan to join a college club that's big on hookup culture. Then I'll hit the campus like a storm."

There are also some people who think of Tokyo as their sole option. It was a very Kazuki-like choice, I thought, but I found myself speaking up as something suddenly occurred to me.

"Wait, you're not planning to play soccer anymore?"

Kazuki shrugged, smiling a little sadly. "I understand my own social position more than you'd think. My soccer game isn't good enough to make a living off it. I plan to wrap it up in high school."

"…I see."

It wasn't that deep a question. When you've been giving your all to sports ever since childhood, this is a decision that you have to make sooner or later. Either to go for it and try to go pro, or to continue it on the hobby level. Or to give it all up entirely.

I guess even a guy like Kazuki knows his limits—even though, in my opinion, he's capable of going for it as a regular at a high-ranked school. Maybe all the more so since he's gotten this far already.

Kenta, who had been listening to the conversation so far, nervously spoke up next.

"I think I'll just go to Fukui U. I can't imagine myself leaving the prefecture, really."

Fukui U was Fukui University, the only national public college in the prefecture. If you wanted to go on to college within the prefecture, it was generally the first choice.

Actually, there's a lot of folks who don't want to leave Fukui even to go to college. Some of them really love Fukui, but a lot of them are just afraid to leave their familiar hometown and live alone.

Then most of the people who stay in Fukui for college end up working in Fukui after that, I hear.

Be born in Fukui, grow up in Fukui, build a family in Fukui, and live in Fukui forever. It's not for me to decide whether that's true happiness. I'm not sure if anyone really knows, come to think of it.

Yua gave her opinion next. "I think I feel the same way as you, Yamazaki. I can't picture myself walking the streets of a big city somehow…"

Asuka smiled kindly. "It's not only big cities that exist outside of the prefecture, right? Every region's got their big-name colleges, don't they?"

"But if I'm going to a regional college anyway, I might as well stay in Fukui, I think. I'm not sure I could live by myself, either."

Yuuko leaned forward. "Whaaat? Ucchi, you'd be fine! You're so put together! I can't even cook or do laundry. If I left home, I'd be a total mess!"

Nanase waved her hand dismissively, interjecting with an impish grin. "You've got to do some home ec training first, Yuuko! Now me, I can already cook and do laundry. Looks like you need to play catch-up!"

Yuuko's eyes narrowed as Yuzuki fixed her with a meaningful grin.

"Hmph! I'll start today! I'll go home and boil an egg or something tonight!"

"What did you even learn in home ec? We've been taking it since elementary school."

I couldn't resist getting that little dig in, and Yuuko puffed out her cheeks in indignation.

Asuka spotted this and spoke up. "What about you, Hiiragi? Will you be staying in the prefecture or looking outside of it?"

"Honestly, I can't even visualize which way to go yet. If I just go with the flow, I'll end up opting for Fukui U by default... But what about you two upperclassmen, then? Have you already picked your first-choice colleges?"

I was a little surprised, but at the same time, it made sense.

Yuuko always seemed like she was galloping merrily along her own path, but apparently, what was happening inside her was more complicated than that. She always seemed willing to leap off at a moment's notice, propelled by a single emotion, but she was actually extremely careful when it came to taking a really important first step. This lack of balance wasn't a sign of weakness in her, though, but strength. At least, that's how it struck me.

Okuno was next to speak, after he'd been following Asuka's lead this whole time.

"Um, let's see... I think I'm like, uh...Mizushino, was it? I think I'll be headed to a private university in Tokyo. Keio is my top choice, but I plan to apply to all the major ones… Meiji, Aoyama Gakuin, Rikkyo, Chuo, and Hosei."

There was no more animosity in his voice. He clearly really wanted to do his bit and give advice, as someone a year older than the rest of us.

For us college-prep-school students, deciding on our future path is a major life step, and it's not the place to go inserting personal agendas. His ability to get serious when the situation called for it had me warming to him just a tiny bit.

Yuuko had another question for him. "Is that because you wanted to go to Keio? I mean, is it like, uh, there's a professor you really look up to at Keio, or is there a specific academic department that's tied to your future career goals somehow?"

Okuno thought for a moment before replying. "I wish I could play it like I've got all the answers, but to be honest, I don't have a well-defined reason like that. It's just that I've grown up in Fukui, so at least once in my life I'd like to try living in the biggest city in Japan. The reason I chose Keio… Well, if I'm going to go to Tokyo, it'd be cool to live that glamorous Keio Boy lifestyle, maybe?"

"Er… Is it all right for us to choose based on reasoning like that?"

"It's not something to emulate. It's just, I figure if I shoot for the best college I can get into with my academic ability, and I choose my fields of study carefully, then I can reassess my future after college, in four years' time."

I figured that was the kind of mentality you'd expect to find in a third-year student with college entrance exams breathing down his neck.

There aren't many people out there who want to have their whole future careers mapped out while they're still in high school, me included.

I mean, deciding where you're going to live, picking a college you like the sound of, then what subjects you're going to study based on your interests and abilities, and making sure to choose one that's not going to be so intense you won't have time to focus on job hunting in your final year... All you can do is pick based on all that.

Yuuko was nodding thoughtfully, and then she redirected her question.

"Have you decided already, too, Nishino?"

Asuka smiled a little bashfully and scratched her cheek. "Ah-ha-ha. I know it seems arrogant of me to attend a talk like this, but to be honest, I still haven't decided for myself, either. Whether to stay in the prefecture or go to Tokyo, that is."

"What! That's so unexpected! Just watching you today, you totally seemed like you had all of that already figured out."

"...Nope, not at all. I'm just as lost as anyone else."

Uncharacteristically, her voice sounded like it was tinged with genuine emotion.

I thought about interjecting with something, but Okuno spoke first.

"I keep telling Asuka that we should just go to Tokyo together, y'know?"

Yes, yes, how nice. Come along, Asuka, come along with me. Let's take a tour of the old sunken barrels rolling around the sea-floor of Tokyo Bay. That's where Okuno's body will be dumped.

Asuka let his remark slide without seeming affected by it in any way.

"Hmm, I'll consider it if you buy me a single-dwelling apartment in Shirokanedai, y'know?"

"You could at least suggest a roommates-type situation."

I watched the two of them banter lightly back and forth like normal high schoolers do, trying really hard not to feel disappointed. I wasn't sure if my disappointment was directed at Asuka or at myself.

Asuka laughed softly then, almost as if she had seen right through how I was feeling.

I looked away, feeling downhearted somehow.

*

After that, Asuka took plenty of time to answer everyone's questions.

At some point, Yuuko realized I was the only one who hadn't discussed my future plans, and she pointed it out.

That's when a certain person decided to say, "You don't have to say anything right now, 'kay?" in a tone loaded with meaning, which stirred the pot even more. That aside, though, it was a good opportunity, and everyone seemed to get something valuable out of it.

Once the talk session was finished, the members of Team Chitose went off to their respective clubs, while Kenta, whose only club activity was going home, left right away, saying something about a new light novel going on sale that day.

—So then, what was I doing, you may ask.

I leaned against the glass door of the entrance, listening to the rain for well over twenty minutes. For some reason, I just didn't want the day to end like this.

Fwump. Fwump. Colorful flowers bloomed, moved past, and disappeared.

The first-year girls, still with that spring in their step, opened up their umbrellas with relish, and the deluge of raindrops fanned out into the air around them like hydrangeas.

I plunged my hand into my pocket and felt the leather of my still-new phone case. When I brought my fingertips to my mouth, I could smell the leather, a scent that resembled a baseball glove. I smiled, just a little.

That was when someone knocked on the glass door behind my head.

Whirling around quickly, I could see Asuka smiling at me through the glass.

"Don't tell me you were waiting for me?" She came around the door and peered into my face as she spoke.

Before I could respond, another voice interrupted. "Asuka?"

Then he appeared behind her, and I saw the face of the guy who was sitting beside her until the talk ended: Okuno.

When it occurred to me that the two of them were probably planning on heading home together, I felt my chest constrict painfully, and I couldn't speak.

Asuka replied in her usual breezy voice. "Hey, Okuno. See you tomorrow. I'm heading home with my *good friend* here."

"But..."

"Tomorrow, okay?"

Her tone was amicable, but it gave him no room to argue. An unreadable expression crossed Okuno's face for a moment, then he snorted through his nose before walking off in the direction of the school gates.

I sucked in a breath as if recalling something and tried to speak as casually as I could. "That's unusual, you referring to me like that."

Asuka sputtered with laughter. "I needed to drive the point home."

"Like you wanted to drive the point home with Nanase?"

"If you can't play nice, better zip that lip."

Asuka reached out and squeezed my lips together as she spoke. Her slim fingers smelled faintly of soap.

I looked away, embarrassed, and she let go as she spoke again.

"Well then, shall we head home? Can I squeeze under?"

"What, you forget your own umbrella?"

What if I wasn't here? Was she planning to squeeze under Okuno's umbrella? My head was whirling with childish thoughts again.

"I was thinking about squeezing under someone or other's."

She saw everything.

"I guess I have no choice but to help you out, then."

"Yep. You're stuck."

I opened up my cheap-looking, nondescript plastic umbrella.

The capricious stray cat of a girl squeezed right in next to me. We started walking slowly, not saying anything. *Pitter-patter, pitter-patter.* The raindrops danced right above our heads, on top of the umbrella.

"Look, your umbrella has polka dots."

Asuka gazed up at the sky through the umbrella's plastic as she spoke.

I used to think I hated rainy days, back in the past.

But now I really, really don't.

✶

We walked along the familiar riverside path, just us two.

Since we had a special eighth period, the peak of home-time foot traffic was long gone, and there wasn't a person to be seen either in front of or behind us. The intimacy of being alone together shouldn't feel this odd, when this girl was the type who never seemed to need anyone else.

"Hey, remember to share."

Asuka seemed to have noticed I was leaning the umbrella over to her side.

Her small shoulder pressed against mine.

I returned the umbrella to center. "You'll get wet, you know?"

"Isn't it supposed to be hot when a girl's all drenched?"

"Speaking of, I heard a rumor that this river is haunted by the ghost of a woman who drowned in it."

"I keep forgetting you have that side to your personality." Asuka chuckled before continuing. "Good, now it's like normal times again."

"…I guess you caught me, huh?"

"You've been kinda distant today."

"Speak for yourself."

"You only think that because you're the one who's been distant."

"You're a high school girl, after all, aren't you?"

"I certainly am." Asuka grasped the hem of her skirt playfully. "Didn't you know?"

I didn't even need to explain to her. I think she just knew everything I'd been feeling.

I twirled my umbrella like those girls I watched earlier did, letting the hydrangea bloom.

On a day like this, what I needed was a really shitty joke.

"And that guy is completely devoted to you."

I spoke pointedly and could feel Asuka's shoulder shaking against mine.

"I think you interpreted the situation pretty well."

"He couldn't keep his eyes off of you. It was obscene."

"So you say, but I spotted plenty of obscene eyes on you, too."

I looked over to her, surprised by her response, her cheeks puffed out like a child.

Now it was my time to snort with laughter.

"What?"

"It's just… You always look so cool and unbothered, but just then…"

"You're the one who's pretending to be cool all the time."

"I'm not pretending. I'm always cool and mysterious, I'll have you know."

This kind of thing was like a ritual, I thought. Goofing off, deflecting, comparing all kinds of feelings between each other.

The rain started coming down harder all of a sudden, and Asuka started walking a half step closer to me.

Our uniforms had changed for the season already, and our

bare arms bumped beneath our short sleeves. Her cool skin pressed against my own, I realized that her temperature ran lower than mine.

"It was a lot of fun, though, talking about our futures. It felt almost like I was one of your classmates."

It sounds obvious when you think about it, but Asuka was born an academic year ahead of me, and she would go on to become an adult a year ahead of me, too. She would graduate and leave school a year ahead of me. We simply weren't both born in that same strictly defined period of time between April and March, and the one who was going on ahead couldn't exactly pump the brakes. No matter how much we might have wanted it, we never would be classmates.

It's completely obvious, something like that.

But Asuka was continuing.

"You've got Hiiragi, Uchida, Nanase, Aomi, Mizushino, Asano, Yamazaki. Why aren't I in with the rest of you? That's what I thought."

"I was thinking how I wouldn't have wanted you in with the rest of us."

"Yep, I know that. I've got to be your amazing upperclassman, right?"

You're the one making yourself say things like that, I thought.

Ever since that twilit day beside the river when we met, Asuka has always been the same Asuka, just for me.

"Hey..."

It's all right. You don't have to be so kind. That was what I was about to say, but I gathered up those words and stashed them in my pocket. I should have responded with those words a long time ago, honestly, but for just a little while longer, I wanted to have this. I was afraid I would lose my grip on her in the meantime, though.

Asuka spoke again, seemingly copying my aborted phrase from moments before.

"Hey..."

Her arm against me grew stiff, squeezing against mine.

"If the two of us were classmates, and we met totally normally at the entrance ceremony, I wonder if we'd be walking home from class like this every day."

"If the two of us were classmates, and we met totally normally at the entrance ceremony, it's possible you wouldn't have shown any interest in me, Asuka."

"Nor you in me, *Saku*."

So then why are we having this conversation anyway? I kept walking along nonchalantly and changed the subject. Also nonchalantly.

"You haven't decided yet, huh? Between Tokyo and Fukui."

"...Nope."

Last month, during that whole issue with Nanase, I had learned about her dilemma when we ran into each other. I knew it wasn't something that could be decided that easily, but when I studied her face during the talk session when the subject came up, I started feeling like I should ask her about it again, more seriously this time.

"Do you have anything you want to talk to me about?"

Not like I can do much, I thought but didn't say.

Nothing to be done about something like that, after all.

"Nope." Asuka's response was brisk. "If I consulted with you about it, I know I'd end up wavering."

"You make it sound like you've practically already made up your mind."

"...Mm-hmm."

I sighed deeply. "If you really want to get me off the subject, I wish you'd learn to be a better liar."

"…Mm-hmm."

I sighed deeply again. Then I spoke in a light and jokey tone. "If there's anything I can help you with, shall we make a pretentious pact? If you start wanting to elope with me at any point, just touch your left ear. That will be the sign, something like that."

Asuka looked shocked for just a moment, then she nodded a little. "Would you come with me, then?"

"I think I've pretty much already answered that question."

Asuka leaned her head against my arm.

It tickled, and it also filled me with a sense of frustration. I pretended like I'd barely even noticed.

★

Back home, I showered and flopped onto the sofa. I was awakened by a distinctive *ding-dong*. Checking the time on my phone, I realized it was already seven PM.

My place isn't fancy enough to have a doorbell camera, so I looked through the fish-eye lens instead and saw two familiar faces side by side, one beaming, one with a slightly furrowed brow.

Rolling my eyes a little, I opened the door.

"Good evening! We're here to deliver domesticity to you!" Yuuko chirped.

"Ah, we don't need any of that, thank you."

I tried to close the door on them, but the toe of a loafer appeared, jammed in the crack. This was no delivery. This was pushy door-to-door sales.

"Now, now, don't be like that. You haven't eaten dinner yet, right? I'm gonna make it for ya!"

"I don't want a dinner that consists only of boiled eggs, thanks…"

I had no choice but to open the door again, and now I could see Yua standing behind her, looking apologetic.

"I'm so sorry to barge in on you. Yuuko was determined that we were coming, you see."

Yua lifted the supermarket carrier bag she was holding and showed it to me. A big stalk of leek poked unpretentiously out of the top. It suited Yua, and I found myself smiling in spite of myself.

"Hmm, well, if you're here, Yua, at least I don't have to worry about her burning the place down."

"That's mean! Just what are you implying?!"

I beckoned them both inside, and Yua began unpacking her groceries.

She had been to my place once or twice, so she knew her way around. She couldn't have done a prior check of my stocks of seasoning or anything, but she had thought to buy some more of what I was in danger of running low on, including refill packs. Yua's housewifely skills were a force to be reckoned with.

On the other hand, Yuuko disappeared into the bathroom clutching a paper shopping bag. *Hey, what about your domestic training? At least watch your instructor while she's at work.*

I switched on my Tivoli Audio stereo system, synced it to my phone with Bluetooth, then put my music on shuffle. Glim Spanky's "Go to the Wild Side" started playing, and just then…

"Ta-daa!"

Yuuko opened the curtain that led to the bathroom's dressing room. *I'm begging you, with an amazing intro song like that, please could you do the cooking to the tune of "Main Street"?*

I turned around, rolling my eyes a little, and then I was at a loss for words.

On top of her familiar uniform, Yuuko wore an apron designed to look like an ordinary dress. It was fairly retro, you might say. The top half had a floral pattern in mostly blue, and the waist was fitted with a large ribbon that was tied tight like a cord. If you lowered your eyes past the ribbon, you could see that the rest of the apron was a simple blue. It looked great on her, with her hair tied up in a ponytail to keep it out of the way for cooking. The cinched waist made her D-cup breasts even more prominent than usual.

Speaking plainly, she looked amazingly cute. And also hot.

"What do you think?"

Yuuko was advancing on me, but I was too embarrassed to give her an earnest compliment, so I answered casually instead.

"You look like a newlywed wife who's immediately started attending cooking classes. But cute."

"Wife!!!"

"It's not a compliment."

"To mark the occasion, why don't you change into a *yukata*, Saku?"

"I'm not seeing the retro connection here?"

At some point, Yua had changed into an apron of her own as well.

Hers was by Chums, an outdoorsy sort of brand. It was made of denim and had several big pockets, with the Chums Booby Club logo in red.

It looked like it was chosen for its durability—very Yua-like. But it lent her an air of authenticity that made her seem like a real housewife. And also hot.

"Guess what Yuuko did after school? She went right off to buy that apron." Yua was chuckling as if she was really tickled by this. "You were that affected by what Nanase said, huh?"

Yuuko puffed out her cheeks indignantly. "Nuh-uh. I just thought that I'd better learn to do housework, or it's only going to narrow my field of options when it comes to my future."

"For a moment there, I was almost impressed to see you thinking things over so seriously. But why do you have to do it at my place?"

"Say what? If I'm going to learn, I'll learn a lot faster if I do it for someone I really love and not just for my dad."

"Don't let him hear you say that. You don't want to make him cry, do you?"

I smiled wryly, looking at Yua, who had her palms pressed together in front of her chest in an apologetic gesture.

She must have tried to reason with Yuuko using all kinds of logic. I could totally picture it.

Hmm, well, it was a bit of a surprise, I'll admit, but having dinner cooked for me by two pretty girls like this—I couldn't really complain.

I shook my head in a "no problem at all" kind of way, speaking to Yua now.

"So what's on the menu for tonight?"

"I was thinking we'd tackle something like meat and potato stew. It's a classic and not that hard to make."

"Amazing. Incidentally, beneath that apron, are you na—? Hey, hey, I was just joking! Chop the vegetables, not me!"

*

Clink, clink. Chop, chop. Bubble, bubble. The apartment was filled with the rhythms of cooking. Finding myself with nothing to do, I lolled on the sofa and listened to the sounds.

When I was a kid, and I was invited to a friend's house, or when I went to stay at my grandmother's, I would remember moments like this.

My own parents stayed at work late on weekdays as a general rule, and even on weekends, they were the type to go right into work if they were needed. So I don't really have any memories of family dinners. Ever since I entered high school and started living alone, I got by with convenience store food, or eating out, and some basic cooking.

Maybe that's why sometimes, on the way home from school, I

get a whiff of curry cooking when I walk down a back alley, and suddenly I'm feeling lonely and melancholy.

I found myself thinking about how nice it was, just sitting and waiting for someone else to make you dinner. Maybe Yua noticed that about me, and that was why she came by every now and then with some excuse to cook for me.

"Yuuko, be careful! Your fingers!"

"It's all right! I can dodge it!"

I found myself thinking idle thoughts like, *If I had a family in the distant future, would it feel something like this?*

Would I be sprawled out on the sofa like this, drinking a beer or something, listening to music and reading a novel?

"Yuuko, don't peel so much! There won't be any potato left!"

"Really? But I'm in the peeling zone!"

This apartment was originally a two-bedroom, one-kitchen affair, but it had been forcefully remodeled into a one bedroom with an eat-in kitchen. It didn't have anything fancy like a big island counter.

I lifted my head, looking at the two of them standing there working away in one corner of the apartment.

I found it hard to look at the girls in their aprons from the front, but to be honest, the rear view was what really got to me. The apron strings tied tight emphasized their butts in a distinctly sexy way, sure, but at the same time, the sight was oddly soothing.

"Yuuko, hold on! One tablespoon doesn't mean one heaping tablespoon!"

"All righty!"

"Hey, are you really sure you can handle this?!"

I was trying to ignore the proceedings and just soak up the pleasant atmosphere, but I couldn't resist the urge anymore to snark at Yuuko.

I got up off the sofa and headed into the kitchen, where I found

Yuuko's special apron smeared with all manner of ingredients until it was a real mess.

But the person wearing the apron—she was chipper as ever.

"Hey, Saku, cooking's loads of fun! ♪"

I briefly met eyes with Yua, who was standing beside Yuuko, advising her while washing up at the same time. She looked dejected, so I gave her a reassuring shoulder pat, which was when she spoke to me with a very weak-sounding voice.

"It's… It's almost ready. Can you set the table?"

"I'm on it."

"Ah, can I ask a favor, Saku? Could you roll my sleeves up for me?"

"Sure."

I stood behind Yua and rolled back her sleeves.

"Hey! Ucchi! That's sneaky!"

"Never mind that, Yuuko! Keep watching the pot! The pot!"

I left the kitchen and laid three placemats out on the table, before spraying some paper towels with disinfectant alcohol and giving the table a wipe. Finally, I laid out the same number of chopsticks and cups.

I didn't have placemats at first, and I only used to have enough chopsticks and cups for one, but thanks to Yuuko and Yua, the place has gotten much better equipped these days. Kazuki and Kaito sometimes shell out for groceries, but these two tend to think of the finer details when they come around.

I opened up the rice cooker and scooped some steaming hot Fukui-grown *koshihikari* rice into three rice bowls, placing them on the table. By the way, Fukui folks all grow up believing that this variety comes exclusively from Fukui, but the truth is that *koshihikari* has a pretty varied history behind it. But once you get on the subject, watch out, because it'll start a rant comparing Fukui and Niigata Prefecture. Don't try it at home, kids.

These days, the *ichihomare* variety of rice is leaving *koshihikari* in the dust, apparently. I really should get around to trying it one of these days.

While I was doing this and that, Yuuko and Yua seemed to have finished up, too. The main dish, a meat and potato stew, was brought to the table, and there was also miso soup and something that looked like a side dish.

Yua took off her apron, sitting down at the table with a hint of regret on her face.

"I'm sorry, Saku. Today we weren't able to make much…"

It seemed like she usually followed the one-soup, three-side-dishes formula, so she must have felt like there wasn't enough variety on the table. I didn't need to ask why; the reason was obvious, and besides, I was more than happy to have dinner made for me.

"No, no, it looks delicious. What's this?" I pointed at the one dish I couldn't identify.

"I had some daikon leaves left over from the ones I put in the miso soup, so I fried them up in some sesame oil with dried red chili peppers, tiny *jako* fish, and some bonito flakes, and seasoned them with a little *mentsuyu* sauce. I thought it would go well with white rice."

"An invention that could only come from a veteran housewife."

"Hey! Watch that tongue!"

Yuuko added another dish to the table just then. "Here, Saku. Eat up!"

"Sure, thanks. If possible, do you think you could shell these? And maybe cut them in half? That would make them look like something you actually made for dinner, you know?"

She literally just boiled three eggs.

Beside us, Yua laughed with amusement.

"Yuuko was desperate to challenge herself."

"Hee-hee. Ucchi told me how to make them! I'm a boiled egg maestro now!"

It's not exactly easy to screw up a boiled egg, I thought, but Yuuko looked so happy, flashing her peace signs at me, that I didn't have the heart to rain on her parade. Incidentally, when I first started living alone, I burned a couple sunny-side ups myself.

"I look forward to trying them. Let's eat up before this gets cold."

"Hey, Saku, do you want dinner? A bath? Or should we go straight to...?"

"I said eat!!!"

*

Everything Yuuko and Yua made was delicately flavored and well cooked. Absolutely delicious.

When it's just me cooking, I tend to go heavy on the flavors and make unsophisticated bachelor-type food, but this kind of good home cooking really soothes the soul.

There were a few veggies in the mix that were a little bit questionable, maybe, but I knew that Yuuko had really tried. I didn't pay too much attention and just let my chopsticks go into shoveling mode. I wasn't sure if it was down to Yua's tutelage or just the luck of the draw, but the boiled eggs were perfectly runny in the middle.

When I gave them my honest feedback on the food, they both gave me drippy smiles, and I felt a little bit guilty for not giving them more, even though I was the one who'd had food made for him.

"Yua, these daikon leaves are really delicious!"

"Want another serving?"

"Yeah." I held out my bowl, and it got refilled.

"Some tea, Saku?"

"Please." I held out my cup, and cold barley tea glugged into it.

"Cheek."

"Mm."

I turned my cheek toward Yua, who plucked the grain of rice that was stuck there off my face before popping it into her own mouth.

"Stop!!!" Yuuko suddenly bellowed. "Ucchi! That is SO sneaky! How can you act like such a brazen...*wife*?! You're not giving me a chance here!"

"Er... I have no idea what you mean." Yua scratched her cheek, looking perplexed.

Hmm, I understood how Yuuko felt. What was with Yua's whole overwhelming tolerance thing? Abandoning the self, body and soul, without a second thought.

"You're really something, Ucchi. I'm not just talking about today, either. You could easily start living by yourself at any moment."

"I dunno. I can do housework, I think, but I'm sure I'd get incredibly lonely if I lived all by myself, after a while."

"Hmm. Do *you* ever get lonely, Saku?" Yuuko redirected the conversation toward me.

"Yeah, I get lonely. To be honest, I'd love it if we could all have a sleepover tonight. The three of us all snug as bugs, sleeping in a row..."

"I'll sleep over!" Yuuko cheered.

"I will *not* sleep over," Yua said.

All jokes aside, though, let's think about this seriously.

"After my parents decided to divorce, and I was given the chance to try living alone..."

As soon as I opened my mouth and started speaking, the two of them got an unreadable look on their faces. Of course, I had already told them both about my family's circumstances.

"To be honest with you, it wasn't nerves I felt as much as a sense of relief, and I wasn't angry, just grateful. Neither of my parents ever seemed to really see me, but they both at least respected my opinion."

As I explained to Nanase not long ago, my parents were extreme opposites.

And yet they both shared a parenting philosophy along the lines of *Think and decide for yourself.* Of course, that came right along with *Take responsibility for your own choices.* But I liked that they didn't just shoot down what I wanted without even hearing me out first.

"When you think about it that way, I decided on this way of living for myself, so I always felt like it was more fun than anything else. It sounds a bit trite, maybe, when they're sending me money to live off, but having my entire style of living completely within my control and my responsibility... I can't say I hate it."

Yuuko and Yua were both listening with solemn expressions.

"Still, I'd be lying if I said I didn't have the odd, lonely night. That's why it's so nice when you guys all come and visit every now and again like this."

With that, I smiled.

Yuuko looked slightly conflicted. "I see... You know, to tell the truth, until I heard what everyone was saying today, I never once thought about leaving the prefecture or living by myself. When I think about how Kazuki and Yuzuki are going to end up leaving Fukui, it makes me feel really, really sad."

Go on to college in the prefecture or leave the prefecture altogether. Yeah, that choice would have a huge impact on our group dynamic.

If we all chose Fukui U, then we'd probably all still be together even after graduating high school. But the ones who left Fukui would go on to new cities and make new friends and homes for themselves. No doubt they would only ever see their hometown friends when they came back to the prefecture for seasonal events like Obon and New Year's.

If Asuka went to Tokyo, I probably wouldn't have any more opportunities to meet with her—or even any reasons to. In fact, since Asuka was already in a different grade in school and had a totally different friend group, that went double for her.

No doubt Yua was thinking along similar lines.

"We're all connected by our phones and social media, but if you or Yuuko left the prefecture, Saku, it wouldn't be so easy anymore for us to meet up and cook dinner together like this, huh?"

"Ucchi, don't talk about that, please. You'll make me depressed." Yuuko's voice was a little choked.

Yua reached out to stroke her hair reassuringly as she continued.

"But you know, we're at the age now where we have to start thinking about these things, don't we? Thinking it over seriously, while we're still able to spend time together, just like this."

I cleared my throat, wanting to keep this conversation from getting any darker and colder.

"All right, I think we should definitely have a sleepover tonight, as snug as…"

"You can sleep on the kitchen floor, Saku."

"Hey! I'm the one who's lonely here!"

*

It was getting late, so I saw the two of them off, then returned to the apartment.

I let myself in with the scrape of the key in the lock, noticing that the warm atmosphere had disappeared as if it had never even been there, and the apartment was cloaked in heavy silence.

—Yeah, sometimes, I do get lonely.

Without turning on the light in the living room, I used my phone's flashlight to make my way to the bedroom. Then I turned the crescent-shaped desk light on my small bedside table on with a click.

The warm light spread out across my cold room, and I felt a sense of relief as I rolled onto the bed.

Gazing idly at the ceiling, I thought about Asuka.

It seemed somehow strange, her vacillating over her future. Hesitating over their future path was perfectly normal for a high schooler, sure, but it weighed on my mind, her stubborn refusal to discuss her reasoning.

Asuka had said she was undecided between Tokyo and Fukui. She also said that she had basically made up her mind, but that if she discussed it with me, she might start to waver.

She had always given off this free-spirited aura like, "I'm just living life on my terms, exactly where I ought to be, and the only guidance I need to follow is my own." This weakness from her just wasn't her.

And yet, I thought.

Maybe I was the one who had been casting her in that type of role and enforcing it.

Once, I told her she was like some kind of phantom lady in my eyes.

And what was it she said? If we got any closer, we wouldn't be able to keep on playing our roles, her as the cool older girl and me as the adorable boy.

"You're a high school girl, after all, aren't you?"

"I certainly am."

What if, what if.

Incoherent conversation, going around and around in my head. My mind was growing fuzzy as I felt myself drifting off into the world of dreams.

Was I pushing my own one-sided fantasy onto Asuka?

I really wanted to believe that wasn't the case.

It would be great if I could smoothly scoop up and transmit to her all the amazing things about her, all the cool things about her, and her peerless beauty, that she herself wasn't even aware of.

—Just like how a young girl in a white dress once told me that I was free.

*

A few days later, we finally had a lunch period with clear skies. Once I was done wolfing down some lunch, I headed to the baseball field with Haru.

Haru asked me to come and play some catch with her, since she had a brand-new baseball glove. I say asked, but this is Haru we're talking about, so it was more of a demand. That's Haru for you.

It was getting on one full year now since I'd quit club sports.

I'd been thinking I should play some baseball sooner or later, just for fun. Maybe Haru was doing me a solid here by giving me the opportunity.

"Chitose! I had no idea high school baseballs were this dense and heavy. Just knowing how hard these suckers could hit, it really gets me all fired up! Watch out for my death ball, now!"

...Yeah, I was just overthinking things, after all. Haru only wanted to add another physical hobby to her repertoire, burn off some of her excess steam.

I put my Mizuno Pro glove onto my left hand. I hadn't been skipping on its upkeep. Then I punched it a couple times with my right fist. It all took me right back. The still-bright bitter orange. The laced-up web. The smell of the leather.

I sucked in a breath, took a whiff of the kicked-up dust in the air.

It was smack-dab in the middle of rainy season, but the sun's glare was strong, which heralded the coming of summer a half step earlier than it usually came.

—Ah. Here I am, standing out on the baseball field.

I signaled to Haru with my hand. She looked like she was ready to roll. A whole mountain of balls came flying my way, and I caught each one in my glove with a clean thunking sound.

That moment, the feeling of acceleration when you run for a fly ball and the instant when you catch it and fire it back home, the sting of excitement when you steal and slide into the next base, the feeling of hitting that game-deciding pitch with the core of the bat—it struck me all at once, and I almost started crying.

Offering a silent *thank you*, I gently threw it back to her.

She really did have a knack for sports. Haru caught the ball neatly in the brand-new glove she said she'd bought for herself, but then she fumbled it. The ball came rolling back to me.

"Agh! I thought I had you just then!"

"Haru, lend me your glove for a sec?"

"Nuh-uh! Blaming my own mistakes on my equipment? I know better, Chitose."

"Just hand it over, you rookie."

Haru handed me her bright-red glove.

It looked like she had bought a generic cheap one from a sports store. It wasn't the kind of substitute glove used by a serious baseball team, but I was surprised by the fact that she'd actually gotten one that was suitable for hard training.

The glove was still stiff, so I tried touching the thumb and little finger parts together a few times to soften it up. It got a little bit more supple, and then I slammed the ball against the palm part a few times to make it a bit easier to catch with.

Once I had it in a shape I was satisfied with, I returned the glove to Haru.

"There, try it now." Haru opened and closed the glove I'd just handed to her. "Hey, it feels more flexible than before now!"

"I can't get it to open and close really smoothly in such a short amount of time, but if you keep using it without bending it the wrong way, it'll start to feel familiar to you soon. When you store it, keep a ball inside it, and use a band to secure it if you can. I'll bring you one."

"Oooh, a present, just for Haru?"

"It's just some string held in place with Velcro." I went around behind Haru's back as I spoke.

"Gonna touch you for a sec."

"Oh my! ♡"

"Not like that. You're the one who told me to pay attention to the details."

"I was kidding, duh. Go ahead."

I put my hand on the glove that Haru was wearing and turned it so its inside was visible.

"See this depression here, where the ball was? Generally speaking, you should try to catch it there. Okay, tighten up your left hand, and… Hyah!"

Whap!!!

I slammed the ball as hard as I could against the spot I just indicated.

"Ouccchhh!!!"

"Good, good, remember that pain."

"You didn't have to go OTT out of nowhere on me!"

"All right, let's move on."

"That still hurts like the dickens (translation: a lot), though, you know?!"

I put my arms around her from behind and took hold of her hands. It's not really a problem if a guy presses his chest against a girl's back, now, is it?

Haru stiffened for a second, then immediately went limp. I tried to ignore the sensation of her body heat as I spoke.

"What a lot of girls do is they throw the ball almost like they're pushing it out, not quite like a shotput throw. Don't do that. Twist your body like this." I guided Haru's body into the correct form. "Pull your opposite arm in conversely at the moment you throw."

I stayed close to her right through to the end of the practice throw and then moved away.

Haru stared at me, looking just a little embarrassed; then, as if she couldn't handle it anymore, she snorted.

Then she was really laughing—clutch-your-belly laughing.

"Ah-ha-ha, that's so funny. You're so proactive today."

"I don't recall trying to lecture you at all?"

"Well, it felt like it. You're so passionate about it. You like this that much?"

"I'm not following. I was simply trying to teach you how to play a decent game of ball."

Little Haru was peering up at me inquisitively. "Yep, I like that side of you. I really do."

"...You're being awfully proactive yourself today."

"Better to hammer it on home, though, huh?"

Then she slammed the ball she was holding into the left side of my chest.

I coughed on the witty retort I had all lined up and grabbed hold of the ball instead.

I laughed, and that laugh had a lot of emotion behind it. "All right, time to practice," I said.

"Bring it on!"

Haru trotted backward, getting distance, and I threw her a slightly faster ball.

It thwacked against her glove with a pleasant sound.

This time, her form was a little better than before, and the ball returned to me a tad faster.

I threw again, just a little bit faster still. Haru caught it with obvious enjoyment and threw it right on back.

This is fun, I thought. *I wish this could go on and on.*

On our fifth volley, Haru threw the ball a bit too hard, and even though I jumped with all my might, I couldn't catch it. It was a real wild pitch.

I landed heavily, and I was just turning around to go scoop up the errant ball, when...

"—Hey, Saku."

* * * *

There were a few of my former teammates from baseball club standing there.

The guy at the front of the group picked up the ball that slowly rolled over toward his feet. Then with a snap, he threw it to me. I caught it side-on, and after a beat of silence, I laughed.

"Hey, Yusuke... Sorry for messing up the baseball field. We'll make sure to rake the dirt back neatly afterward."

Yusuke Ezaki, Fuji High baseball club's glorious batter number four, seemed almost deaf to my words. Instead, he frowned. He seemed sad for some reason.

"You're still doing baseball?" I replied, my frivolous smile never slipping. "We're just playing. You caught me about to put the moves on this sports-loving girl."

I looked over at Haru and threw the ball at her as if to resume our practice session, but it went right over her head and ended up rolling off into the distance.

She must have picked up on something. She ignored the ball completely and came dashing over this way.

"Chitose, who is this?"

"Some old teammates."

Yusuke ignored my casual tone and took a step forward.

The familiar faces standing behind him were all watching the proceedings nervously.

"Saku... Are you sure you don't feel like coming back?"

"God, no. It's been almost a year since I quit, you know. I'm sure my skills are totally rusted over by now."

"A year away isn't long enough to get that rusty."

"Remember what you yourself once said? A batter's sensitive intuition can slip out of his fingers if he lets even three days go by without touching the bat."

"Yeah, but when I saw your face just then... You love baseball, don't you?"

"—Do *you* guys love baseball?"

I flipped it back on them, then mashed my lips together. I knew I'd messed up.

"We can all try talking to the coach this time. It won't go down like how it did before. Now we know what it's like without you, Saku; we…"

"Hey, listen here!!!"

I was just starting to grind my teeth when Haru cut Yusuke off mid-sentence, her voice high and loud.

"I have no idea what happened here, but it seems clear that you guys are the ones who didn't—or couldn't—stop Saku from quitting, huh?"

The small girl with the ponytail stood in front of me, almost as if she was trying to cover for me or protect me somehow.

"Chitose quit baseball. It's obvious something happened. I don't know if you guys were part of the problem, or if it was something you turned a blind eye to." Haru slapped the glove against her chest. "But what I can say is this. Right now, *I'm* the one he's practicing with."

Instinctively, I reached out to try to touch her slim shoulder, but…

"Hey. Chitose."

Someone was calling my name loud and clear from behind us.

I turned to see someone there winding up for a pitch, and I took two, three steps backward out of reflex.

The ball left his hand with a whump, then shot through the air like an arrow, releasing a hissing sound. It was flying at top speed, right toward my chest.

Thwackkk.

I caught it with my mitt, slightly enjoying the sting against my palms and the way the shot rocked me back on my heels.

"Nice throw… Atomu."

The pitcher was strolling over as if it wasn't even a thing.

"Nice group you've got here. Let me join."

The sight of this intruder made Yusuke scowl for a second, but then an instant later recognition dawned.

"You… You're Uemura, from Youkou Junior High, right?"

"Hmm, so even guys who didn't register on my radar know me on sight, huh?"

"I know practically everyone who played junior high baseball in my hometown."

"Well, Chitose didn't remember me at all." Atomu snickered self-deprecatingly, then grew serious. "Anyway," he continued, "what are you bunch of losers doing here? Come to blub over losing your star player or what?"

Yusuke narrowed his eyes in annoyance. "What's it to you?"

"Not much. Just saw Chitose out here trying to put the moves on a girl with a friendly game of catch, so I came to give him a hard time about it."

The two of them stared at each other with silent animosity, until Yusuke finally huffed air out of his nose and turned away.

"Another time, Saku."

Sure, I shrugged, raising a hand in parting as he turned and started to walk away.

I watched and waited until Yusuke and company had all left, then I spoke.

"Wanna play catch, Atomu?"

I held out the ball to him, and he took it, but then after gazing at my hand for a moment, he slammed it back against my palm.

"You gotta be kidding. At least teach Aomi here how to hold the ball, man."

"…Will do."

Come to think of it, I spent a lot of time fussing over proper form and never got around to telling her how to handle the ball. Even from a distance, this guy knew what he was looking at. No wonder. He was a former pitcher, after all.

"And you. How long are you going to keep on like this, huh? Not knowing how to let go."

"…"

Maybe he'd lost interest now, or maybe he had other reasons for coming over in the first place. At any rate, that was all Atomu said. After that, he walked off the field without even a backward glance.

"Ugh. He is so weird."

I held the ball between my middle and index fingers, then held it out toward Haru.

"This is the proper way to hold the ball. Also…" I slammed the ball into the cup of her mitt. "Thanks. For being my partner in a game of catch."

Haru blushed for a moment, then grinned.

"Hammered it home, did I?"

"A stake right to the heart, yup."

The bell rang, signaling the end of lunch period. To deal with our mutual feelings of sudden awkwardness, we devoted all of our attention to raking the dirt back nicely, and then we ran off to class.

*

After school that day, Year Two, Class Five finished up homeroom and started getting ready to go to their respective clubs or to go home. I threw my textbooks and pencil case into my Gregory day pack as I chatted with the other members of Team Chitose.

Yuuko had already packed up her stuff and was now talking excitedly. "Hey, Saku. You got any plans for after school today?"

"Nope. Why?"

"Thought I might come over and cook dinner again."

"It started with a domesticity service and turned into a pushy wife delivery service, huh?"

"Wife!!!"

"It's not a compliment! Crack a dictionary, will you?"

Nanase came over, sports bag already slung over her shoulder, on her way out to club practice. "Chitose, if you don't have any other plans, why not come and watch our practice? Misaki said to bring you along anytime."

"No way. Miss Misaki scares me."

"She wants you to take the responsibility you ought to take."

"What's that supposed to mean?"

"Remember what you did to me that day, hmm?"

"Don't phrase it like that! I thought there was some huge misunderstanding going on for a second!"

Ever since the stalker incident got cleared up, she and I had gone back to being just Chitose and Nanase again. Our classmates, who had clearly picked up on our temporary closeness, all seemed to treat it as a taboo topic, a tumor that shouldn't be prodded.

Incidentally, the school underground gossip site was filled with choice posts on the subject. They all said things like: Class Five's Resident Man-Slut Chitose has pumped 'em and dumped 'em yet again! ...Tch.

While we were all chatting away, the classroom door slid open on its tracks, and...

"Hey, friend. Wanna go on a date with your upperclassman?!"

Asuka came bounding in, her voice loud enough to wake the dead.

By reflex, I jumped to my feet, my eyes sliding over to the other two girls.

Ah! What beautiful smiles, ladies! But please, don't forget to involve the eyes as well! You're seriously scaring Saku here!

Asuka came floating over, as if she were weightless.

"So. Date?"

She crouched down in front of my desk, resting her chin on the backs of her hands and blinking up at me naughtily.

"And why're you barging in here all of a sudden?"

"I told you, didn't I? I hate having to make plans in advance."

"Indeed, but you also said something about how we should avoid dating at all costs."

"That's ancient history. I've forgotten all about that now."

"And it absolutely has to be today?"

"I never plan for after tonight."

"Was that supposed to be *Casablanca*?"

This exchange reminded me of something I'd seen in an old movie. The next moment, Asuka stood up.

"So then, Hiiragi, Nanase, may I borrow him?"

"That's... I mean..."

Yuuko's expression contorted; she seemed terribly conflicted.

She had only met Asuka recently, during the future plans session, and Asuka certainly did feel older than us. It was difficult for Yuuko to be her usual self in front of her. Besides, she was supposed to be going off to club practice right now, so she couldn't even come up with a plausible pretext for stopping our date.

Nanase, however, was a cool customer. She waved a hand airily. "Be my guest. Help yourself to my old ex."

"Hey! Who are you calling old, huh? And I don't remember giving you permission to pass me along like a possession!"

"...No offense intended."

"What was with the loaded pause just before you said that, then?!"

Just then, a hand squeezed mine—but Asuka's voice was peppy and breezy, as if to discourage anyone reading too much into it.

"All right, that's enough. Come on. You're mine now."

And she yanked me by the arm.

I got up from my desk, and with a cheery "We're off!" Asuka started running.

""Hey! We didn't say you could have him!""

We left Yuuko and Nanase complaining behind us as we flew out of the classroom and rocketed into the hallway. Departing students turned around to see what the commotion was. Nearby teachers all started talking at once, making protests, but we ignored them all and shot off again.

For some reason, the whole thing was really funny, and the two of us choked with laughter as we ran.

*

I had no idea where we were going, so I swung by the boys' basketball clubroom and borrowed the key to Kaito's old granny bike before leaving the school. I was just pushing the bike for now as the two of us walked along the same old familiar riverside route.

"So then, what kind of big joke is all this, huh?" I asked.

Asuka, who had been walking a little ways ahead, whirled around happily.

"Why, it's the famous School Uniform Date, of course."

"That's not what I meant."

"Listen…"

She fell back a little, until we were walking shoulder to shoulder.

"Once you become a third-year student, you start thinking more about the path ahead, you know? When I saw y'all in your classroom, I started going over all of it in my mind. I thought even more on the way home. This is the only time we all have to be high school students together. Ten years from now, we can wish all we like, but we'll never, ever be able to return to this time."

"That's why you want to go on a date wearing a school uniform?"

Asuka scratched her cheek, looking a little embarrassed.

"I mean, you and I only ever meet by chance on this river path. We chat and say good-bye, and that's it. We don't even know each other's phone numbers or LINE IDs. That kind of relationship is poetic and romantic, sure, but we can't stick those memories in photo albums. I don't want to look back and regret missing chances in my youth. There's such a strict time limit. That's what I've been thinking."

That just strikes me as cheap sentimentality.

Take any ten high school students. Probably at least eight or nine of them will have moments when they think the same thing.

And yet Asuka will be leaving here soon. I still have more time. The speed at which time is going by is probably completely different for each of us.

For me, this is just another ordinary day. But for Asuka, it's one of a dwindling number.

"That surprises me. I figured I was the one who'd end up cracking first and saying something like that."

"Yeah, I thought so, too. I probably shouldn't have gone to your class's future talks session, but I was curious. If I never found out anything, I could have just gone on being your mysterious girl right up until I disappeared into thin air."

Her voice was tinged with weakness, loneliness.

"...Asuka, you really are that mysterious older woman I admire." I tried to speak with as much emphasis as I could.

I mean really, this was something I should have been the one to say. Back then, I was trying to be strong, but I was so weak. I'm still weak. Here I was again, letting her be the adult.

"I mean, think about the way you felt watching me and Okuno banter together. Seeing you getting along so well with Hiiragi and Nanase, I ended up feeling the same way."

I recalled the touch of her hand on mine, just before.

"To be honest, I couldn't sleep very well the night after that talk. I couldn't put my finger on why. I was tossing and turning on my bed, like how you roll an almost-empty tin of Sakuma Drops candies around to see how many are left. Once I finally took the lid off my feelings, the answer came right on out."

Asuka's face crumpled, and then a transparent smile appeared on it.

"I realized that, aw, man. I'm just a regular high schooler, Asuka Nishino, and I want to experience youth…with you."

My heart started beating faster as I gazed at that look on her face. I'd never seen it before. My lips moved to form a dissatisfying sort of response.

"Like if you and I were just regular old schoolmates in different grades."

"You don't like regular?"

"No, it's just that it's kinda hard to picture it."

"But don't you think, if that's how it really was, it'd be our time to test it out? Wouldn't we have reasons to give it a shot?"

I relaxed my shoulders and smiled over that.

"Oh, I get it. You're a lot more into me than I thought you were, Asuka."

"Oh, you didn't know?" Asuka continued, her tone playful and teasing.

"I've been totally in love with you right from the start."

*　　*　　*

A vacuum formed in time, for just a moment.

A breeze blew, almost as if it was blowing straight toward tomorrow. A stray cat streaked across the path in front of us. From somewhere far away, a crow squawked. The river gurgled and burbled.

We looked at each other. And looked at each other. And looked at each other.

Asuka refused to look away. So did I.

Up until this point, we'd drawn a very clear line in the sand when it came to our relationship.

Ah, it would be more accurate to say that I was forced to draw it, at least.

So I knew this wasn't really a confession of love. This was Asuka's way of bringing our strange and unusual play to its end. Her gentle good-bye.

I had no reason to say no. I didn't need to be rolled around like a candy tin in order to fall right out into her hands.

The two of us were in the last year we would ever be able to spend together in high school. The next thing we knew, we'd be strangers. We wouldn't even get to pass in the street.

And so I responded with the tritest line of dialogue you could think of.

"Well, for now, want to do something with me that high schoolers do?"

"Sure!"

The two of us shared a totally normal high school smile, possibly the first since we'd met. Asuka tugged her tie loose, as if somehow she was feeling released.

*

On National Highway 8, the same road that the Lpa mall is on, there's an arcade and internet café located pretty close together where Kazuki, Kaito, and I often hang out. With Asuka riding double on the bicycle behind me, I pedaled us both in the direction of the internet café.

I say internet café, but it actually has all kinds of attractions inside, like a karaoke room, darts, billiards, and stuff like that.

I first suggested that we split up, take individual booths, and read some manga or something, but...

"The only thing that should be *split up* on a date is a Papico or Chupet popsicle—when it's a summer's day, that is!"

...she turned me down outright.

Trying to resist at least a little, I attempted to select a booth that had a roomy sofa for two, but Asuka turned to the staff person and, without hesitation, ordered a booth with a couple's loveseat that reclined all the way back.

Once we were installed on the loveseat, which resembled nothing so much as an actual bed, I tried to adhere myself to the wall. But I couldn't keep it up as I explained the features of this internet café and found myself leaning in. I couldn't breathe, Asuka's lavender scent was filling the tight space we were in, and I knew that I couldn't last a whole hour in here without announcing my defeat.

We went to report our intentions to the staff person before we headed into the room where the dartboard and billiard table were set up. Then I could finally breathe again. But it was a tight fit in there as well, and we were alone.

"Tch, give me a break."

As I muttered to myself, Asuka stopped fondling the long, narrow billiard cue and turned to look at me.

"I thought you'd have more chill than this, you know."

Then she gave me a mature-looking grin, as if the past few seconds had never happened.

In the dim, indirectly lit space, that smile looked really good on her.

I sighed, muddling the brightly colored balls about on the blue felted surface of the table.

"I'm on a date with the older girl I've idolized—and with barely a second of advance notice. If you know any guy who wouldn't be a little on edge in that situation, I'd like to hear names."

"But you must be used to this? Being in such close quarters with girls, I mean."

"I'm not used to being in such close quarters with you."

"Is it cozy? Or irritating? Or are you just flustered because you're not sure what to do now?"

"Now, that's not a very thoughtful question. That's like asking a newborn baby, 'So what do you think of the outside world?'"

Asuka chuckled, removing the cue stick from its holder. In her enthusiasm, though, she tugged it out a bit too hard.

She quickly bent down and scooped up the fallen cue, before whirling back around to me with a "Did you see that?" sort of look on her face, giggling and scratching her cheek.

"Hey. Have you noticed yet?" she asked shyly. "There aren't any girls out there who wouldn't be a little on edge during their first date with an amazing younger guy they know."

Asuka said she'd never played billiards before, so I taught her the rules for nine ball.

Short version is: You line up the balls marked one through nine, and whoever pockets the nine ball first wins. Basically, you have to hit the cue ball first and hit the smallest number on the table, and you keep doing that until someone pockets the nine. It's a very simple game.

But to be honest, I don't know any other way to play billiards.

I put the number one ball at the top and placed the nine ball in the middle, then put the others all around them in a diamond shape. You have to hit the one ball first—that's called a break shot—and then you scatter the other balls, and that's how the game starts.

While I was still explaining things, Asuka started practicing with the white cue ball, but she was so terrible at it that I couldn't help snorting with laughter.

"It's not fencing. You won't get anywhere trying to do it one-handed."

She pouted in response. "Hey, it's my first time at a place like this, remember?"

"That's unusual for a Fukui high school student, isn't it? Not ever having come to a place like this? Someone usually always suggests stopping by here at some point, in my experience."

"Well, in my household…"

Asuka leaned her butt against the billiard table and looked up at the ceiling, as if reminiscing.

"My household's pretty strict. My mom's a junior high school teacher, and my dad's a high school teacher. They're both as straitlaced as they come. I wasn't allowed to buy any food from street stalls at festivals, and I wasn't allowed to sleep over at my friends' houses. Wasn't allowed to go anywhere that wasn't totally safe for kids."

To be honest here, this confession took me by surprise.

To me, Asuka was like a paragon of freedom, and while it never seemed like she was the type to openly defy her parents, I certainly never imagined that she had grown up under such a strict set of rules.

Of course, there's a world of difference between how different sets of parents place restrictions on their kids. My parents, now, they're pretty lax, since they allow me to live by myself and all. But some parents keep their kids on lockdown, giving them a strict nine PM curfew when they're not at club practice or cram school.

I guess I always assumed that Asuka's parents were more like mine.

I wasn't sure how to respond to her now.

Maybe she never mentioned it before because the subject had never come up. Maybe she just felt like saying it right now, in this moment.

After hesitating for a while, I came out with a pretty glib response.

"You're saying you've never had the pleasure of gobbling down some *marumaru yaki*, or a huge tray of *yakisoba*, cooked by some old person at a festival stall, then washed it all down with a bottle of Ramune? Man, you've only half lived."

"Like you did the other day, with Nanase?"

I looked away, cowed just a little, then she continued by saying: "And yet…"

"The truth is: I did actually get taken to one, just once. Way back."

"By your parents?"

"…Wouldn't you like to know?" She gave me a loaded smile. Then she hopped off the billiard table and picked up the cue. "That's why I want you to show me the bad ways of having fun."

"It's just billiards."

"Well, it's a first-time experience for me."

"Are you sure you want to be giving up your precious firsts to a guy like me, you bad girl?"

"It has to be you."

I wasn't expecting that answer, and I couldn't find a reply.

"You mean…?"

Asuka broke into a devilish grin. "'Cause, I mean, if it ends up not being a great memory, I can just block it out and forget it, right? Like getting bitten by a dog."

"It's fine, sheesh. Go back over there. I'm going to drill this into you until you can't stand it anymore."

If I was playing against Yuuko, or Yua, or Nanase, or Haru, I could easily dismiss this as an extension of everyday life and make a bawdy joke. But I never expected that I would be having typical high school banter with *this* girl.

But it's funny. The Asuka in my mind never crumbled and fell. I let out the breath I'd been holding and unlatched my own cue. "First, try holding it with your left hand."

I showed her how to make a basic bridge and to steady the cue with her hand.

Asuka moved her fingers like I demonstrated. "...Like this?"

"You're not making a fox shadow puppet, here. Make a ring out of your index finger and lower your little finger."

Ah, I felt shy about touching her hand again. Still, I found myself reaching out and taking her hand.

"No! Like this, not like that! Then you place your left hand outstretched and rest it on the table. Place the cue alongside your index finger and then with the right hand hold tight to the..."

I felt Asuka's soft and shiny hair brushing my nose like raindrops. Her slim neck gave off a girlish scent, and I leaped backward, startled.

Yikes, that was close. I accidentally started manipulating her into position like when I was showing Haru how to play ball. What was I thinking?

Faced with the gravity of my own actions, I found myself mentally replaying the sight of her bare neck in front of me, the short hair there, her small ears, the slight bumps of her vertebrae.

"Okay, so then... What now?"

Asuka turned, cue in hand, and I thought her cheeks appeared just a little pink. I couldn't look right at her, though, turning to the side.

"Now...you aim for the center of the cue ball and jab the cue forward with your right hand."

She nodded in the corner of my vision, then faced the table, seemingly deep in concentration.

"Like this?"

I looked back and found her leaning right over the table. Her small but pert, round butt was sticking right out, and her skirt, which wasn't even that short, was now several inches shorter at the back.

I could see her thighs, and they were surprisingly soft-looking for an androgynous type of girl such as Asuka. They were so enchanting, so youthful and vibrant, and even though Asuka was the upperclassman I admired, she was still a girl first and foremost. I couldn't ignore that fact.

I glanced around to check whether any other guys were watching, but we were still the only two people around.

"Y-yeah, just like that."

I stammered out my response, going around the table so I was facing Asuka instead.

If Asuka was some other girl, some girl I'd seen around but didn't know her name…or even if she was Yuuko or Nanase, I'd be counting myself lucky right about now. But I just couldn't look at her in a sexual way like that.

With a clunk, Asuka hit the cue ball badly, sending it ricocheting against the cushioned side of the table and rolling wildly away.

I grabbed it and returned it.

"Good, good. That's much better than before."

"I think I've started to get the hang of it. Watch this." Asuka replaced the cue ball and readied her cue.

That's when her shirt front gaped open, and my eyes were arrested by the sight of white material, a turquoise blue bow in the front.

I felt myself go numb, from my lower body right up to mid-back. I quickly averted my face, but the carnal afterimage was burned into my brain.

"Asuka! Your tie. Tighten your tie, will you?"

"Hmm?" Asuka sounded oblivious, and there was a space of

silence that lasted maybe three seconds before I could sense her quickly whirling around, her back to me. Finally safe, I allowed myself to look in her direction once more.

Fiddling rapidly with her tie, Asuka spoke over her shoulder.

"...Did you see?"

"I tried my hardest not to."

"How much did you see?"

"Enough to guess you like turquoise blue."

"...Ack!"

Asuka covered her face dramatically and sank to her knees, hiding behind the cover of the billiard table.

Her response was so silly, and so adorable, that I couldn't help laughing.

"Ohhh! Now I can never be a pure bride." I could hear her moaning quietly.

"Want me to step up and take responsibility?"

"...You mean commit ritual seppuku?"

"Could you please calm down just a little?"

Hands gripping the edge of the table, Asuka popped her head up, but her eyes were still downcast.

"Fine then; let me hear you sing," she mumbled. "And make it good. Like you're saying hello for the first time, with the knowledge that one day, we'll have to say good-bye."

"That's an easy enough deal. I'll sing. Like I'm saying hello for the first time, with the knowledge that one day, it'll be over."

I knew she wasn't trying to goof with me just then, but I still responded like a smart-ass.

With a clunk, Asuka hit the cue ball wildly, hitting the number one ball and sending all the balls rolling around the table. The nine ball fell neatly into the pocket.

*

Pocketing the nine ball with a break shot was serious beginner's luck, but Asuka let it go to her head, and we played three games after that.

In the end, I won one game and lost three. What the heck? How did I end up losing so badly?

"Does not compute," I said.

Asuka chuckled in response as we stood in front of the soft drink bar.

"Why? Why is it that, while I pocketed more balls in general, you always just happened to manage to pocket the nine ball?"

Even if I sunk every ball from one to seven, Asuka would hit the eight ball and send it ricocheting into the nine ball, and both of them would go spinning into the nearest pocket. After I scattered the balls with a cool break shot, Asuka would plunk her cue against the two and sink the nine.

I kept on losing in that kind of fashion, and we ended up in an immature sort of death match, until I managed to snag just one win in the final game.

Asuka filled up her glass with melon soda, a nonchalant look on her face.

"Well, whoever pockets the nine ball first wins, right?"

"I know, but... I mean, yes, but...you were more surprised than anyone every time you did it!"

"Now, now. That's not a manly way to speak, young man."

"Hnnnng! Did you just pat me on the shoulder?!"

I slurped my iced coffee as the two of us headed to the karaoke room.

The room had sofas lining three walls, and Asuka took a seat right next to me without hesitating. As instructed, I sang several songs, and even though I kept pressing her to sing something, she made no attempt to pick up a mic.

She was fiddling with the touch panel screen (I had to show her how it worked), clearly enjoying herself. "I want you to sing this one next. 'Guild.'"

"The song you say reminds you of me, right?"

"To be more precise, it reminds me of how you were back then."

Back then? She probably meant when I had just quit baseball and was feeling totally despondent.

Which meant last fall…when I first met her.

"Do you still remember?"

"How could I forget?"

I mean, if I had never met Asuka, I'd probably still be an empty shell of a guy right around now.

—Watching something I'd poured my heart and soul into since elementary school just crumble and fall through my fingers—those days when I felt so helpless and resentful toward the environment that had caused that to happen, the people involved, and mostly importantly, myself for accepting defeat.

The Asuka I met that twilit evening on the riverbank—to me, she was as beautiful as the faraway moon I always felt like I was reaching for.

If I was just listing facts, all she really did was join a circle of kids who'd taken a joke a step too far and steered them away from what seemed to be a case of ganging up on one of their own. That was all.

But even so, to me, back then, she shone so bright it almost hurt to look at her.

She ignored other people's gazes, their dirty tricks, their weaknesses, their faults. Asuka was walking her own path, believing it to be the right one for her.

She wasn't clad in strong armor, putting on an act like someone I could mention. She was fine being herself, like a free-blowing breeze, like a stray cat strutting down the main road, going ahead without ever even checking the compass.

If only I could be more like that. Then this would never have happened to me.

So after that, I was always looking for Asuka. On the way to and from school. During the school day. And after classes let out, too. Every time I spotted her, I would call out to her and head over. And when time permitted, I would try to find some reason to chat with her. Because I wanted to talk to her.

To be frank, I believe it was the first time I ever went out of my way to approach another person like that. Before that, I preferred to just go up to people on a whim and move on from them just as freely.

Maybe Asuka was a little put out at first, being shadowed by a younger guy like that. She didn't welcome me so much as she just got used to me over time, I guess, until I became just another expected part of her day.

Then as time went by, I started to feel saved by her insight and her eloquent way with words.

We would have real conversations, like this:

"Asuka. When you have to act lame now and then so you can live a life that's generally cool…what should you do?"

"I guess it depends on the individual's concept of what's cool. Something you think looks lame might not to another person."

"So do you think a stray cat who sucks up to an old lady to get food thinks he's being lame? After all, he's acting just like a pet."

"No. He's just doing what he has to do to survive as a stray cat."

"So you have to stop being what you are, in order to keep on being…what you are?"

"You'll figure it out eventually. I have faith in you."

*   *   *

And like this:

"Asuka. If you know you're just going to get betrayed in the end, don't you agree it's better not to trust anyone in the first place?"

"I think you'll find your life has less color in it if you only think about it in terms of return on investment. If you feel that way, then why bother studying if you won't use what you learned in the future? Why bother dating anyone if you're just going to break up? Why bother fighting if you're not going to win?"

"So in other words, if you're not going to live a beautiful life, you may as well be dead?"

"That way of phrasing it is much more your style."

And she would hand me little notes, like this:

Hey friend,

I believe that words have power.
Along with music. Music that can permeate your soul, when you're feeling mentally tired out.
I hope this can help you find a sense of peace to fill the void within you.

Asuka

And with the note, there was an album. *Yggdrasil*, by Bump of Chicken.

I went home and played it on my portable stereo system. And I cried, the tears streaming down my face.

The music and the lyrics—they were wonderful, of course, but more than anything else I was touched by the warmth of Asuka's words, chosen and delivered just for me.

Thinking back to that time, I tapped a different song into the remote control unit Asuka was holding. Not the song she had requested at all: "Bye Bye Thank You."

It's a song about leaving one's hometown and heading off to the big city you've always longed for.

No matter how far away you wander, there will always be this place to return to. I'll be thinking of you, beneath a sky we both share.

And I prayed that my sentiment would reach her, using the words that she had shown me.

*

When we left the internet café, the curtain of night was descending, almost dividing the sky in half. The restless crescent moon was showing its face. We had been having so much fun that the time got away from us.

I suggested that we ride double on the bicycle, but Asuka said she wanted to walk a little.

I pushed the bike as we made our way past the small park and the rice fields, walking alongside one of those little culverts you see all over the place in Fukui.

"So how many points do I get for the first date?"

Beside me, Asuka chuckled. "Let's see. Ninety points, my junior friend."

"I was hoping for a hundred. Maybe even a hundred and twenty."

"You lost points for annoying me with that final song. And your cheekiness." Asuka stuck her tongue out at me adorably, then a rather solemn look settled over her features. "Hey, can I ask something I wouldn't normally ask?"

I nodded a little, signaling her to continue.

"Do you have a dream?"

"To be the king of a beautiful harem and rule the world."

"No! Be serious!"

"Up until last year, I guess my dream was to be a major-league baseball player."

I could hear her breathe in, a little sharply.

"...Sorry, I shouldn't have asked that."

"Don't sound so upset. If it wasn't for you, I wouldn't even be able to talk about the past like this. I guess my dream is to be able to find a new dream for myself, maybe."

Something told me that she wanted to talk right now, so I shrugged and turned the question back on her.

"What about you, Asuka? Is it all right if I ask?"

Asuka nodded emphatically, as if she'd been waiting for me to say that. "I want to do a job that involves words. Bringing words to people."

"Like a novelist?"

This time, she shook her head no.

"Hmm, when I was younger, I did think about it a bit, but that's not what I want to do. I prefer to think of myself as a reader, so I'd like to be involved in bringing books to publication while still staying true to that. So I was thinking of going into literary publishing."

Publishing. I rolled the word around in my mouth.

I was dimly aware of what that entailed. Dealing with novelists and manga artists, taking charge of their manuscripts, and then finally polishing and editing them.

I knew that Asuka loved novels, so it wasn't really a big surprise to me, but I would have thought that such a book lover would first think of writing novels herself.

Asuka continued, as if guessing what I was thinking.

"Since I was young, I've immersed myself in stories and the words they're made up of. They've brought me such joy, and such sadness. Made me braver, encouraged me, propped me up, saved me. Even if I couldn't be the hero myself, I could at least know what it felt like to be close."

"I think I get what you're saying."

"So I want to help in drawing those stories out and bringing them to people."

She paused then, scratching her cheek with some embarrassment.

"I guess maybe this sounds kinda…cheap?"

I shook my head slowly, emphatically. "It sounds perfect for you. I think you're probably well suited to a role like that."

And I meant it.

After all, I was saved by the words this girl brought to me.

"But you know, it's not about encountering that one novel that saved your life or meeting that editor who changed your life."

I silently indicated for her to continue, and Asuka looked down awkwardly.

"In other words, I guess it's as simple as—I want to work in publishing because I like books. But it's reading I like, not writing. That's why I want to be an editor. I do really want to become one, but at the same time, I feel like I'm pretty easygoing about it."

Her voice was growing quieter and quieter. I knew there was something she was hung up on here.

Maybe you need to have a bigger, more convincing reason behind your life's dream to discuss it.

I wonder how many people start high school with a defined dream for the future.

It's one thing to have one when you're really young.

I want to be Kamen Rider when I grow up. I want to be a professional sports player. I want to be a manga artist. I want to be an astronaut. I want to be a pop singer.

No one's going to raise an eyebrow or snort with laughter at you if you talk about having some ridiculous dream like that.

But when you get to this age, talking about your dream for the future means your future job. Or otherwise the kind of lifestyle you want to live. We stop talking about it in such grand terms.

It gets a little lonely, when you talk about your dream.

To be frank, back when I used to tell people I was going to play major-league ball one day, I was often met with looks of slight derision or smiling frustration. Some other people looked at me warmly and said things like, *"You're getting too old for such childish statements..."*

An editor, now—that's not as divorced from reality as becoming a pro baseball player, but it's also not the kind of job that just anybody who feels like doing it can do.

So no doubt Asuka felt a little hesitant about it.

Maybe she felt like she needed to prepare some tangible basis for talking about having a dream at this age. Something theatrical and dramatic, something convincing.

I could kinda understand how she felt there.

So I chose my words carefully.

"In my case, I love baseball, which is why I wanted to go pro. So if you want to be involved in books since you love reading, well, I think that's a good enough reason to go after it."

Asuka's expression evened out, as if she was experiencing relief.

"I see... Thank you. To be honest, I wasn't that confident about it. I thought my feelings about books might just be on the hobby level. I wasn't sure it was something I could make a profession out of."

I looked at her, and then I voiced another thought I'd been having.

"So you're considering moving to Tokyo; is that because you'll need to be there to pursue a career in publishing?"

"…Yeah." Asuka nodded firmly, then continued. "Like I said before, I haven't had a lot of the experiences that other people take for granted. And yet I think I've got a pretty good idea of what it's like to stay over at a friend's place, hang out at places like that internet café, and go on first dates."

"Because you've read about all those things in books."

"Right. But you know, actually experiencing them—it's so much more fun, exciting, and enjoyable than just reading about it. I've found that out, for sure. It's made me start thinking about how it's so, so important for both novelists and editors to actually have firsthand experience of things in life."

"There's a world out there that can't be experienced in a countryside town, huh."

"Hence, Tokyo. I know it sounds a bit simplistic. But there's still so much I don't know. I thought I could start from there."

I think that's a very smart first step to take toward a dream like hers.

If you want to bring words and stories to other people, then you need to believe in the sentiment behind them, the weight of them, their worth, your own kindness and strength. You need to know true frustration to reach the hearts of those who are frustrated. Like how someone who knows how to grip the ball knows how best to throw it far, far away.

Asuka giggled bashfully. "Heh, that's what I'd like to say. But the truth is that Tokyo is where all the best media colleges are. That's the pragmatic reason. If I want to end up working at a major publishing house one day, I'll have to move to Tokyo eventually either way."

She was right there. Fukui had its local newspapers and town magazines, but if you wanted to edit novels, you'd have to go to Tokyo to find work even if you went to Fukui U initially. So it would probably make more sense to go straight to Tokyo for college.

Essentially, deciding between Fukui and Tokyo was the same thing as deciding whether to go ahead and aim for a publishing career or to give up on it entirely.

Asuka muttered in a low tone. "Remember when I said I love this town…and hate it, too?"

"Yeah."

She was referring to the last month, when we ran into one another at the bookstore near the station.

"Fukui is such a warm place. You know all your neighbors. You go to the supermarket, and your friend's mom's there and says hi to you. And wherever kids are goofing off and doing something dangerous, you'll find some stubborn old geezer giving them a tongue-lashing."

"When I was in elementary school, there was this crusty old guy who watched us on our route to school. We all knew him. Once, I was walking home snacking on some leftover bread from my school lunch, and he was all, '*Hey, sonny! Watch your manners!*' Boy, he sure told me off."

"Yeah, like that." Asuka chuckled. "It's like…like this town is so deeply intertwined with its own past."

"Fukui Station finally got around to installing an automatic ticket gate, you know."

"Hmph! I'm not talking about surface-level stuff like that!" She slapped me on the shoulder. "It's more a sense of continuation, I guess? Like, our parents, and grandparents, they all lived the same kind of lives, in the same place."

I thought I had a pretty good idea of what she was getting at.

My house is full of slightly weird people, a little out of the norm, but I had the same impression, living here.

Asuka continued. "Time flows slower here... I guess that's a clichéd expression, but you know, there's this concept of on time and off time, right? What do they call it...? Work-life balance. But Fukui people seem to live their lives just going with the flow all the time. Work, home life, weekdays, weekends, every day the same."

"Generally, yeah. People aren't too stiff here. In both a good way and a bad way, people here are like, 'That'll do.' Like, it's pretty laid-back."

But that doesn't mean that Fukui people never give things their best effort, or that they slack off, or anything like that.

Everyone works hard and lives decent lives.

But the city people we see on TV and in movies, and read about in books, they always feel too frenetic, in my opinion.

I wonder if those guys and girls ever meander along a riverbank at twilight listening to music? Do they ever smell the scent of other people's households when they walk home through the back alleys? Can they tell the change of the seasons by the smell of the air at night?

"But you know...," Asuka continued. "I do love this town, and hate it, for those reasons. I can easily picture what it'll look like if I stay here forever. Graduate from Fuji High, use that stamp of approval to enter Fukui University. Apply for jobs at places like city hall, the local TV station, newspaper, the bank... Then become some guy's wife. Some guy whose name I don't even know yet."

I felt my chest tighten painfully, but I tried to hide it as I inclined my head, encouraging her to continue.

"Have two or three kids. Take maternity leave, become a Fukui mom with the help of my parents and relatives and the neighbors. It's so commonplace. But to me, it will seem like I'm living a life that's unique."

"I think there's happiness to be found in a life like that."

I gave a rote response, something very surface level.

"Yes, of course. I don't intend to deny that. I respect people who choose that path. And yet... And yet... If I do that, it will mean I never strayed off the beaten path. It might sound horrible of me, but to think of a future me so deeply steeped in the countryside life...scares me."

It was my guess that this was what was on the flip side, the second choice to Asuka's publishing dream.

Living a life sending out dreams to people whose names you'll never know, or living a life spent cherishing the people close to home.

Of course, there are a lot of people who manage to do both at the same time.

She could choose Fukui now, and then she'd have an extra four years in which to think about it at her leisure. She still had that backup option.

So it's not an issue of whether or not she could realistically do it. If she chose to stay in Fukui at this moment, then perhaps the passion driving her to chase after her dream might disappear, fade away into the noise of everyday life. I think that was what she was afraid of.

When I spoke next, it was to confirm to myself what I was already feeling.

"So then, when you said you'd already mostly made up your mind before, you were talking about choosing Tokyo?"

"I think... I think I'd like to let my answer to that one rest for a little while longer."

"I see."

She hopped on the back of the bike, preventing further questioning.

She settled herself down on the bike's rack—and then, as if to cautiously take stock of the distance between us, she put her arms around my waist.

I touched the tiny bundle of interlaced fingers resting just below my stomach, and then I stepped on the pedals.

"Maybe one day I'll start talking about trying to become a novelist."

"And in that scenario, your editor would be…me?"

"Who knows."

"I go to Tokyo, and the distance is too great, so we stop seeing each other. Then one day I happen across a novel you've written under a totally different pen name. I have no clue it's you, but your story is so amazing it moves me to tears, and I push the author for a meeting to discuss publication. And then you appear."

"Like some sort of fairy tale."

"Sometimes fairy tales come true. Sometimes sooner than you expect."

I realized that night had already enveloped us.

There weren't many streetlights. The roads were as quiet as only the countryside can be. No other cars, no other people.

With my toe, I nudged the lever to the dynamo bike light attached to the front wheel, and the going got harder all of a sudden. With a cheap squeaking sound, the light cranked into life, illuminating only a couple feet in front of us at a time.

I think… I think our futures will unfold like this, too. Bit by bit, searching our way forward through the darkness.

"Asuka."

"Yeees?"

I sucked in a breath and then spoke again.

"If you do go to Tokyo, then let's make sure to see all kinds of things we can only see here, first. Let's have conversations we could only have here. Let's shed tears we could only shed here.

That way, even if we end up far apart, we'll always have this place in our hearts to come back to."

"…Yeah!"

I spun the pedals like mad, and Asuka clung to my back for dear life.

As if the two of us could pedal up into the sky and fly all the way to the moon.

CHAPTER TWO
Illusions, Drop-kicked

The Sunday after my first date with Asuka, I went to Lpa, the shopping mall everyone loved, with Kaito, Yuuko, and Haru. It was a rather unusual ensemble cast.

Haru only had morning club practice and was already finished, and she was the one who initiated this group hang when she said she wanted to try hitting a few balls this time. I suggested a trip to the batting center or something, but Yuuko picked up on the plans somehow and jumped in: "I want to go on a date with Saku, too!" And then Kaito, who was in the vicinity, got on board as well.

So why did we all go to Lpa? Well, Yuuko said she wanted to do a little shopping. Haru didn't seem all that interested, but she didn't say no.

When Yuuko appeared at the meeting place, she wore an expensive-looking glen plaid jacket with a matching pair of shorts. Today, her long hair was pulled back into a braid that flowed over the front of her shoulder.

Haru wore a baggy Champion parka. It was in a bright shade of aqua blue with a hem that covered barely half of her thighs. Her healthy-looking legs stretched out beneath the hem. When I asked her, without thinking, "Are you sure you can move around in that?" she stuck out her tongue and replied: "Duh, I'm wearing short shorts underneath, of course."

I certainly didn't expect a sight like that when I showed up.

So we cooled off inside Lpa, and now we were accompanying Yuuko as she looked at clothes. Well, we two guys were hanging back with nothing really to do.

Yuuko picked up a floral-print dress and looked around. "Haru, do you always wear such casual clothes?"

"Yeah. I like stuff that's easy to move around in."

"What? You should totally try wearing something like this! I swear it would look so good on you!"

"Those are clothes for feminine girls like you, Yuuko. Although I think Yuzuki would look just right in them, too."

"No, that's not true! I'll prove it! I know you have your style, so I'm not saying you have to wear this every day, but you should have at least one outfit like this for special days!"

"Special days?"

"Like when you have a date with a guy you like."

"No, no, no, no. Yuuko, what is it, exactly, that you think of me?"

"I think you're a cute girl, why?"

"Don't act so deadpan about it!"

Thinking about it harder, these two were sort of an unusual pair to see together.

I think this might be the first time I've actually seen the two of them have a conversation.

Yuuko slowly turned to me. "Hey. Saku, Kaito, what do you two think?"

Kaito put his hand behind his head, fingers interlaced, as he responded. "Hmm, I don't see it. This is Haru we're talking about here."

"What did you just say, huh?!!" Haru leaped on the offense, but she looked half relieved as she did so.

I watched her, the corners of my mouth twitching upward.

I mean, even if you know something about yourself, having

another person pointing it out can really rile you up. Haru said that, once before.

Haru rounded on me, perhaps misinterpreting my smile.

"Yes, yes, I'm sure dearest here has the same opinion. Excuse me for not being sexier."

"It's not that…" I coughed a little before continuing. "To be honest, I think I'd love to see it. You, in feminine clothes."

"…What?"

Haru went red and took a few tottering steps backward. Maybe it would have been better to act uninterested in the idea.

"Listen, you. What kind of weird adult videos have you been watching online? You picked up some weird kinks, or what?"

"Okay. Would you like me to coat that in a few more layers of sugar, Milady?"

I was actually speaking from the heart there. I wasn't trying to spare her feelings or anything.

To begin with, Haru was the kind of girl who, based strictly on looks, was perfectly suited to being part of Team Chitose. She had this casual personality that led her to being treated more like one of the guys, that was all, but it wasn't like she was being purposely self-deprecating.

Still, if I went around saying things like that, it would embarrass us both, so I usually refrained. So then why did I go ahead and run my mouth today, huh?

I spoke again, casually, trying to push down feelings that were too much for me to handle.

"So then, Yuuko, if you please… Make her beautiful! ♪"

"You got it!"

"H-hey! Hold on!!!"

Haru tried to make a break for it, but Yuuko grabbed her and dragged her deeper into the store.

*

"Yes, yes, attention please! Check this out!"

The two of them had gone into the large dressing room together, but it was Yuuko who opened the curtain a little and slipped out. Apparently, she wanted to show off a new outfit of her own as well.

She struck a model pose.

Beside me, Kaito went: "Whoa!"

They weren't exactly hot pants, but she was wearing a pair of damaged denim shorts that barely covered the important areas. And she wore a baggy gray sweatshirt on top like the one Haru had worn, but this one was tucked in. She was also sporting a navy baseball cap pulled down low and round sunglasses with deep-purple lenses.

It was an unusually boyish style for Yuuko, and the contrast was quite appealing. That wasn't all, though. Her curvaceous thighs and ample bust contrasted with the distinctive curve of her waist as well, making her look like a Hollywood A-lister on their day off. Even in the boyish clothing, you could see her feminine form. It was hot. Very, very hot.

"What do you think? Huh?" Yuuko shook her butt like an excitable puppy.

Kaito threw his hands in the air and bellowed, not missing a beat. "Whoa! Amazing! So hot! So cute! Marry me!!!"

"Heh-heh! Something like this isn't so bad every now and again, is it?"

Still talking, she turned to check out my reaction.

I gave her a thumbs-up, and she let her face fall into a silly grin.

"But you know, this isn't even the main dish for today. You're gonna be so shocked! Haru, are you ready?" Yuuko turned and called back into the dressing room.

"No!!!"

"Great, I'll count down from five, then. Five, four..."

"Why even bother asking?!"

"Three, two, one," counted Yuuko, before grasping the curtain. "Zero!"

She yanked the curtain open with a flourish.

...*Nng.* I swallowed reflexively.

Haru wore a semitransparent blue dress. It was embroidered with tiny flowers in a complementing color scheme, and for some reason it made me think of the coming summer. Her bare shoulders peeked out of the off-the-shoulder straps, the nontransparent parts of the fabric hugged her bust, and her bare legs could be seen below the miniskirt part. The overall impression was supremely feminine.

Her hair had been done, too, in the same braided style as Yuuko's, only hers was gathered in a small bun at the nape of her neck. There was a soft yellow scarf tied around her head. I think she was also wearing lipstick, in an orange shade.

Haru stood there with her arms crossed and her head hanging, looking uncomfortable.

"Don't stare so much. It's...embarrassing."

Kaito responded with jaunty nonchalance. "Yuuko, you've got a magic touch! It's like she's not even Haru anymore. She's a girl! A real girl!"

I slammed my elbow into Kaito's side, and Yuuko gave him a karate chop to the top of the head.

"What was that for?"

Haru glanced at me just once, before grinning and responding to Kaito. "Hmm, you know, I really do think boyish clothes that you can freely move around in work well for me. To be honest, even I think I look a bit odd."

"...Haru." I had to speak. "You look really beautiful."

"Huh?! How dare you stand there and make fun of me?!"

Based on her expression, I think I got through to her. Haru was bright red, as she clamped her lips together and turned her back.

Yuuko smiled softly, patting me on the back. *It's things like this that make Yuuko equally popular with boys and girls*, I thought.

I continued. "No, that look really suits you. I really like your usual look, of course, but sometimes it's nice to put on a dress like that, isn't it?"

Haru responded, her back still turned to me. "S-stop... I mean it... No more of that."

Beside me, Yuuko took charge.

"You should totally buy it! We can go and pick out a new lipstick together after, too!"

"Ugh..."

"You're not going to buy it?"

Haru turned around slowly, sneaked a glance at me, and then immediately looked away. "...I'll buy it."

"You gotta!"

I made eye contact with Yuuko, and we both grinned.

Kaito, who was still trying to process what was going on, almost found himself completely left behind.

*

"Hyaagh!"

SMACK.

"Gyaah!"

CLUNK.

"Darn you!"

WHACK.

"Don't take it out on the ball, Haru."

After we were done shopping at Lpa, we headed to a batting center located around ten minutes away by bicycle.

Yuuko had been dropped off at the mall by her parents in the car, so she rode double on Kaito's bike. In her usual style, she stood on the hub step and hammered on Kaito's back, yelling,

"Hurry it up, slowpoke!" Kaito kept saying, "Cut it out!" but he was grinning and obviously wanting people to check him out, which really turned my stomach. *Give it a rest, dude.*

I gave the girls a simple lesson on the basics of batting.

Unable to wait, Haru had already stepped up to bat. She quickly got the hang of it, and soon she was able to hit seventy-kph balls.

Incidentally, she had her new outfit in a shopping bag, and she had changed back into her initial shorts and parka for ease of movement. Her hair was back in its usual short ponytail. Oh, and she had wiped the lipstick off in the bathroom as well.

"Ah, I feel so much better. The batting center is amazing, Chitose."

"Tch, you sports maniac. You ruined my plan of showing off how cool I am. You were supposed to miss every hit."

"You wanted to show off in front of Haru, eh? ♡"

"In return for you showing off something good to me, right?"

"Any more cute quips from you, and I'll swing this bat at you next. ♡"

"I forgot to teach you one very important thing… You never swing the bat at a human being, okay?"

While we were goofing around, Yuuko and Kaito came back from buying us all drinks at the vending machine. Kaito chucked two bottles of Pocari Sweat at us, and Haru and I both caught them one-handed.

"Saku, aren't you batting?"

"I'm playing coach today. Yuuko, you want to hit some?"

"Yeah!"

Yuuko answered perkily and bounced into the batter's booth. Her sophisticated outfit was a mismatch with her bright-red safety helmet, which looked kind of adorable. Holding the elementary schooler bat by her waist, she almost looked like she was posing for a fashion magazine shoot.

The copy would read something like: "On a date with my

boyfriend, who's in the baseball club! Wearing a sophisticated outfit for a cute contrast! ♡"

Incidentally, Haru was swinging an adult-size bat that was a free rental.

WHIRR. CLANK.

The lever of the batting machine went around, spitting out a whole heap of balls.

"Hyup!"

With a hearty grunt, Yuuko swung the bat and hit only air, which sent her spinning around until she fell flat on her butt. Her helmet, which looked to be a bit too big for her, fell over her eyes. She giggled comically, scratching her cheek.

The sight of it was so adorable that I couldn't stop chuckling myself.

"Now listen here, Haru. To be a proper girl…"

"Don't say it. I was just thinking the exact same thing."

Beside me, Haru scrunched her face up into a big frown.

I turned to Yuuko.

"Hold your bat a bit higher up and swing from above the shoulder. You need to hit it more like a tennis ball and rotate your whole body."

"All righty!"

The comparison to tennis seemed to have helped Yuuko grasp things a little better, and she made a vast improvement.

WHIRR. CLUNK.

SMACK.

A foul tip bounced off the bat and flew behind her.

"I hit it! I hit it!"

"Great! Wonderful. You were just a touch too fast on the bat. Try hitting it a bit higher up?"

"Okey-dokey!"

WHIRR. CLUNK.

CLONK.

This time, she hit the ball nicely and sent it flying high over the machine's head.

"I did it! Did you see it, Saku?"

"Perfect."

"Hee-hee, the power of love."

I watched Yuuko, who was shooting me a sparkling smile and a peace sign, and then I turned to Haru beside me again.

"Now listen here, Haru…"

"Agh! Shut up, shut up!"

Bristling and pouting, Haru stomped off to the eighty-kph booth this time, which was faster than her previous one.

…But I was only pointing out the obvious?

✳

After enjoying a pitching game together at the batting center, we all decamped to the nearby Hachiban ramen store to eat a slightly early dinner. That's how much we Fukuians love Hachibans; we never eat anywhere else.

I had my usual spicy noodles with extra noodles and green onions and a double serving of Hachiban gyoza dumplings. Yuuko had salt-and-butter-flavored vegetable ramen, and Haru had pork-broth vegetable ramen and a side of fried rice. Kaito had the C-set, pork broth vegetable *chashu* ramen with plenty of *chashu* pork and a side order of fried chicken.

I was originally planning to order just an ordinary-size side of dumplings, but after hearing Haru's and Kaito's orders, I changed it. I knew they would both be after some of mine.

Once all our orders were delivered, we talked about this and that as we ate. And as I expected, Haru and Kaito both stole three of my dumplings apiece.

"So by the way," Haru commented. "Do you have a crush on Nishino, or what?"

""Whaaat?!""

SPLORT.

"*Gack, cack, agh.*"

I wasn't expecting a question like that from a person like Haru, and I ended up shooting out the mouthful of water I was drinking all over the table.

"Ew, gross! Look, wipe that up, will ya?" Haru shoved a damp towel into my face and began scrubbing.

"Can you stop that? You're acting like you're scrubbing dirt off with a wet dishrag."

"So then, what's the deal?"

"You're unusually persistent."

Now that it had come to this, the other two could hardly be expected to remain silent.

"What's all this? I haven't heard anything about it." Yuuko leaned forward in her seat beside Haru.

Kaito, who was sitting beside me, looked at Yuuko and then narrowed his eyes and brought his face close to mine.

"You. Are you serious about this, Saku?"

"You're the one acting all serious here. Calm down. I haven't even said anything yet."

I took another sip of water and then spoke to Haru, once I'd regained my composure.

"Why are you bringing something like that up all of a sudden?"

Haru dipped one of the dumplings she'd stolen from me in the sauce as she answered. "It's just a hunch. It just struck me as weird that there was this pretty older girl you apparently know right in front of us, and you managed to refrain from making a single terrible joke the entire time."

"You don't have to say they're terrible, you know."

"Besides, I've seen you multiple times since last year. After school, by the riverbank, talking all friendly. I never see you make a face like that any other time."

Oh, that's all it was? Hmm, well, it's not like we were meeting in secret or anything. It wasn't so odd for us to have been seen.

Yuuko, who had been leaning forward, let her shoulders slump. Kaito turned his head to look at me. "Listen. Saku."

"…You be quiet. You'll just make things even more complicated." Still, maybe it was time. I'd caused these guys enough worry.

"Last year, I met her by complete coincidence after quitting baseball club. You've all been trying to spare my feelings by not asking me about the reason why I quit, right?"

Yuuko finally looked up when she heard this. Kaito saw this and seemed a little relieved, which was maybe why he straightened up and responded.

"Yeah, 'cause you were radiating this 'Don't ask me about it' aura."

"You're exactly right. I just didn't want you guys to see my weak side, I guess. Even without me saying anything, you looked like you were going to have a breakdown every day I saw you, Yuuko."

Thinking back on it made me chuckle, but Yuuko pouted.

"I mean…! You weren't yourself back then, Saku. And you wouldn't tell us anything. I had no idea how I should approach you…"

"I know, I know. I appreciate your kindness. And besides, I think if you'd asked, I would have just isolated myself. To me, you guys were the reassuring part of my everyday life. But there was a part of me that just wanted to scream that 'the king's got donkey ears,' you know?"

Below the table, Haru kicked her toe against my Stan Smiths. "So you're saying Nishino was the one you could open up to?"

"The thing about her is, she represents the non-everyday parts of my life. Part of it is that she's older than us, maybe. With her, I can be a kid again, at least a little bit."

In other words, she spoils me.

I can talk to her about anything, and she listens carefully to everything, thinks it over, and offers her own conclusions.

Haru mumbled to herself, gazing out the window with a sort of sad look on her face. "Oh, I see."

Beside her, Yuuko appeared conflicted. "I kinda don't like it, but I guess it's thanks to Nishino that you managed to cheer up, right, Saku? I should be grateful to her, I think."

Everyone seemed satisfied with this, and I was able to resume slurping up the last of my spicy noodles.

✶

Yuuko's mom was picking her up in the car at a nearby convenience store, so we all split up outside of Hachiban.

Haru was heading home in the opposite direction, so we parted ways with her, and then Kaito and I headed off, pushing our bikes side by side.

After a period of silence, Kaito spoke first. "Sorry, Saku. I got a bit heated just then."

"You're always getting heated about something or other."

"Ouch, man!"

"Listen, Kaito…" I paused for effect. "It's better for me to pretend like I don't know anything, until you bring it up, right?"

There was a pause while Kaito processed what I meant, and then he gazed at the red-tinged, distant sky and spoke through his teeth.

"You don't know, Saku? You can't begin the race until someone says 'Ready, set, go' and fires the pistol."

"If you're not on the starting line, you can't begin running even if the signal comes."

"You're not the only one who's got the right to run this race straight from the start, you know."

"You're good at getting all heated up, right?"

"Hotheaded guys aren't popular these days."

We were approaching our separate ways now. Just a little farther, and we'd both be saying "See ya" and going in opposite directions.

I cleared my throat. I wanted to get things straight. "Playing the good guy all the time will make you into someone who just goes with the flow."

"If anyone thinks they can treat me that way...then I'll punch them into next week."

"Uh-huh. I chose the wrong words before."

"I understand that you chose those words for me, not for anyone else."

"Listen, Kaito. You really love me, don't you?"

"I love you *all*."

"Ew, gross."

"Huh?"

Then we both laughed like we were going to bust a gut.

"See ya, Saku."

"See ya, Kaito."

We turned our backs to one another at the T junction and never turned back around.

The path we came by. My path. Kaito's path. Would they meet again? Collide again? I decided not to think about it any further.

*

Monday morning after school, I didn't have anything in particular planned, so I headed up to the rooftop.

I had nothing much to do up there, either, but I had the feeling that if I lay on my back staring at the blue sky, the kind of sky that floats puffily over the ocean, then maybe the dust on my soul would be washed away a little. Or something like that.

I was letting my thoughts roam as I twisted the doorknob and discovered that it wasn't locked. Evidently, someone else was already up here.

Maybe Kura—or even Asuka.

I opened the door expectantly and found that the answer was both of them.

Kura was up on the roof's housing unit puffing on a cigarette, and beside him, Asuka was sitting swinging her legs idly. I knew that he had been her homeroom teacher in first year, but this was my first time seeing the two of them chatting like this.

Asuka noticed me and waved, a little awkwardly.

Kura was his usual Kura-like, laid-back self.

"'Sup, Second-Generation Rooftop Janitor?"

"Did I interrupt something important? Because if so, I can leave."

"Nah, we were pretty much finished. Come on up."

I did as I was told and ascended, taking a seat beside Asuka.

Kura ground his cigarette out in his ashtray.

Then he pulled a crumpled pack of Lucky Strikes out of his pocket right away and lit up another one. After that, he started muttering like it was all no big deal.

"There's the parent-teacher meeting tomorrow, of course, but it looks like Fukui's a done deal, huh?"

For a moment, I couldn't make sense of his sentence.

While I was still lost, Asuka responded. "Hey! Kura!"

"He'll find out sooner or later," Kura said. "Or is it the kind of choice you don't want your little junior classmate who looks up to you so much to hear?"

"…It's not that."

Their back-and-forth made something fall into place. Asuka had chosen Fukui instead of Tokyo for her future, right?

Kura continued. "She's going to be a Japanese teacher. Not a bad choice if you're going to live your life in Fukui."

"Hmm, stellar advice from a Japanese teacher who's nothing but a collection of bad choices in human form," I said, keeping it light for now.

Why was Kura talking about this? Why was Asuka so silent? How did they expect me to react to this? I had no idea.

"Chitose, what have you heard?"

I sneaked a peek at Asuka, who was looking down. Her hair was hanging over her face and making it impossible to read her expression.

Recalling that conversation we had about dreams, I wondered what on earth was going on.

Would it be permissible for me to speak freely about Asuka's life?

Usually, you would reckon not. It was for Asuka to choose whether to discuss it with Kura, though, and maybe the feelings she had gently handed to me were meant to stay between us.

And yet…

If that was the case, then why had Asuka not tried to stop this question from being raised? She wasn't the type to cower before a teacher, much less Kura, with whom she had such a long association.

And why was Kura asking me this question anyway? He was a crazy old dude, for sure, but he was absolutely not the kind of guy who would treat his students' feelings inconsiderately.

My best guess was that Asuka and Kura were at some kind of an impasse, with neither able to take the next step forward.

In that case, what they wanted me to say was, "You want to go to Tokyo, right? In order to become a novel editor."

…Right?

Asuka's shoulders twitched, and Kura exhaled, a sigh mixed with purplish smoke.

"I thought so."

Kura stubbed out his cigarette and got up, sliding his feet into his straw-soled sandals from the random places he'd left them.

"Listen here, Nishino. I don't interject when my students have decided something for themselves. For themselves, you get that?

Remember what I said when I gave you the key to this place? I'm giving it to you because you're freer than anyone else, but also more constricted. You should think about what I meant by that one more time."

Asuka nodded, and Kura shot me a brief but loaded glance before strolling down the stairs with a totally carefree air.

Freer than anyone but also more constricted.

Could I reach the truth behind that contradiction?

Right now, all I could do was place a supportive hand on Asuka's back as the lonely wind blew.

✱

Asuka and I sat side by side on our usual riverbank, by the same old sluice gate.

We were listening to music, old favorites, one earbud each.

I got the feeling it had been a while since we'd last spent time together here like this. I had told Kaito and the others that Asuka had represented the non-everyday parts of my life, but at some point she had blended in to the regular parts. For a moment, I forgot the position I was in and dwelled on that realization instead.

It was so strange but also kind of lovely. I couldn't stop myself from smiling.

Asuka took her earbud out and looked at me, a quizzical expression on her face.

"Why'd you have to say that? In front of Kura, I mean."

"You were begging me to say it. Both you and Kura were."

"Cheeky. But…" She plucked my earbud out, too. "…But I'm glad you were there."

I pretended not to notice the element of weakness in her voice as I responded.

"So why were you talking to Kura?"

"He's taken on the role of guidance counselor for the third-years as well as your homeroom teacher."

"He's not such a bad guy, despite…everything. When I look at Kura, I get to thinking that no matter which path I eventually choose, I can make something fun out of it."

Asuka smiled wide.

I felt like I was watching a performance. And it was a real dud.

"Yeah. I feel like I'm here struggling to choose colleges…"

"Yeah, but—"

I didn't let her continue. "But Kura's being like this because he's actually walking the path he chose for himself, right? I think the guy actually really likes teaching, and he's giving it all he's got."

"…Yeah."

"Is there something you'd like to talk to me about?"

"…Yeah. Since I guess you already asked." Asuka stretched her arms way up. "To state it plainly, my parents—mainly my father—are against it."

"Against you going to college in Tokyo?"

"Yeah. Remember what I told you? My household's actually a pretty strict one. They don't like the idea of a girl living alone, or aiming to become an editor, or leaving Fukui to begin with."

When she said it, I realized you hear this kind of thing a lot.

That's why it's such a difficult issue.

In the end, we're all still children, and it's impossible for us to just ignore our parents' opinions when we make decisions.

"What is it that you want, Asuka?"

"I think you know, right?"

I did. Nobody can oppose your plans until you express them out loud. Asuka continued, just throwing it out there.

"There's nothing to be done about it. I owe them for raising me, and besides, they're really stubborn. If arguing about it isn't going to get me anywhere, I figure I should just accept it and start adjusting my attitude. And hey, if I stay in Fukui, then you and I can go on more dates anytime."

I sighed. She was forcing herself to be cheerful.

"I wouldn't be caught dead on a date under those circumstances. I'm not some consolation prize you get for giving up on your dreams. You're not being you, Asuka."

When I said that, Asuka looked a little despondent. "Not being me?" she said quietly. "What does that even mean? That's just you putting your expectations on me."

Asuka stood up, as if she was trying to put distance between us. She took several steps forward and stared at the river.

Not being you. What *did* I mean?

It was true that I was probably placing my own ideals on her in some ways.

She always acted so much more mature than I did and even her name indicated freedom, gentleness, and strength.

But the real Asuka agonized over things, felt lost, and grew despondent. She was just a high school girl.

"I told you: You romanticize me too much. The real Asuka Nishino is much more ordinary. Like a castle made of papier-mâché. At home, I'm your typical good girl who never disagrees with her father. I had a feeling this day was coming, and if you're just going to be disappointed in me, then…"

But now I was convinced.

I stood up and softly approached Asuka before she could say any more.

I looked at her back. So fragile, liable to break or disappear at any moment, an ephemeral, beautiful back that I had been watching for so long, wanting to be more like her. And then…

I kicked her hard.

"Agh!"

KASPLOOSH.

With a girlish scream, and a huge clap of displaced water, Asuka plunged into the river.

It wasn't deep enough for her to go under, but the shock of it seemed to send her into panic mode. She flailed about for a few moments but eventually managed to scramble to her feet, although she was soaked to the skin.

"What? What the hell?"

Asuka looked up at me, an expression of complete incomprehension on her face.

I sucked in a breath before speaking. "What's with all the bellyaching?! You're saying I romanticize *you*? Quit going back and forth; you're giving me a headache! Just go ahead and turn into a drowned river witch, why don't you?!"

Asuka responded, her voice showing clear anger. Very, very unusual for her.

"The heck? You're the one who kept saying I was like your dream woman or something! Pushing your ideals on me, putting me on a pedestal, and now you're acting all disillusioned with me?! I thought you hated when people did that!"

"…You're wrong." I spoke crisply.

Yep, now I knew for sure.

"First off, I was captivated by the sight of you making that soggy, bullied kid smile right here in this river. Yeah, I idolized you, but it was grounded in reality from the start."

"That was just a random thing that happened…"

"Right—random, and therefore *not* random. Whether I was there to witness it or not, whether I was around to idolize you or not, from the start you were living your own way. Free. Gentle. And strong."

"You're wrong. The only reason I could be like that is…"

"I don't care about your reasons. Think of those precious words you gave to me. You filled up the gaping hole in my heart. Don't go throwing words around carelessly now."

"…Or life will turn monochrome, huh?"

I grinned.

"I still honestly don't know the difference between admiring someone and putting them up on a pedestal. The one thing I do know is that I can say much more of what's good about you than you could." I faced her and held out my hand as I spoke. "Is that not allowed?"

Her surprised eyes were fixed on me, as a smile spread across her face like a flower slowly blooming. She wiped at her eyes, which were streaming either as a result of river water or sudden emotion, and then she took a little breath, readying herself to speak.

"I guess you really are kinda like my hero, aren't you?"

"Don't be ridiculous. You're *my* hero, Asuka."

She took a firm hold of the hand I held out to her, and then—

"Hyah!"

She yanked me down with all her might.

"Whoa!"

KASPLOOSH.

I tumbled headfirst into the river as well.

"Now, you listen here…"

"Watch out! It's dangerous to open your mouth right now!"

Then she began splashing me with water.

"*Glub!* Eurgh, that's gross!"

"Well, I did tell you."

"Say it before you start splashing, then!"

"Your reflexes are surprisingly kinda dull, aren't they?"

"All right, don't move. Or I really will become the river witch and be added to the Seven Wonders of Fuji High (official name TBD)."

After that, we both started splashing each other at the same time.

Splash-splash. Splosh-splosh.

Splash-splash. Splosh-splosh.

We were goofing off and chasing each other around like children.

The spray of the water refracted the sunlight, imbued with color in this one sparkling moment.

As if to guide us home that day. As if to guide us to tomorrow.

"Hey!"

Asuka grinned at me as she spoke.

"Can I hug you right now?"

"Huh?"

But I didn't have time to say anything back. Before I knew it, she'd grabbed me in a full-frontal hug. Not the romantic hugs grown-ups share, but the innocent bear hug a young girl might give her father as she leaps into his arms.

And so I obliged by patting her on the head.

I could detect a fishy stink, the smell of searching for river crayfish as a kid.

"Asuka, you stink."

"Speak for yourself, mister."

"Got any gym clothes?"

"Nope!"

"Me neither. How are we supposed to get home?"

"We let the wind carry us."

"Hmm, well, that's not a bad idea."

I peeled Asuka off of me, since she showed no inclination of letting me go, and her smile was bright and dazzling—and somehow newly unburdened.

"Death is better than an unbeautiful life, right? I'm going to try living like you. Like a glass marble, floating in a bottle of Ramune soda."

"You don't need to be like me. Just be like Asuka, the Asuka you've always been. If you want to do a job that involves bringing meaningful words into people's lives, then you need to start by using them to tell your father that."

After that, we walked home, both of us dripping water.

Behind us, we left a trail, like Hansel and Gretel.

The people heading to town all turned and looked at us with odd expressions, but neither Asuka nor I cared about that. We just kept on laughing.

As I watched her walk through her own front door with a refreshed sort of expression, I knew she was going to be all right.

I could just feel it.

*

"...Hold on a second. What do you mean by that?!"

The following day after school I stopped by the staff room to return some questionnaires I was in charge of gathering up in my role as class president.

It was six PM already. I'd completely forgotten about the deadline for the questionnaires, so you could say it was my fault, but once I remembered, I also had to chase down the sports club members who'd slacked on handing them in, and that had taken me a considerable amount of time.

Kura wasn't there, so I left the stuff on his desk and was just turning to leave when I spotted him sitting in the little alcove used for greeting visitors. If he didn't look too busy, I planned to say hi, so I went over there, and that's when I heard a conversation.

"We've already decided that Asuka will go to Fukui University and then become a civil servant."

Whoever was speaking sounded angry.

There were three people sitting in the alcove, and they were all looking at me. On one of the two facing sofas sat Kura, and on the other sat Asuka and a man in a sharp suit.

He was slim and well muscled, his tie meticulously done up without a hint of slack. He looked like a capable, business-minded guy.

Behind his wire-rimmed, square-framed glasses, his eyes were intelligent but cold as he regarded me.

Asuka had her head hanging low, as if she was embarrassed.

"Ah, Chitose." In contrast to the man opposite him, Kura sounded positively breezy.

"Thanks. Just put the questionnaires on the desk and head home for the day."

"But…"

"I told you to head home. *What right do you have to insert yourself into this conversation?*"

"…"

His voice was firm and invited no argument.

Besides, Kura was overwhelmingly in the right.

Any way you sliced it, I had no right to say even a single word here.

I mashed my lips together and was just about to turn away, when…

"I see. So you're the one, huh?"

The other man was speaking.

"You're the one who's filled Asuka's head with all these wild ideas."

He shoved his glasses up with a forefinger, giving me a look that was almost a glare.

"All right, then, Iwanami. Why not take a seat, then, if you feel like it?"

"Dad."

I'd heard that a parent-teacher meeting was going to be held today, so I figured that's what this was, but now Asuka had given me confirmation. Usually a meeting like this would take place in an empty classroom, but maybe they went over time, or perhaps there was some other reason. Either way, it hardly mattered.

"Excuse me. I'm one of Asuka's juniors. My name's Saku Chitose."

I sat down beside Kura without hesitating.

The man opposite me raised his eyebrows as he scrutinized me. I couldn't make any sense out of what he'd said moments before.

Asuka was hanging her head even lower, looking more and more embarrassed. Beside me, Kura breathed a heavy, dramatic sigh. I ignored them both and looked at Asuka's father.

If I tried to look away now, I got the feeling I'd never have a chance to speak to this man face-to-face again.

Kura sighed again, then cleared his throat. "Come on, Nisshi."

"That's Mr. Nishino to you. Don't mix friendships and work. Right now, you're Asuka's guidance counselor and a teacher, nothing more."

"Tch, you've always been such a stickler for the rules. All right then, Mr. Nishino. So this decision has been made after listening thoroughly to what your daughter has to say, right?"

"There's no need to discuss it. I know Asuka better than anyone else, and I made my decision after first carefully discussing what would make her happiest in life."

"...Pfft!"

I snorted, and Asuka's father looked at me.

"Chitose, was it? It looks like you've got something to say."

I coughed, then responded. "Excuse me. Have you asked Asuka why exactly she wants to go to Tokyo?"

"Apparently, she wants to become a literary editor."

"You think ignoring that dream will make her happy?"

While I was talking, Asuka continued staring at the floor.

She had her hands resting in her lap, but they were bunched into fists, gripping the hem of her skirt.

Asuka's father responded in a bored tone.

"Her dream. That's a convenient word, isn't it? You young people think all of your choices can be justified by claiming you're following your dreams. So you heard from Asuka, then? About why that's her 'dream'?"

"She said she wants to do a job that involves bringing words into people's lives."

"So then let me ask you this. Why can't she just become a teacher of Japanese? Or a librarian? They both involve bringing words into people's lives. And she can make either of those two career paths a reality right here in Fukui."

"Well…"

I wasn't able to come up with a rebuttal, and I found myself falling silent.

"Do you know the chances of success involved in becoming a literary editor?"

"I imagine pretty slim."

"Even more so if you're aiming to enter a top publishing house. More than a thousand new graduates apply and only a few get accepted. The world isn't a kind place, you know. You can't get ahead just because it's your 'dream.'"

"…Maybe she could start off working somewhere smaller and work her way up. That's possible, right?"

"You think the other hopefuls won't be doing the same thing? There are more applicants than positions at any publishing house, a lot more. In order to make Asuka's ideals become a reality, she'll need to get into a place with a good novel publishing department. That's the minimum. And there aren't endless publishing houses like that."

"Even so…"

"You're saying it'll still be worthwhile for her to work her way up? Enter a small publishing house and wreck her mental and physical health working for low pay? It'll be too late when she's worked herself into a corner and finds there's no chance of switching companies. Are you going to step in and take responsibility when that happens, Chitose? Are you going to be the one to take care of Asuka?"

I was suddenly, painfully, aware of my own naïveté.

This man wasn't holding Asuka back because he was exercising his parental rights. He'd been telling the truth when he said he'd considered carefully what would lead to a happy life for his daughter.

"There's a reason they say that you shouldn't make your passions your career. It can make you end up hating your passions. I think it's far better for Asuka to continue to enjoy literature as a hobby, like she's been doing."

Asuka's dad saw that I wasn't going to say anything in response, and he continued, in a matter-of-fact tone.

"If she stays in Fukui, then she'll have her family home nearby in case anything happens. She'll have us. The civil servant exam won't be any trouble for a girl like Asuka to pass. Then all she has to do is find a nice man and build a home, live a long and happy life. Is it so wrong for a parent to want such things for his daughter?"

I couldn't withdraw.

If I conceded now, then Asuka's future would be all but decided.

I had to say something, anything, keep the conversation going.

"When I was sinking into despair, and every day seemed gloomy and cloudy to me, it was the words that Asuka brought to me that saved me. I believe she's got what it takes to beat the odds, no matter how stacked against her they are."

"How many students do you think ended up failing to get admitted to Fuji High after believing they had what it took to beat the odds? And aren't you that baseball kid who thought you were going to go pro, only to end up quitting? Baseless confidence. Nothing but delusion."

"…"

Those words cut me deep.

This time last year, I was filled with that exact kind of confidence. I never could have dreamed that I'd end up quitting baseball the way I did.

"Listen here, Chitose. If it's a parent's duty to respect their child's wishes, then it's also their duty to guide them along the right path. I've already had this same conversation with Asuka that you and I are having now. It's done. Neither you nor Asuka have been able to say anything to sway me."

What this guy was saying, as a parent, was right. I really thought that.

But it wasn't the only correct option.

He was right, in his point of view—but who gets to decide when there are multiple correct answers?

The one who has to live with the responsibility for the choice.

I could line up a bunch of arguments against him, but that would only make him say, "What's it got to do with you anyway?"

What right do you have to insert yourself into this conversation?

"You're a smart man," said Asuka's father. "I think you've seen how this conversation is going to end. Asuka's always been a smart girl as well. When the logic lines up, she's never once defied me. That's why I was a little surprised when she dug in her heels over this. I guess that's your influence, Chitose?"

No, I wanted to say.

I just gave Asuka a little push. A little push for the feelings that were smoldering inside her.

Asuka's father continued. "Right. If a conversation could have been had with both you and your parents, then maybe you'd have a little more of a leg to stand on."

He stopped talking then and looked at Asuka, who had been silent all this time.

"But this is *my* daughter's future we're talking about."

I didn't have anything left to say.

Kura patted me on the shoulder.

"Then it's settled. We'll go ahead and provisionally pencil in Fukui U as Asuka's first-choice college."

Asuka's father let the corner of his mouth twitch up. "I thought I told you to put it down as her final decision."

"You shouldn't underestimate how fast these kids grow up. You should know that better than anyone, Nisshi. One day they're a little chrysalis, the next they're a full-grown lion."

"That's Mr. Nishino to you, Kura. You never change, do you?"

"Well, you have. You've become a strict and logic-driven father."

"When you've been a teacher long enough, you'll come to understand it someday."

Then Asuka's father rose from the sofa and exited the alcove.

Asuka followed, whispering "I'm sorry" as she passed me by.

"I guess the version of me you saw really was just a phantom after all."

Give me a break.

As I listened to her footsteps walking away, those words repeated in my head like a refrain.

*

I didn't seem to be able to get off the sofa somehow. Then Kura spoke to me.

"Chitose, you got any plans after this?"

"…No, I'm free, but why?"

"Come for a drink, then."

"Huh?"

It would look bad for me to be seen getting into a teacher's car on school grounds, of course, so I waited for him a little ways off.

As if to mirror my inner state, the damp, depressing rain that had been falling since morning soaked me through to the skin.

The water droplets that had looked so beautiful to me yesterday now seemed like black ink trying to smear the world. I would have given up if it was a heavy downpour, but it wasn't really coming down that hard. Carrying an umbrella would have just been an annoyance in this weather. The kind of rain that couldn't commit.

A car horn blared stupidly.

I looked over toward the sound and saw Kura's blue Nissan Rasheen stopped with its hazard lights on.

When I opened the passenger-side door, there was already a plastic convenience store bag full of garbage sitting there. I tied the handles and tossed it onto the back seat. It made a rustling thump as it landed among a pile of other similar bags.

"Can't you be less of a slob? Maybe straighten up and find a girlfriend?"

"Still so naive. If I could get a girlfriend, my car wouldn't look this way in the first place."

"I think perhaps the fact that you're a self-deprecating old fart who leaves a disaster zone like this untended is the reason why the ladies aren't exactly knocking down your door."

"Hmm. It's a real chicken-or-egg conundrum."

"It's a 'clean your damn car' conundrum!"

Kura released the emergency brake, put it into drive, turned off the hazard lights, and then pulled away.

Had he customized the car, perhaps? The interior was all in blue, the same as the exterior paint job. As Kura pressed down on the accelerator, the needle moved on the classic-style tachometer.

After driving for around five minutes, Kura parked the car haphazardly at a metered parking spot in front of Fukui Station. I followed as he meandered along, and blue neon lights and red lanterns with familiar logos came into view.

I spoke up sarcastically. "You're taking a student to Akiyoshi?"

"It's the best place in Fukui to grab a drink."

Akiyoshi is a grilled-chicken-skewer chain, real soul food for the locals, up there in popularity with Hachiban Ramen, sauce katsudon, and soba with grated daikon. Every now and then, it gets reported that Fukui has the highest grilled-chicken-skewer consumption in Japan, and whether that's true, Akiyoshi's presence is definitely a significant one.

We passed through the automatic doors, and the shop staff greeted us with lively voices.

"Welcome, Presidents!"

By the way, this is an Akiyoshi quirk. They refer to all the male customers, from elementary schoolers to old folks, as President (as in, company president) and to all the ladies as Madam.

Kura and I followed the waiter in and sat down at the counter.

"Kura, I'm wearing my school uniform."

"Relax. People will think we're brothers."

"More like father and son, old man."

A dude with a big chest that strained underneath his waiter uniform took our order.

"What'll it be?"

"A pint of beer, and what'll you have to drink?"

"You're a teacher. You're *driving.*"

"Relax. I'll call a designated driver service."

"Then, get me a ginger ale."

"You're boring. Let's see, then, we'll start with ten *shiro* pork, ten *kei* chicken, ten deep-fried, ten spring onion, ten *piitoro* pork, and then cabbage with salt, and…" Kura looked at me.

"I'll take an assortment."

"Comin' up."

The waiter responded cheerily, turning to report our order to the folks back behind the grill.

Now, that might sound like a lot of food, but the special thing about Akiyoshi's grilled chicken skewers is that they're small enough to eat in one bite even if your mouth isn't huge, so it's normal to order several units of ten skewers at once.

Incidentally, *shiro* is a kind of pork offal, *kei* is a kind of chicken with a nice texture, and *piitoro* is fatty pork. Cabbage is literally just raw cabbage pierced on a skewer; then you can choose to have it with salt, Worcestershire sauce, or mayonnaise. I asked for an assortment, which comes with both Worcestershire sauce and mayonnaise on it.

The beer, ginger ale, and cabbage were delivered right away, so we clinked our glasses together in a toast.

Kura glugged his mug of beer, draining half of it like there was never anything more delicious. Then he went "Ahhh" and lit up a Lucky Strike.

"So then." He sucked in a joyful mouthful of smoke before speaking again. "How are you feeling? The father of the girl you're after just told you, 'I'm never giving you my daughter…'"

"I didn't realize I was there asking for his daughter's hand."

"Well, how do you feel? After acting the big, brave hero and getting defeated?"

"…I haven't been defeated. Not yet."

"Ah, that's the spirit. A gutsy response." Kura crunched on a cabbage leaf.

The waiter returned, putting ten sticks each of *shiro*, *kei*, and *piitoro* down on the counter's silver hot plate.

We were also handed little dishes containing several kinds of sauce and mustard. Another Akiyoshi special feature. *Shiro* and spring onion goes well with one kind of sauce, *kei* and *piitoro*, another. Basically, you have to pair up sauces with different skewers in combinations that work. I usually drench everything in one sauce, except for the breaded ones and the *piitoro*.

I dipped my *shiro* in the sauce that was full of minced garlic and took a bite. It's offal, but it doesn't have that offal stink, and it goes down easy. I reached for my second skewer. I was pretty hungry. Probably caused by all that tension back there.

I used to come here every now and then with my family, but it's not really the kind of place high school kids come to eat. It must have been three years since I ate here last.

Kura dipped his *kei* in mustard and began gnawing away at it.

After eating a *kei* and a *piitoro*, I cleared my throat.

"Do you agree with what Asuka's dad...Mr. Nishino was saying?"

"Does it look like I agree with him?"

"I mean, it seemed like you two were acquainted."

I didn't think it was the right time to bring it up during the talk, but the two of them didn't seem like just a parent and his kid's teacher.

"Nisshi was my high school homeroom teacher."

"I see. So that's what that was about."

During the summer Koshien high school baseball tournament, Fukui always gets introduced as the prefecture that has the second-fewest number of participating schools in the country. In this kinda place, it's not so unusual for a former homeroom teacher to reencounter one of his old pupils, grown and now a teacher themselves. It's not a rarity for your daughter's homeroom teacher to have been one of your former pupils.

"I'm a teacher at a fancy college prep school now, but during my own high school days, I was pretty wild. It wasn't quite at the level of Yan High, but my school at the time was pretty low in the rankings, lots of delinquent students. And I guess you could say I was one of them."

"It's really lame for an old man to be bragging about being a delinquent in high school, you know."

"Did you say something, my bro?"

"Like I said, no one would believe we're brothers."

It was hard to picture it, with how easygoing he was, but then again, he did easily manage to block Yanashita's kick when I came to him for help with Nanase's stalker incident. He was probably telling the truth about being a tough guy in his youth.

But we were getting off the subject.

"This is just a guess, but maybe it was Mr. Nishino who turned you around back then? Maybe back then he used to be more of a passionate educator or something?"

"You're right about the first part. Way off on the second. Yeah, he's the reason I straightened up, but Nisshi's always been the type to block off all of someone's escape routes with the violence of reason."

"I thought it'd be the start of negotiations, but it's just how I guessed it."

"However..." Kura slathered his deep-fried breaded skewer with sauce and mustard as he continued. "He's never been the kind of guy to block someone else's decision with his own reasoning. He kept telling me how miserable my life would be if I carried on the way I was going, but he also said that in the end the most important thing is to find your own way."

"Your own way, huh."

"Nisshi was still a young man back then. I don't know whether the years have changed his mindset, whether he's just overly protective of his daughter, or if there's another reason behind it..."

"Still, I don't think he's wrong in what he's saying."

When I said that, I got a quick grin in return.

"The birth of a youth with a rapidly widening point of view, eh. And here I was thinking you were going to throw a punch at the man. Hmm, I would've had to toss you out by your ear if that happened, though."

"I couldn't do that. The thing he said about considering his daughter's happiness first—I didn't get the sense he was lying."

"I agree."

Kura hailed the waiter and added on another five sticks of *shiro*, five sticks of *kei*, five sticks of tongue, five sticks of tripe, some shishito peppers, some fried tofu with grated daikon, a *shochu* on the rocks, and another ginger ale. Then he continued.

"Being a teacher's a tough job, you know."

"Can't you talk about that in another setting, maybe? One where you'll sound a little more convincing?"

"Just listen."

Kura took the glass of *shochu* from the waiter and chugged it down.

"When you think about it, you shouldn't have to take responsibility for a bunch of kids still wet behind the ears, unless it's your own kid. But in this job, every year, you've gotta take charge of hundreds of them."

"Hmm, well, that's certainly true."

"It'd be nice if they could all graduate smoothly and go on to make their dreams come true, sure, but the world's not made that way. In the shadow of the kids who succeed, you've got an uncountable number of kids suffering setbacks, failures, regrets... And in this job, you've got to be right there witnessing all of it."

"So you're saying we should just trust whatever the teachers say?"

"Hah! No way." Kura snorted, then drained his glass of *shochu*. "There's a ton of teachers, myself included, who don't have the life experience or ability needed to guide every single kid. The thing is, just like how you and Nishino read books and get to thinking you know what it's like to live all these different lives, teachers see their students and get to thinking they know what it's like for humankind."

I'd never usually admit to it, but I actually did trust Kura a lot, and I respected him, too. There aren't a lot of teachers out there who really take notice of their students the way he does.

To be honest, the things he was saying were really resonating with me right now.

I ended up voicing a question that had been on my mind. "Kura, why'd you decide to become a high school teacher?"

"Because I knew I'd get to live in a kind of heaven, with

daisy-fresh high school girls delivered to me in fresh batches every year."

"You'd better not say something like that again, or you won't be getting into heaven. Tch. I'm asking here if you were influenced by Mr. Nishino, you know, like he helped you change your life, and then you started to idolize him—something like that."

"Gah." Kura lit up another Lucky Strike and chuckled a little. "I did decide to straighten up and fly right, but it's not like I started wanting to be a teacher right away or anything. It's more like, Nisshi was the only decent adult template around that I had to go by."

"Something like that, huh."

"That's life. Not everything unfolds dramatically like a play."

"Have you ever had times where you had regrets, as a teacher?"

"Obviously. When I have to deal with brats who haven't shown growth since elementary school despite being full of smarts and leadership, and when I have to deal with brats who've got talent but keep on underestimating themselves. Wasting their youth, chasing their tails. Fools."

"That first one can't possibly be a veiled reference to me, right?"

"But the odd thing is: I've never once looked back and wished I'd never become a teacher. You picked your path. Take responsibility for it and get on with it. Like that."

This old dude really is cool, I thought, not that I'd ever say it out loud.

Even if he was drunk and wouldn't even remember this talk tomorrow.

"All right, Chitose. I'm feeling pretty good. For our next pub crawl stop, I'll take you along to my favorite titty bar, Don't Make Me Take Off My Blazer."

"I recently saw the bare boobs of a beautiful high school girl, so I'm good."

"Stick a grilled chicken skewer up your nostril and die."

"Watch your choice of words, Japanese Language Teacher."

After that, we had a great time engaging in bawdy talk, and after finishing off our meal with some of Akiyoshi's finest crispy fried rice balls and *akadashi* miso soup, we left the restaurant.

*

The next day, and the day after that, I had zero chances to talk to Asuka.

I looked for her at school as much as I could, and I waited for her at our usual riverside spot, reading books to pass the time, but it was starting to look like she was avoiding me intentionally.

Three days had now passed since the parent-teacher meeting, and I was leaning against the glass of the entryway door, the same way I'd done not so long ago, reading a copy of Yoshinaga Fujita's *Aisazu ni wa Irarenai* that I'd picked up at the bookstore in front of the station, waiting for Asuka.

The sky was clear outside, unlike that day, and a hint of twilight was beginning to mingle with the air.

I must have been standing there for close to two hours. It wasn't like anyone was watching me, so I guess I didn't need to feel self-conscious about it, but I still felt like a stalker.

"Chitose?"

Hearing my name, I lifted my chin from my book to see Nanase standing there in a baggy T-shirt and long shorts, her practice gear, looking at me with a curious expression on her face.

Her hair was disheveled, cheeks colored, and she was wearing sweaty workout clothes.

It was such an unreal sight that I couldn't help staring.

"What are you doing, standing around here?"

I slipped a bookmark between the pages of the book I'd been reading and closed it before answering her nonchalantly. "Just waiting for someone."

"Oh, you are, are you?"

"What are *you* doing? Isn't it a bit soon for practice to be over?"

"I lost against Haru, playing one-on-one, and the loser had to go and buy sports drinks."

She was holding a couple of plastic bags from the convenience store, and I could see the 500 ml bottles of Pocari Sweat inside.

"Ms. Misaki's pretty lax, huh, letting you goof off like that during club practice."

"She was all for it. She said it'd be a nice change of pace, get that rival spirit going."

"Yeah, but you could have just bought two or three of the big bottles, you know?"

"It's supposed to be a punishment… Darn Haru."

I pictured Haru bossily giving orders while grinning, and I snorted air through my nose.

"Still, I guess that's the jock code of conduct. Losers don't get to complain."

"Hmph. She won't get me next time. The instant she lets her guard down, she won't know what hit her."

"You're talking about basketball, right?"

Nanase came to lean against the door beside me, putting the bags down with a heavy clunk. Rustling around, she grabbed one of the bottles and pressed it to my cheek. "Here. Share the wealth, I say."

"Are you inviting me to do a sweaty workout with you?"

"No way. I don't want to see my ex-boyfriend crying. I've got a samurai's compassion, you know."

"Is that how you see things?"

"You and I are alike, remember?"

I grinned wryly, remembering similar conversations we had.

"Darn, we never should have broken up."

"Face up to your feelings. They're important. That way, you won't wallow in regrets after you end up losing someone. That's the lesson."

It felt like she knew everything, saw everything.

"You know, Yuzuki, you really are a serious catch."

"Thanks, Saku."

Then Nanase heaved both bags off the ground and disappeared in the direction of the gym.

I was chugging the bottle of Pocari Sweat I was still holding, when...

Clunk, clunk.

Someone knocked on the glass behind my head.

I knew without turning around that it was Asuka.

But when I did turn around, she seemed almost sulky, different from what I'd been picturing.

Looking away, Asuka said, "It's not what we talked about!"

"What isn't?!"

"When I came down to the shoe lockers, I saw you from behind. I felt a mix of fear, melancholy, and also somehow relief... I pictured it going like this."

"Knock-knock."

"Asuka."

"I guess I can't keep running from you, huh. I've been thinking... I should really talk things out with you one more time. Let's go... to our usual spot."

"Or something like that!"

"How was I supposed to know?" I shot back, and she pouted even more.

"But why? You're supposed to be waiting for the older girl you look up to, but instead I catch you flirting with the cute girl from your class you've got history with?! I was so taken aback, I missed my chance to storm off, you know?!"

"Calm down, Asuka. This isn't your character at all."

Asuka coughed loudly, her expression growing fragile. "I guess

I can't keep running from you, huh. I've been thinking…I should really talk things out with you one more time. Let's go…to our usual spot."

"It's a bit late to start over now, don't you think?"

✳

Then, at our usual riverside spot, Asuka began to talk, her head hanging low.

"I'm sorry I caused so much trouble for you."

"It was my choice to join in. You shouldn't feel bad, Asuka." I kept one eye on her as I continued. "Actually, I guess I'm the one who should say sorry. To be honest, I came barging into that situation without even really being prepared."

"That's why you're so wonderful."

"No, not at all. Your father raised you with a lot of love, and I had no right to stand there and talk like that."

Asuka smiled with some embarrassment and hung her head again. "He's not…a bad guy."

"I know. If he was a bad guy, I never would have backed down the way I did. Your dad's decent. A good father."

"If you say it, then it must be true."

I was sure that Asuka already knew it was true herself. That was why she was drawing the line.

Maybe she would've been happier if she could have stayed an honest, open little kid. In this world, there's a lot of kids who go barging into situations and pushing for their own selfish whims for the flimsiest of reasons, and there's an equal number of parents out there who cave in and just accept it.

But Asuka wasn't like that.

She was the type to feel indebted to her parents for raising her, the type to understand the logic behind what her parents were saying. The type to seriously consider real-life issues like financials.

"But you know," I said, "you really can't just give up on your dreams."

Asuka looked at me but didn't speak.

"I think your father's right in what he's saying, sure. The majority of people come up against situations in their lives where they have to give up on things. But I think it's really wrong to give up just because someone else is making you do it."

"You're one to talk," she muttered.

I tried to smile as gently as I could. "That's right, Asuka. I *am* one to talk."

Asuka's eyes widened suddenly, and she looked down, still mumbling. "I'm sorry… I'm the worst."

I shook my head slowly. "It's okay. I think you must be a little tired. But don't worry about me right now. Worry about yourself."

"I thought I could be more like you, only…"

I felt a little guilty.

More like me. It was kind of her to say that. But in this type of situation, my parents certainly wouldn't be kicking up a fuss. They were the kind of parents who were fine with their high school–age son living completely alone. As long as I had a good reason behind it, they'd accept my post–high school plans, whether I wanted to go to Fukui U or Tokyo or wherever. They wouldn't comment. They'd just send money, like it was a foregone conclusion.

So I really couldn't share Asuka's troubles with her on the same level.

I had a sense of limitless freedom that I'd gained through letting go of my own dream. People who were still pursuing theirs didn't have that luxury.

Somehow, I got the feeling that really wasn't fair. But we all have to swim in that sea of unfairness. All of us.

While I remained silent, Asuka continued. "You know, when

you turned to me back then, you said you admired the way I live, that I seemed so free. I was so glad to hear you say that. I've always wanted to be that kind of person. I felt like I'd gotten a little bit closer to who I wanted to be. I felt validated."

I was about to say something, but she cut me off. "Thing is, though... I guess I've got a long way to go still. The way I am right now...I can't show you anything better. I'm all out. I watched how you got back on your feet after a much, much more painful experience, and I don't want to drag you into this any further... I wasn't trying to be like a big sis to you just for it to end up like this."

With an endlessly sad smile, Asuka got to her feet.

The sunset-colored wind blew past.

It blew too far, as if it was trying to blow all the way back to yesterday. Or maybe it was trying to blow toward tomorrow. Either way, it was a strong wind.

Asuka tucked her hair behind her left ear and spoke.

"So this is where I say good-bye to you."

"Asuka..."

"I won't forget the time we spent together. Our chats by the river, the music we listened to. Our first and final date. I'll keep my memory of you tucked up in the photo album of my heart, and I'll never forget those fleeting moments of youth I shared with that amazing guy one year my junior."

She turned and started walking away, and I stared at her back. Always one step ahead of me, always the one I looked up to.

Give me a break.

The words kept repeating in my head like a refrain.

I felt a sharp pain and unclenched the fists I'd been holding as I found myself completely lost in the night.

*

The next day, I dragged myself around like a deflated balloon and made it to the end of the day somehow.

I caught a glimpse of Asuka in the library room once, but she seemed to be in the middle of studying with Okuno. That sight made me even more depressed.

Haru and Yuuko, who were by my side, kept asking if something was wrong, but it wasn't the kind of thing I could turn to my friends for advice about. Besides, I still wasn't sure if I should try to do something about this or not.

Until Asuka herself asked me to help her, I knew I had to keep my nose out of it.

The only thing I had left was the vestiges of a small promise I wasn't even sure she remembered making.

After homeroom, I wanted to find something, anything to do and reset myself mentally. That's when I caught sight of Kenta, getting ready to head home with a surprising amount of pep.

I flopped onto my desk and called out to him. "What are you looking so happy about? You got a hot date?"

Kenta whipped around in surprise, then came right over with a spring in his step. "It's not a date, King! It's far more serious! I'm talking marriage! I'm off to collect my new wife!"

"Hold on; you're not making any sense."

"It's the release date for the newest volume from my biggest-ever fandom! And there's even a special Animate limited-edition version! You read it, too, King, remember?"

Then he reeled off a title, one of those light novel series that I did indeed own copies of myself. When I was trying to convince Kenta to come out of his room, I read every book in the series so I could build some common ground with him. To be honest, I was a little curious to see what was going to happen in the next volume.

"What do I have to lose?" I found myself muttering. "Maybe I'll go with you..."

Kenta's eyes lit up.

"Are you serious?! Let's go, let's go! And there's so many great series you haven't read yet, King; let me show them to you! If you spot any series with great illustrations that really grab you, there's a good chance I can lend you my own copies! I'm happy to do it! I've got backups! I'm like a missionary distributing vital texts; that's how I see it! Heck, I'll give you a whole set to keep for free if you like!"

"Ah... Uh-huh."

I'd heard of this, the fabled otaku info dump.

And it was starting to sound like the rumors I'd heard of otaku buying multiple sets of the same thing wasn't just an urban legend, either. Apparently, they bought one set to read, one to preserve, one to display, and another for handing out to others they wanted to get hooked on the series. I couldn't quite process the concept of buying a separate set to keep on display, much less any of the other stuff.

As I gave in to Kenta's enthusiasm, Kazuki came over, laughing obnoxiously.

"What's the commotion? What are we talking about?"

"Uh, Kenta's heading to Animate, apparently, so I was thinking I'd go with."

"Really? Maybe I'll come, too. Then after, we can grab dinner on the way home."

"Huh? Don't you have club practice?"

"The coach has some business outside of school today, so nope."

He was right there, listening to our conversation, eyes sparkling all over again.

"Seriously? Let's go, let's go, Mizushino, let's go! Now, I get the impression you don't usually read light novels, so I'll lend you a series I believe would be the best pick for a first-timer! But I think you should take a peek at the artwork and the blurbs for a couple of series as well and see what speaks to you; that's the beauty of it, you know, the discovery, and—"

""All right, all right.""

Kazuki and I both took a step backward as Kenta began rambling passionately again.

And so the three of us ended up heading to the Animate in front of Fukui Station.

I'd hung out around this area tons of times before with Kazuki and Kaito, but we usually went to eat or to the Loft inside the department store, or MUJI, or to one of the fancy clothing stores Kazuki liked. Either that or we hung out at the nearby general bookstore. To be honest, I'd never even realized there was an Animate here before.

Okay, if I'm being really honest, I did recall seeing that blue storefront before, but the only thing that registered with me about it was, "There sure are a lot of capsule toy machines in front of that store."

I was expecting something a little more for the hard-core otaku, since this was the spot Kenta was bringing us to, but the shelves were actually filled with mostly normal shounen manga, which Kazuki and I both read. It turned out it was more of a bookstore with a strong emphasis on manga, light novels, and anime, rather than some sort of otaku heaven.

There were even some totally normal-looking high school girls there who didn't look the least bit weebish.

Before, when I was seeking out the light novels Kenta read, I'd needed to go to four different bookstores to find them all, and it was a real pain. But this store had all of them under one roof.

I felt like going back in time and whacking the culprit on the head, saying, "You shoulda told me about this place earlier!"

Present-day Kenta seemed to quickly locate the book he was

looking for, and then he dragged me to the light novel section and began proselytizing.

Incidentally, Kazuki had escaped after sensing the danger and was busy browsing through the free previews in the manga section.

"King, King, what about this one? *I Was a Huge Shut-in Nerd, but Now I'm Hanging with the Cool Kids?!*"

"I've had enough of the 'dorky kid gets popular' trope," I responded wearily.

"Then what about something from the opposite angle? *I Started Off a High-Spec Popular Kid and Carried on Living a Peerless High School Life Surrounded by Babes?*"

"What kind of ridiculous title is that? Who the hell would read that?"

"I don't think the author would be pleased to hear that from the likes of you."

*

I ended up buying two books that Kenta recommended, and then we left the store.

"Who wants to eat?"

I posed the question as I stashed the books in my day bag, and Kazuki replied.

"Hachiban or katsudon?"

"It's not like those are the only two options available in this town. Let's eat something different for once."

Kenta, who was walking a few steps behind us for some reason, continued. "What about Burger King, then?"

"Hmm, not bad. We only get the chance to eat it by the station, after all."

Kazuki was down, and I had no reason to object, so we headed to the Happiring shopping mall near the station.

We arrived at the building, which had a strange ball-shaped structure attached to it that brought to mind a well-known TV station. I still hadn't been there, but apparently the ball thing was some kind of planetarium with ultra-high, 8K resolution.

A thought flashed through my mind, that this would be a great place to come to with Asuka for a little recreational fun, but I cut it off. First, I had to focus on my own recreation.

We entered Burger King on the second floor, and I ordered a bacon cheeseburger set, while Kazuki ordered a double cheese-burger set, and Kenta had a teriyaki Whopper Jr. set.

There were some seats by the glass wall, which offered a full view of the rotary in front of the station, so we sat there. Then we all started eating.

Tossing a french fry into his mouth, Kazuki said, "Unusual group we've got today, huh."

"Hey!"

It wasn't me who answered, of course, but Kenta.

Kazuki chuckled and continued. "Who'd have thought you'd end up eating fast food in a group after school like this, Kenta."

"I mean, you're not wrong. If I was still the same guy I was before my shut-in incident, I wouldn't even register on your radar, Mizushino."

"Not so. I would have noticed you. With scorn, of course."

I jumped in then. "That's right, Kenta. This angel-faced, secret playboy of a wicked prince once said, *'That kid isn't the type who belongs in a group like ours. I don't discriminate, but I do differentiate.'*"

"Really?! But when I first tried talking to him, I thought he was a total gentleman on the inside as well as out… I was totally impressed, dammit!"

Kazuki waved a hand, aloof. "Well, I'm fine with anyone socially as long as I'm fine with them personally. In terms of pri-orities, I place cute girls first, then my guy friends. But it struck me as a fruitless endeavor to go out of our way and add an ex-shut-in to our circle."

"I get it."

"No, you don't."

Kenta was nodding understandingly, and I had to knock him down a peg or two.

"But you know…" The guy with the angel face was still talking. "Right now, I think of you as my friend, Kenta. I like people who are doing their best to improve themselves and move forward."

"Heh… I like you, too. ♡"

"Kenta, want to go somewhere after this where we can get cozy?"

"I'm down. ♡"

"Quit swooning over him! Don't fall for his tricks."

I had to jump in again, and then the three of us burst out laughing.

Then a thought came to me, and I changed the subject. "By the way, Kazuki. Did you ever go through a rebellious period?"

"Nope. Too low-return."

"That checks out. For you."

"Does this have something to do with why you've been moping all day?"

Taking my silence as a yes, Kazuki chuckled and continued.

"The thing is, when you get to our age, we're capable of considering things for ourselves, taking action for ourselves, and so on. Maybe not as capable as adults, sure, but we *are* capable, and we *want* to do that. Your parents are kinda unusual, Saku, in that they really respect that. But a lot of parents, their image of their kids seems to be frozen around elementary school–age."

"There's a huge difference between a boy in elementary school and one in high school."

"Right. You grow pubic hair, you learn how to jack off, some even start having sex. But to our parents, we're just obnoxious kids they need to take charge of and guide. Until we can find a way to bridge that gap in perspective, there's no talking to them."

Kenta continued, looking apologetic. "I guess when you put it that way, I certainly can't deny it. I've sure acted like the brattiest brat who ever needed guiding."

He's right, I thought. "That reminds me, we've got the poster boy for the rebellious period right here. I bet your parents were like, 'Get your butt back to school' at first, huh? But you stayed shut away in your room. How did that feel?"

When I asked him that, he looked down in embarrassment and cleared his throat.

"The main crux of it was that I just didn't want to go, but… now, with the benefit of hindsight, I can see that if my parents had really pushed to find out the reason, I would've felt really isolated, like I was the only one who really understood how I felt."

"Hmm, I see."

"An adult could have seen the correct answer immediately, but we tend to suffer in silence, and debate the right way to go, and feel really bad about things. We may reach the same conclusion in the end, but none of us want to skip over the soul-searching and have the answer just thrown in our faces."

"It's the age where the simplest romantic rejection feels like the end of the world, after all."

Kenta was shrinking down in his seat, but we weren't trying to make fun of him here.

To be honest, what he was saying had actually given me an epiphany.

When parents look at us, they see the past. But to us, that's the future. I think that's the key here.

"Maybe this is a hindsight is twenty-twenty kind of opinion, but…"

Kenta was continuing.

"Even if we're going about things the wrong way, we need to wade through our complicated feelings and face up to ourselves in order to come out the other side. That's how I ended up here, meeting you, King, and the rest of the group. To be honest, I've got zero regrets. I guess in the end, no matter what kind of choices are ahead, as long as you can be sure you've made the choice you truly wanted to make, then that's how you end up constructing your future self... I dunno, I'm not putting this well."

"It looks like being dumped and shutting yourself up in your room awakened the philosopher inside you."

"I wish I hadn't said anything now!"

Kazuki grinned. "You really are an amusing guy, Kenta, aren't you? Saku was right all along."

"Right?" As I answered, my expression grew serious. "I'm so much smarter and sharper than either of you two."

"Two? Don't lump me in with Kenta."

"You've gotta draw the line early on. Draw the line here... You're probably not going to be a pro baseball player. You're probably not going to be able to fix being a shut-in at this point, so draw the line there. Even if you've fallen for someone, there's no guarantee they'll like you back. Draw another line. That way, you'll never get your feelings hurt; you'll never have to struggle. You'll feel confident that you can keep living well in the future, too."

"When you're not the type to get fired up about anything."

Kazuki smiled, a little bit sadly. "I don't think that's such a bad way to be. I like to see other people getting fired up, but I don't want to be one of them—the kind of person who gets so fired up they stop being able to see the ground beneath their feet. Instead of a high-risk, high-return venture, I prefer a low-risk, low-return venture that's close by."

I thought about Asuka's father.

I was still dealing with a lingering feeling of annoyance after the parent-teacher meeting, an unwillingness to accept it. But now, hearing the same kind of story from friends I respected, it was sort of a punch to the gut.

It was like Kura said. That guy, as a teacher, must have had to watch over countless students who tried to bite off "high-risk" mouthfuls only to find they couldn't chew them.

Kazuki spoke then, as if wrapping up the conversation.

"But the weird thing is, in this world, there *are* some people who get those high returns when they go after something high-risk. You might say those people have something special, but one thing's for sure: I don't have it."

I couldn't think of anything to say in return. I just stared at the dark rotary in front of the station down below.

The illuminated, animatronic dinosaurs were moving, just like they always did.

*

That night, I had just gotten into bed and was planning to go to sleep when I got a message on the LINE app.

Are you free tomorrow night?

Yeah.

Can I come to your place?

Sure.

She sent a stamp back, but I closed my eyes without responding to it.

*

"'Sup."

"Hey. So what did you want to come over for?"

"Well, what would you like me to come over for?"

"How did you make that sound so suggestive?"

The following night, Friday, Nanase showed up at my place.

She must have come straight from club practice. When she passed me coming through the door, I got a whiff of sweet deodorant.

She put down her sports bag in the corner of the room and gave me a flirtatious look. "Just thought I'd better check that there aren't any telltale signs of another woman around."

"There aren't any signs of you, either."

When I said that, she chuckled and pulled out a crinkly plastic bag.

"I thought we could eat dinner together. Look, a jumbo-size *gyudon* beef bowl with lots of spring onions and an egg on top."

"That's an unusually masculine choice. If you can't whip up a home-cooked meal, at least go for something like a fancy pasta dish. There are plenty of options."

"You're already getting home-cooked meals from certain ladies I could mention. Besides..." She stopped then and looked up at me with languid eyes. "Guys like this kind of food, don't they?"

"Ah, I can't argue with you there!"

I chopped up some carrot, daikon, and leek and whipped up a simple miso soup, which I brought to the table.

Looking pleased, Nanase put her hands together. Her expression was radiant.

"Thanks for the food!"

"Thanks."

I put some dressing on the salad she'd bought to go along with the *gyudon* and took a sip of miso soup. It had a slightly lighter flavor than the soup Yua always made, but it wasn't bad.

"It's so good! It's warming me right through."

Nanase slurped her soup, too, as she spoke.

"If I lived with you, Chitose, I bet I'd stop cooking altogether. Wouldn't be good."

"Wouldn't be good for you to bring up living together so casually like that in the first place."

I plopped the boiled egg and spring onion on top of the beef bowl and mixed it up lightly.

"You didn't say anything when we had that future plans session, but have you decided what you're going to do after high school, Chitose?"

"To be honest, I haven't given it a single thought," I replied.

Nanase looked a bit surprised, but then she nodded as if she understood.

"The thing is, back when I was doing baseball, I only ever thought, 'All right! I'm gonna try to get into the Koshien high school baseball tournament!' and that's it. I thought if I did that, professional scouts would all want to talk to me. That was my plan. If it didn't work out, my backup plan was to go to a college with a good baseball team and try to get ahead that way."

I think, that day, Asuka must have realized I wouldn't have wanted to talk about this, so she smoothly turned the conversation away from me.

Enter the Koshien tournament on some small-town school team, attract attention and distinguish myself, then go pro.

You might think it was childish, but I honestly believed I had a shot at grabbing hold of a dream like that. The kind of dream that you only read about in manga.

"Ah, you're still on summer vacation, right?"

"Hmm."

That's a strange way of putting it, I thought.

After baseball left my life, I found myself incapable of even being able to picture what kind of future I might have.

I had the feeling this whole year had just been me killing time until the hole in my soul filled itself up, but recently I felt like I was pretty much there.

That said, when you peeled off the thin cover, there was still a large gaping hole left behind.

I would probably have to find something else to fill it with at some point.

This is why I didn't want Asuka to have to go through the same thing.

Nanase didn't ask me anything else, so I decided to turn her question back on her. "You said you're planning to go to college outside of the prefecture, right?"

Nanase paused and neatly swallowed her mouthful of beef before responding. "That's right."

"Is there some kind of special reason for that?"

"Hmm, nothing major, really. Remember how I told you that I didn't want to talk to my parents about that stalker incident?"

"Yeah."

At the time, I didn't think too hard about it. Just typical high schooler things, I thought.

"I think I've done a good job meeting most of my parents' expectations. I haven't caused them any major worries. But you know, it's a little bit stifling having to live like that, right? At least during college, I want to live more freely, have some independence, you know. I guess that's my thinking."

"I think that's reasonable enough for a future path."

When I said that, Nanase frowned a little.

"Ah, sorry. I didn't mean to imply that it was boring or anything."

"I know. You're not the kind of guy who'd say something like that, Chitose. I guess I was on the mark about the reason you've been kind of down lately, too."

While she was still talking, Nanase had finished eating and was crushing the *gyudon* and salad containers flat. Then she brought our soup bowls to the sink and started washing them.

After wiping them dry with a towel, she seemed to have a sudden thought about something, and then she snapped off the room lights.

She stepped closer, relying on the mellow light of her phone to guide her.

"Hey. C'mere."

*   *   *

She whispered in my ear.

Her sweet breath sent a shiver down my spine.

She headed to the bedroom, and I followed her.

She opened the door and shone her phone screen into the room, then with a little chuckle, she turned on my crescent-moon-shaped lamp.

Then she sat on the bed and patted the space beside her.

Illuminated by the soft light, her white thighs were on full display.

I sat down beside her, just as she invited me to, and she gently touched my neck.

I could smell a feminine scent, distinct from the deodorant.

Nanase leaned her face in close to mine, and then—

—she squeezed my neck menacingly.

"Come on. Spit it out."

"Nanase, that's Yua's special move. And what is it you want me to spill?!"

"The thing that's been on your mind, Chitose, that's what."

"…Can I ask one thing?"

"Hmm?"

"What was that sultry setup all about?"

"I thought you'd feel more comfortable spilling your secrets in dim light."

"I'll fling you down on my bed again if you're not careful, little missy."

"Ooh, don't! ♡"

Dammit. I had to go and get all excited, didn't I?

*

After that, I talked about Asuka.

About how I wasn't sure what to do, after everything.

Nanase listened carefully, nodding solemnly.

I got to the part where Asuka said good-bye, and then I sighed.

"So that's what happened."

When I looked back on Nanase's little visit this evening, I realized she'd already cottoned on to all this.

She clearly knew I wouldn't spill unless she handled me skillfully, with kid gloves.

"You know," Nanase said, her voice soft and kind, "you're really a much bigger idiot than you realize, Chitose."

Scratch that.

"You act smart and always make things sound so complicated, but you worry about very simple things. You agonize, and then you just sweep it all aside and play the fool."

"Better wrap it up there, or poor wittle Saku will get his feelings hurt, you know?"

"Take me, or Mizushino, for example. We're better at concealing our feelings. But you can't do it, Chitose. That's why you're an idiot."

Get it? The beautiful girl tipped her head to one side, watching me.

"There's only one thing you *can* do, and it's the same thing you've always done."

Then Nanase grabbed me by my shirt front, as if she was itching for a fight.

"Face that wall that's in front of you and kick it down with all you've got. Smash it."

She clapped her hand onto my face, almost hard enough to call it a slap, and then she smooshed my cheeks together.

"You're a man, aren't you, Saku Chitose?"

It took every inch of self-control I had not to fling my arms around the girl sitting next to me.

"Otherwise"—Nanase licked her lip lasciviously—"I'll throw you down right here and have my wicked way with you. ♡"

"Man-eater."

"Do you want to stay the night, Nanase?"

"Don't go putting words in my mouth!"

I looked at Nanase, who was cracking up, and realized that all the thoughts whirling in my head seemed to have quieted down.

In the eyes of the adults, we really are all just kids, I guess.

So what was wrong with acting childish? Being a bit wild and impulsive?

"Thanks, Nanase."

"Uh-huh."

She was still lightly smushing my cheeks together. I knew I looked bizarre, but I didn't care. I just kept staring at that beautiful face.

⋆

"Ah, looks like I gave some damning ammunition to the worst possible person…"

Someone's faint sigh disappeared into the night sky of the countryside town.

⋆

Fwish. Clack.
  Fwish. Clack.

The following day, Saturday. Early morning, five AM.

Bathed in the first light of sunrise, I was practicing pitching.

It reminded me of my baseball practice days. Of course, we didn't get up quite this early. But the memory was pleasant.

Fwish. Clack.
  Fwish. Clack.

*　　*　　*

For the past few minutes, I'd been picking up tiny stones—you wouldn't even really call them pebbles—and throwing them against my target.

Fwish. Clack.
Fwish. Clack.

I was glad it was early morning on a weekend.
If anyone saw me right now, they might think I was up to no good.

Fwish. Clack.
Fwish. Clack.

I'd been at it for around twenty minutes or so.
But finally, I was getting the result I wanted.
The second-floor window rattled open.
A sleepy head emerged, and when the person saw who it was, I sucked in a big breath.

"A new dayyy-ayyy has dawned!"

I started singing the song that goes along with the calisthenics program they play on the radio.
Asuka stared at me blankly for about ten seconds, still trying to process what was happening. Then...

"Huh? ...Yeek!"

Quickly smoothing down her bedhead hair, she wrapped her arms protectively around the front of her satin pajamas and ducked below the window frame.

After another ten seconds or so, her head popped back up again, and she peeked down at me. She was still flattening her hair with her hand.

"Wh-what are you doing?"

The morning was so still, not even a single car had come by. I could hear Asuka perfectly without her even needing to raise her voice.

She still appeared to be in a state of panic, and I couldn't help snorting with laughter.

"I told you this day would come, right? I said I'd ask you on a date by standing beneath your window and singing the radio calisthenics song."

"But…the other day…I told you…"

"It hasn't taken me my whole life up until now to realize that, when a girl tells you good-bye, what she really means is for you to chase after her." I faced the window and stretched out my hand.

"Come down, Asuka. I've come to spirit you away."

Asuka looked like she was going to cry for a second, then she seemed to swallow it back. She lowered her head for a moment, then, as if gathering her resolve, she met my gaze and held it.

"Half an hour! Or it might be a bit longer. Wait for me in the park over there!"

That was all she said, then she closed the window briskly.

I quietly fist-pumped.

When Asuka said good-bye that time, she *tucked her hair behind her left ear*, you see.

✳

I bought a black coffee at the vending machine and sat down on a bench in the nearby park, within sight of Asuka's house.

I started grinning, wondering what I thought I was doing.

I thought I was acting childish and impulsive, but perhaps I was going too far.

Last night, after I made up my mind to take Asuka to Tokyo, I hurried to Fukui Station. But after buying the tickets, I remembered I didn't know Asuka's LINE address or phone number.

I had taken her home many times, so I knew her house and the approximate location of her bedroom. But I couldn't exactly ring the doorbell and say, "Excuse me, I'm just borrowing your daughter for a bit."

That left only the old-school method.

Still, the risk of being discovered was too high while her parents were awake. Even worse, a neighbor might spot me and raise the alarm.

It takes about three hours by train to go from Fukui to Tokyo anyway. I wanted to leave plenty of time to return before nightfall, so I planned to set off first thing in the morning.

I pulled the tab on my can of coffee and took a slurp.

I guess I really am an idiot, just like Nanase said.

✳

I wasn't used to getting up this early, so before long, I found myself nodding off on the bench.

"...Hello?"

Someone tapped me on the shoulder, calling out to me.

I dragged my heavy eyelids open, and...

"Good morning."

...a beautiful girl was standing there in a pure-white dress, smiling beside me.

"Asuka..."

For a moment, I felt like I was on the verge of remembering

something, but the memory slipped away, too vague and indistinct to grab hold of.

"Good morning. You look great."

Asuka scratched her cheek bashfully. "Is it too much? I may have gone overboard."

"Not at all. You look like you stepped out of a dream about a young boy and girl."

"Really?"

"If it wasn't for the residual bedhead, you'd look perfect."

"What? No! But I thought I fixed it?!"

"Just kidding."

"Hmph!"

She was wearing a sort of old-fashioned white dress, the kind that might make you think, *In this day and age?* But she looked great in it, like something out of an old portrait.

That looks amazing on you, just as I thought.

I remembered a fragment of a conversation we'd had.

Asuka stood up and faced me. Her skirt blew around just a little, as if portending the coming of a far-off summer's tale.

"Will you spirit me away now?"

She held out her hand, smiling softly, and I took it and gripped it tight so I wouldn't lose sight of her.

CHAPTER THREE
The Blue Night of the Faraway Sky We'll Remember Someday

We were at the back of the Shirasagi, getting rocked side to side.

The Shirasagi is a special rapid train that connects Kanezawa, Fukui, and Nagoya, kinda like the Fukuians' answer to the Thunderbird.

A few years from now, it seems they'll extend the Hokuriku Shinkansen line, but as of right now, the Shinkansen still doesn't go through Fukui.

If you want to go to Tokyo, you have to take the special rapid to Kanezawa Station in Ishikawa, then get off and change to the Hokuriku Shinkansen. The other option is to take it to Maibara Station in Shiga, then get on the Tokaido Shinkansen.

Either route would have been fine, but I heard that the Hokuriku Shikansen goes through a lot of tunnels, so I opted for the Tokaido Shinkansen so we could enjoy the view.

We could even have taken an airplane if we wanted, but Fukui airport is mostly used for private planes, and there are few scheduled commercial flights. If you want to go to Tokyo by plane you have to go to Komatsu airport in Ishikawa Prefecture, so it actually works out faster to take the special rapid and the Shinkansen.

Incidentally, back at the park, Asuka got into a panic about not having the money for a Shinkansen ticket until I told her, "I've already bought them, so you can pay me back whenever."

It was my idea to drag her to Tokyo, after all, and I rarely spend my money, so I had plenty to spare. If I told her it was my treat, though, it wouldn't feel fair to my parents or to Asuka herself, so I refrained.

Since we obviously hadn't eaten breakfast, we stopped at the Imajo Soba inside Fukui Station. I ordered hot plum and seaweed soba and two rice balls, and Asuka had hot soba with grated yam.

Incidentally, even though this Imajo Soba is the narrow kind where you stand up to eat, it's pretty popular with the locals, so some people even come to the station just to eat there. It's nothing too fancy or refined, but it's the kind of reassuring, comforting food that makes you want to immediately eat it whenever you think about it.

We left Fukui and passed through stations in Sabae and Takefu, making our way through the prefecture.

Asuka leaned her head against my shoulder and nodded off like a child.

I couldn't blame her, not after I'd woken her at the crack of dawn and then sprang this unexpected journey on her.

Every now and then, in rhythm with her sleepy breathing, her hair would tickle my collarbone.

I could smell a waft of lavender, and it wasn't just my collarbone that was being tickled.

I looked over at her and was taken aback by the innocence on her face, an innocence hard to imagine when you thought of Asuka's usual dignified beauty.

She was leaning against me, which made the neck of her dress gape open a little, and since she had her hands folded on her knees, the soft mounds of her chest were pronounced.

I spotted a tiny mole there and quickly diverted my eyes to look out the train window.

I could see rice fields soaked in water, small mountains and hills ringing the vicinity, and an endless sky overhead. Your quintessential countryside scenery.

I recalled family vacations from long ago.

The time I rode the night bus for the first time.

There were quite a few couples sitting nearby who looked like they could be college students, faces close together and whispering happily. There were even some wrapped up all snuggly under blankets together, and I remember thinking how grown-up they seemed.

I wondered if I'd ever take a trip like that with someone special.

Strange for a young kid to be imagining such a far-off future for himself.

I felt a weight on my shoulder, and before long another weight was laid against that, and I began to drop off, too.

Maybe one day I'd be looking back on this moment wistfully.

The train shook and rattled, bringing the two dreamers to the far-off city.

*

"Time to go, Asuka! You were really asleep, I gotta say."

"Huh? *Satsukigase*?"

"No, not the well-loved Fukui confectionary! Darn it, this isn't the time to be cute!"

I grabbed a still-sleepy Asuka by the hand, and we left the train, clutching our bags.

Asuka was yawning. "Sorry, my bad. I guess I fell all the way asleep."

"You even drooled on my shoulder."

"Wait, really?!"

"Nope!"

"Oh, you suck!"

We went down the stairs and joined the crowd lining up for the transfer gate.

I led the way, but then I heard a dinging noise behind, and I turned to see that Asuka had gotten held up at the gate and was holding her hand out to me with desperation.

"Wait! Don't leave me behind!"

"Calm down, Asuka. It looks like you need to feed all three tickets into the gate at once."

We got through the gate without further incident, bought drinks at the vending machine, then went in search of our allocated seats.

I put my backpack and the retro-style leather Boston bag onto the overhead luggage rack, and then Asuka piped up, sounding excited.

"Which seat do you want?"

Ah yes, we missed out on this sort of quintessential train journey back-and-forth earlier. It just ended up with Asuka taking the window seat and me sitting on the aisle.

I didn't hesitate to answer.

"Window seat."

"Let's do rock-paper-scissors..."

"You're not going to give me my turn?"

"Come on, I swear I'll play rock."

"It's been a while since I've engaged in rock-paper-scissors-related psychological warfare!"

"...One!"

I threw scissors, and Asuka threw rock.

"Aw, I told you I was going to throw rock. You tried to out-think me."

"Oh, shut up!"

In the end, Asuka ended up getting the window seat again, and I sat on the aisle.

"Oh, I almost forgot! Could you get my bag down for me? Sorry, I know you only just lifted it up there."

I did as she asked, and she rummaged around inside before pulling out a plastic convenience store bag.

"Snacks!"

"Suddenly, your bag seems much less sophisticated."

"But isn't it exciting to have stuff like this on a journey?"

"You made sure to stick to the five-hundred-yen spending limit, I presume?"

"Of course!"

As we bantered back and forth, I decided to bring up something that had been on my mind.

"Asuka, your mother and father..."

"I left a note. It said, 'Stay calm and don't try to find me.'"

"They wouldn't report you missing or anything, would they...?"

Asuka chuckled. "Just kidding. I hate lies. I wrote, 'I'm going to see Tokyo, and I'll be back tomorrow.'"

I had been planning to be back that same day, but I didn't say anything just then. "Did you say who you were with?"

"Nope. No way."

I breathed out a sigh of relief.

I'd prepared myself to ask her father straight-up if I'd been caught when I went to wake Asuka. But to be honest, I was really relieved I'd managed to make it without encountering him.

If I had to go up against her father, I had a feeling things would get pretty tough.

"You know, it's a bit late to be bringing this up, but..." I paused. "Sorry for...all this craziness."

Asuka put her head to one side and smiled warmly at me. "You picked up on the 'come help me' signals I was transmitting, right?"

"I certainly did."

"Who could condemn a neighbor for watering a plant in his neighbor's garden if it was obvious that plant was going to wilt and die without water?"

I looked away. "But now I've already done everything I can do for you," I said quietly. "Even after visiting Tokyo, the situation will be unchanged. I think this time away, what it's all about, is letting you finally face up to yourself, Asuka."

Asuka put her hand gently on top of mine. "Thank you. The

version of me you talk about... I'm going to try to find her for myself this time."

As we gazed at the scenery whipping by outside the window, I thought about mundane things.

That old house nestled in the mountains. It must be so full of someone's memories. But we can't appreciate its value as we whip past it in the span of a second.

Where does the scale upon which dreams can be weighed exist?

Who gets to decide what the counterbalance weight should be?

The scenery continued to whip by outside the window.

*

Then, just after ten AM, we arrived at Tokyo Station.

On the journey, I remember us feeling excited about getting to see the actual Mount Fuji. We even took photos.

But once we passed Shin-Yokohama Station, we started seeing all these huge apartment buildings everywhere, the kind you'd never see in Fukui, and we started murmuring to each other: "Wow, it's really the capital city." And then we started seeing actual skyscrapers, some stacked three together, and we were astonished.

Then when we passed Shinagawa Station, the huge buildings seemed to touch the sky, higher than anything we'd ever seen, and the two of us pressed our noses to the glass like a couple of country bumpkins. "Wow," we said, over and over.

As the train ran over a raised section of track, I gazed down at Tokyo, shocked by how densely packed everything was.

There was barely any space at all between houses, or between apartment blocks. They were close enough for the residents to look right into their neighbors' homes.

Nothing felt quite real; in fact, it looked like some sort of miniature town.

We got off the Shinkansen together, quaking a little, and Asuka spoke first.

"Is there some kind of event going on today?"

"I completely get what you mean, but I don't think that's it."

I knew this was the last stop and all, but the Shinkansen seemed to vomit out an unbelievable number of passengers.

Neither of us had any clue where the exit was, so for the time being, we decided to join the flow of the crowd and descended the escalator.

We passed through the gate that was marked TRANSFERS, and then a whole ocean of people appeared from the platforms.

The air felt thin, mingled with unidentifiable smells.

"Asuka, you're really going to live in a place like this?"

Asuka was shaking her head, clutching hold of my arm weakly.

"I think I can see what your father was so concerned about now."

But even so, I had no idea where to start, where to go.

"It might be a bit late to think of this now," I said.

Nod, nod.

"But why didn't we make a plan during the Shinkansen ride?"

Nod, nod.

"Er, hello?"

Was there no getting through to her?

Anyway, we needed to decide what to do next, or we wouldn't get anywhere.

Tugging along a frozen Asuka, I tried to find a less crowded spot. You had to stride forward decisively, or you'd end up getting stuck in the crowd and bumping into people.

And why did all these Tokyoites walk so fast?

It wasn't like they were all running late for a train, but I couldn't figure out why they were all walking at such a speed. I was getting frazzled and out of breath, like I was fleeing some evil organization with the female love interest by my side.

Just when I had given up on getting to the side, I spotted a bookstore tucked away by the escalators. There was a signboard outside advertising curry, of all things.

Apparently, it was some kind of bookstore slash café.

I headed inside for somewhere to catch a breather, and that was when Asuka's mouth started working again.

"Wow, this is amazing. You can bring books you haven't even bought into the café to read, apparently."

"Aren't they worried about people splashing curry on them?"

"Right? I wouldn't feel safe doing it myself."

The spicy scent was inviting, but it was still a little too early for lunch, so I ordered a cold brew coffee, and Asuka had a cold brew tea.

The interior of the restaurant felt a little cramped from a Fukui perspective, but we managed to find an empty table and finally sit and relax a little.

Asuka took a sip of her iced tea and then exhaled slowly.

"I feel exhausted already, somehow..."

"And we haven't even left the station yet."

"We've barely even gotten to the T of Tokyo, huh."

"Exactly." I nodded. "We came here on the spur of the moment, but what should we actually do now?"

"Honestly, I'd just like to walk around Tokyo and soak up the atmosphere. I think that would be more than enough. Only..." Asuka began rummaging around inside her bag, pulling out a red book. "I guess I'd like to go here."

The cover of the book was emblazoned with the name of an extremely famous private university, a name every high schooler in the country knew.

"That's your first-choice Tokyo college, then?"

Asuka nodded a little hesitantly. "I heard it's got good job prospects for media work. And it's known for its student clubs, the ones centering around literature. A lot of my favorite novelists have actually gone there."

"All right, then we'll go check it out."

I looked up how to get to the university using my phone. The names of stations I'd never heard of popped up. I had no reason to use one in Fukui, but last night I'd downloaded an app that helps guide you around Tokyo by the rail network. I searched for the best route from Tokyo Station to the station we wanted, and several different choices came up for the same two stations. My head swam.

"Do you think we can handle the subway?"

Asuka shook her head anxiously.

"You think we can smoothly transfer between lines?"

Wobble, wobble.

"Then the only choice is this Yamanote Line. We can go there without needing to switch lines, apparently. Then we have to walk a little to get to the university. Does that sound all right?"

Nod, nod.

Apparently, that sounded all right.

It'd be easier to walk it and rely on a GPS map than wrestle with an unfamiliar subway system.

"We got one ticket back from the gate, right? It says we can go anywhere in Tokyo with this, right?"

Wobble, wobble. Yes, that's right.

I checked, and apparently we could use this ticket to get to Takada Baba.

We finished up our drinks, quickly located the Yamanote Line heading to Ueno, and got on board.

The seats were already full. In fact, there were so many people we couldn't even see any seats.

The pressure from the people boarding behind propelled us forward, and both Asuka and I found ourselves being pushed into the middle.

Even the straps had all been claimed, so I grabbed hold of the bare pole.

There was no chance of putting our bags up on the racks, so I sandwiched mine between my legs to avoid inconveniencing other people. Asuka followed suit.

We're way too close together, I thought.

I had complete strangers pressed up against my chest and back, and I tried to inch away, feeling awkward and apologetic, but the other people didn't seem to care or even notice.

Being this close to someone in a public space—not even a romantic partner but a total stranger—was unthinkable in Fukui. You got more personal space at Lpa on a national holiday.

Crammed into this tiny box, young and old alike, men and women alike, all thrown in and jumbled up together.

And Asuka was going to live in a city like this?

I flicked my gaze to the side.

There was a handsome dude in front of me and one to the side.

Just then the train set off with a jolt, and Asuka suddenly lost her balance.

Gripping the pole with my right hand, I scooped my free arm around her waist without thinking and pulled her to me.

I held her tight, like you'd hold someone really important to you. As if begging her not to leave and go far away.

"Sorry, Asuka. It was just a reflex."

She looked up at me, her beautiful eyes glistening. "It's…totally fine."

"Um, should I let go?"

"Could we just stay—? I mean, it's fine to stay like this. I feel more comfortable knowing you've got me."

Her words made me tighten my hold on her.

We were standing there flustered, but there were plenty of other passengers who seemed to move and sway comfortably with the motion, even without a strap or pole to hang on to.

We're not from around here, clearly, I thought.

This was just another normal weekend for these people. The only ones overwhelmed and out of place were us two.

"Hey, look outside." Asuka nodded toward the windows.

The view outside was like some sort of science fiction world.

Everywhere you looked, there were massive buildings. If any one of those buildings had existed in Fukui, they'd be major landmarks known to everyone in the prefecture. And the streets were crammed with people; if there were ever that many people out in Fukui, you'd be like, "Uh, is there some major event going on today or something?"

Just how many people lived in this city, anyhow?

And all with their own dreams, either living them or chasing after them, or dealing with the broken pieces of them.

"It's hard to believe this is in the same country as Fukui."

"But they're all just looking at their phones," Asuka mumbled.

"This amazing scenery has become unremarkable to them. That's Tokyo, I guess."

Asuka gripped my T-shirt. "I think I'm...really excited."

"I...I think I know what you mean."

I didn't want to admit it fully to myself, but I was feeling it, too.

This city had to be full of all kinds of experiences you could never have in Fukui, just waiting to be uncovered.

As I gazed out the train window, we reached Akihabara Station.

There were girls in cosplay strolling along the platform, and my eyes widened in amazement.

When Asuka talked about wanting to experience all kinds of things in order to become an editor, I'd agreed with her that it was necessary. But I didn't truly understand what she meant.

I'd been like, but couldn't you have all kinds of experiences in Fukui, too?

However, as I watched the girls in the maid costumes sashaying along, I felt like I was in a completely different country.

I was still thinking about that when I felt a sharp pinch on my side.

"Ouch! Stop, stop, I swear I wasn't staring at the cosplay ladies with the big boobs."

Asuka eyed me with suspicion as I let my thoughts continue to run freely.

Whether or not Asuka was able to convince her parents, I knew that by the end of our short trip, Asuka would have made up her mind to live in this city.

A person like her, who delved into novels seeking worlds and lives unknown to her—a person who wanted to be on the inside helping to make those stories a reality—no way she wouldn't want to dive in and immerse herself in this amazing city.

Which would mean that our opportunities to spend long amounts of time together like this—those opportunities would soon be gone for good.

I clenched my hand tight on the pole, determined not to let my feelings of sadness and loneliness ruin this day for Asuka.

＊

Takada Baba was reassuringly small-scale compared to Tokyo Station, but it was as crowded as everywhere else we'd seen so far. Although, there did seem to be quite a high proportion of college-age people about.

Incidentally, when I saw the station name placard, I realized it didn't read TAKADA BABA as I'd thought, but TAKADANOBABA, apparently. Where did the *no* come from? Were they mocking country bumpkins with that country-sounding name or something?

We exited the station, and my first impression was: Is this a circus?

Brightly colored billboards and advertisements jostled for attention. My eyes slid over them. People and cars were going every which way. I felt on edge and out of my depth.

Asuka seemed to be feeling the same way, and she was blinking rapidly at everything around us.

I fired up my map app and entered our destination. It didn't look like such a complicated route, which helped reassure me a little.

"So it seems we head down this big street and just go straight."

Nod, nod.

"Let's try to acclimatize already, okay?"

We started walking, and while there were plenty of convenience stores and chain restaurants that we also had in Fukui, there were also a lot of establishments I'd never heard of before, all crammed in together and lining the road.

There was a Yoshinoya and a Matsuya almost right next to each other, both fast-food beef bowl joints—there was just one other store sandwiched between them. How did they survive the direct competition when they were so close together? I wondered.

"Asuka, what's this Hidakaya place? Is it a ramen shop? Chinese food? I like the lantern hanging outside; it's kind of cool."

"Oh yeah! I wonder if it's a long-standing establishment? Let's add it to the list of lunch candidates!"

"And why are all these restaurants so small?! No parking, either. Fukui's Matsuyas and Yoshinoyas are so much bigger."

"Y'ain't kiddin'. Fukui ain't to be beaten." (Translation: Indeed. Fukui can certainly hold its own.)

"Oh look, there's a Starbucks, too! That's the big city for you."

"Wow! You can get coffee to go on your way to classes!"

"By the way, aren't there a lot of convenience stores around? There's a 7-Eleven right here—and then another one just over there."

"Tokyoites must be too busy to cross the street, I guess?"

"I thought all these restaurants might just have been concentrated near the station, but they just keep on going along with the road."

"With all these choices, I feel bad not trying every single one."

"Oh, apparently we turn here. Asuka, look, there's a cool vintage clothing store here! I bet it's pretty popular! Shall we take a look inside?"

"Yeah!"

…And that's all the excited babbling from two Tokyo newbies you're going to get out of me.

We entered the small side street, gushing excitedly together, and stepped into the store.

The smell of old clothes was in the air.

It reminded me of summers spent visiting my grandmother's house, a smell I actually kinda like.

The store was tiny. A few steps inside was all it took to reach the back wall. It didn't have random racks of old clothes but instead carefully curated selections arranged artfully.

There seemed to be a lot of retro blouses and dresses for women, and I thought this style of clothing would look really good on Asuka.

I gazed at the selection for a moment, then I picked up a cute dress.

"What about this?"

It was a short-sleeve number with a little bow at the neck, in a summery cobalt blue with little polka dots.

I don't know much about women's fashion, but it seemed like the kind of thing you'd expect to see on girls who appeared in old movies, like *American Graffiti* and *Back to the Future*.

"Oh, that's cute!"

"Why don't you try it on?"

Asuka went to ask the shopkeeper in the back, then headed to the changing booth.

I waited outside the booth, thinking.

She was changing from a dress into another dress...

I remembered the flash of turquoise I'd seen when we played billiards and moved away from the changing booth in a hurry.

I didn't give it a second thought when I was waiting outside the booths for Yuuko and Haru. Maybe it was because Asuka and I were alone on a trip together like this.

Pushing away the thoughts that kept tugging at the corners of my mind, I flipped through the racks of men's clothing.

Of course, the only thing that registered with me about them was that, yep, these were indeed clothes.

After I did that for a while, the door to the changing booth opened.

"What do you think?"

It was Asuka, a little embarrassment in her voice.

"It's great. You look like Ingrid Bergman in *Casablanca*."

"Is that a compliment? Or are you saying it's too old-fashioned?"

"I'm saying you look like you could have just stepped out of a black-and-white movie."

"That doesn't answer my question, you know?"

I was goofing around because I felt awkward giving her two straightforward compliments in one day, but of course it looked good on her.

Asuka pouted and continued.

"I'll wear that next time, and we'll go on a slightly fancier date, okay?"

"...I'm down."

Seeing her shy smile, I was glad I suggested stopping by this store.

"Okay, now it's my turn to choose clothes for you. We can give them to each other as presents; how does that sound?"

"I'm fine, thanks. This kind of stylish clothing doesn't really work for me."

"Just leave it all to Big Sis Asuka. I'll make you look just like Humphrey Bogart in *Casablanca*."

"What does that mean?"

"A good, old-fashioned egotist who makes women cry."

"Hey! And what do you mean by *that*?"

In the end, I agreed to let Asuka use her skills to choose a few things for me to try on.

*

After buying clothes for each other, we headed back out and made our way along the narrow street.

I was interested in a used bookstore that was close by the retro clothing store, but we'd already used up more time than I'd bargained for, so I decided to prioritize heading to our main destination.

We'd entered a residential area that was extremely quiet compared to the hustle and bustle nearer the station. There were some old-looking houses and apartment buildings. The kind of scenery a few country kids like us were more comfortable with.

Walking alongside me, Asuka commented, "Nice to see even Tokyo has these kinds of neighborhoods, huh?"

"It's kinda reassuring. It's like, wow, people really do live here."

It didn't need saying, perhaps, but I voiced that thought anyway.

"It's almost noon," she said. "Smell that? Curry. Light novels and movies always focus on the big-city parts of Tokyo, but there's also these residential neighborhoods where people are just living normal lives, too."

"Us country rubes grew up thinking Tokyo was cold and impersonal. I guess we were brainwashed."

Asuka giggled at that.

After walking for a while, we came back out onto the big street.

There was a building up ahead that looked like it was part of a college campus. Apparently, we were close to our destination.

We walked along the main street, me checking my phone map, and then finally, we reached the university campus…except the main gates were shut.

"Aw, man. Are you serious…?"

"Ah, darn."

I knew it was the weekend and all, but except for the female-only colleges, I thought it was common knowledge that the campuses were open even on weekends for anyone to enter.

I couldn't believe we'd come all the way to Tokyo only to end up unable to visit our number-one destination. I was embarrassed about my lack of preparation as well.

"I'm sorry, Asuka. I should have checked ahead."

"No, I'm the one who should be apologizing. But it's enough just to be able to see it from the outside."

While we were standing there in bewilderment—

"Hey there. You here visiting?"

—someone was speaking to us.

We turned to see an old man smiling at us with a Shiba Inu. He looked to be in his seventies and had good posture. His white hair was neatly cut, and he somehow made me think of a fish market manager.

"Hello." Asuka lowered her head politely.

"Hello, hello," the man responded.

"May I pet your dog?"

"Go ahead, go ahead."

Asuka crouched down, and the Shiba put its front paws on her thighs and licked her face.

"Hey, whoa! You're tickling me."

Seeing that fluffy tail wag back and forth, I wanted to shout, "Down!"

After receiving the dog's affections, Asuka stood back up. Losing its source of attention, the dog came and sniffed my leg before turning its nose up and trotting back to its owner.

I bet you're a boy, aren't you?

"We came to see this college, but we can't go in since it's the weekend, huh." Asuka's voice was filled with disappointment.

"Ah, you can't go in from here. But if you head over that way, there's the main campus. You can enter from there."

This must be what they call the Tokyo dialect. It was a little fast and a tad rough, but his accent was sort of kindly at the same time.

"Really?! We came from Fukui, actually, so we really don't know anything."

"Fukui? Never been there. You students?"

"We're in high school right now."

"Going to college in Tokyo?"

"I'm still trying to decide…"

"It's a bit crowded, sure, but it ain't half bad, around here."

Asuka smiled a little. "I was just thinking the same thing."

We were the only ones who understood the significance of her reply.

The old man patted the dog's head. It seemed antsy, either because it wanted to continue its walk or because it was desperate for more attention from the pretty young girl.

"You kids brother and sister?"

""Whaaat?""

We both yelped in surprise. In unison.

"Oh, was I wrong? Just thought you looked alike."

While we hesitated over what to say, the older man continued.

"Well, enjoy yourselves."

I thought we were in for a long chat, but the old guy walked off, waving a hand airily.

Asuka and I looked at each other. She was the first to speak.

"Brother and sister."

"Not boyfriend and girlfriend, huh."

We both burst out laughing.

It just seemed so funny for some reason. I laughed until I choked.

"*Do* we look alike?"

Asuka put her head to one side, considering. "No, we do not."

After she said that, I continued.

"I'm surprised. Tokyo's actually kind of a friendly place."

"It *is* friendly, isn't it? Tokyo."

I hoped, from the bottom of my heart, that the friendly warmth of Tokyo would embrace Asuka's future like a warm and protective blanket.

*

After that, we headed to the main campus, using the map app to guide us.

Just as the old man had said, we could enter the campus grounds freely from here.

When we tried to go in through the main gates, I spotted this building that looked like a church.

Was that a university building or something totally unrelated? If it was the former, then what was it used for? I couldn't imagine.

When we stepped inside the campus grounds, we found that there were plenty of students around despite it being the weekend. Some were sitting on benches reading and relaxing, clutching coffees, and others were talking animatedly.

I'd thought a Tokyo university would be somehow stuffier and less laid-back, but it was nice, with tall trees dotted here and there and big wide pathways.

Some of the buildings were traditional-looking, but then right opposite them you'd find more modern-looking buildings in glass and concrete. The contrast was pretty fascinating.

Asuka was looking around, her eyes sparkling.

I smiled a little as I spoke. "It seems much more laid-back than I'd thought. It really does feel like a literature-focused campus."

"I think I could see myself going here." Asuka beckoned me over to a nearby bench. "Look, try picturing it."

We sat down side by side and closed our eyes.

"We're both university students. I'm wearing the dress you bought me, and you're wearing the shirt I bought you. Maybe we've both dyed our hair. I can't really picture that part, though."

"I think you look amazing just as you are, Asuka. But what about me? Maybe I should try going bleached blond?"

"You'd look like a real player on the outside, too, you know."

"Don't say that in such a serious tone. You'll hurt my feelings."

Asuka giggled. "You'll enter the lit department as well, I guess. We'll sit side by side like this and chat about which classes we're taking."

"We have to choose a college club, too."

"You won't want to be separated from me, so you'll join whatever club I join."

"So that I don't end up getting taken home by hungry ladies after the club nights out."

"You're not that innocent to the ways of the world." She slapped my thigh. "Hope I can get a part-time job at a publishing house."

"What'll I do? Become a seedy club host?"

"Your big sis would never allow it."

A cool breeze blew by.

The dappled flecks of sunlight wavered with the rhythm.

"On weekends… Let's see. We'll walk around town together like we just did and practice our terrible cooking in a tiny kitchen."

"Just to point out, I'm actually a pretty decent cook, you know?"

"…First, we'll start off with something like meat and potato stew."

"Don't pretend like you didn't hear me."

But Asuka continued, "That kind of future isn't going to happen. Because I'm a year ahead of you at school."

I had to agree. "Even if I did choose the same university as you. By the time I enter, you'll already have picked your department, you'll be busy with studying and your part-time job at the publishing company, and you'll have made all new friends in your college club. You'll even have mastered cooking meat and potato stew. You might even have a boyfriend by then."

"We're not in the same place, are we?"

"We're miles apart."

Asuka touched her pinkie finger to mine. "Even though right now, we're this close."

A year was a long time to us high schoolers.

In the interim, so many things would change. Too much would change.

Asuka linked her pinkie with mine, as if making a promise.

"But I have to face forward and keep going. Or I won't be able to keep up."

With what? But I didn't ask.

Maybe it was still just a half-formed dream. The hand of a clock you can't stop ticking. A phantom, an illusion of a person who you built up and idolized.

All of us, we're just moving forward every day, living a youth that won't ever, ever come back.

*

Asuka said she wanted to go to Jinbocho.

Even I had heard of it, but apparently, it's an area where there are a lot of publishing companies and bookstores, a sort of mecca for bibliophiles.

I looked it up on my phone and realized it was pretty far. We really should have gone there first. Still, we embarked on this trip without any plans in place, so it couldn't be helped.

If we walked from a station called Kanda, we could avoid having to change trains. In that case, all we'd have to do was take the train we came by but in the opposite direction.

I wanted to give Asuka the chance to see different areas of Tokyo, though, so I decided to take on the challenge of the subway and switching various train lines.

It was total hell.

I tried looking for big buildings that might be stations, but for some reason all the subway entrances were tiny.

And switching train lines in the subway was so darn confusing.

Also, I had no idea how you were supposed to buy tickets.

I ended up having to ask station assistants for help at least five times, but finally we managed to reach Jinbocho.

We picked one of the many exits and emerged on the surface. I felt like we'd traversed a huge video game dungeon, and the sense of completion made me feel slightly tearful.

"Tokyo is freaking scary. I can't even."

Nod, nod.

"Hungry AF. Need food."

Nod, nod.

And so we found ourselves at Jinbocho's best-rated curry house. By the way, this place was also a total country bumpkin killer.

Even after we arrived at the spot indicated on the map app, there was no entrance in sight. We walked all around, and eventually we had to ask a passerby for help.

How were we supposed to know you had to go around the back of the building to find the entrance?

Also, even though it was past two PM, and the lunch peak was long over, there were still about ten people waiting ahead of us in line.

Finally, we were shown to our sofa seat, and slightly frustrated, I ordered a large beef curry, extra spicy. Asuka ordered a chicken curry, medium spicy.

After waiting for a while, we were each served two baked potatoes dripping with butter.

Asuka and I exchanged looks.

"Asuka, what are we supposed to do with these?"

"Well, there's butter on them, so I guess we're supposed to just eat them? You know, like the baked potatoes you get at festival stalls."

We looked around, trying not to look too much like a pair of rubes. Some people were eating the potatoes as is, while others were mixing them up with their curry.

"Looks like you can do either," I said.

Asuka smiled wryly.

"You know, you and I really are just country bumpkins. No one's stopping us from eating these any way we want."

"It's funny to think that a girl who jumps in a dirty river without caring who's watching would stress out about the correct way to eat a potato."

"Ah, there you go again, being all snarky."

Asuka tried to cut her potato in half using her fork, but she was doing a bad job of it. Eventually, she gave up and picked it up in her hand. With shaking fingers, she tried but failed to split it, so I jumped in to help her and managed to split it with my fork. Asuka grinned with delight.

Picking up half of the potato, she dipped it in the butter and then spoke.

"But you know, didn't you realize it, when we were walking around? No one here seems to take much notice of each other. And they didn't take any notice of us, either."

"For sure. I spotted some people walking around in pretty outlandish clothes, and even that guy playing a harmonica on the street. But no one seemed to care or say anything."

I shook some salt on my potato and bit into it. Oh, man. Steaming hot and super delicious.

"The place where we live is doing well, for Fukui, but it's still pretty country, isn't it?"

"You mean how everyone knows everyone else's business?"

You often hear that small towns have pretty firm surveillance societies in place.

Now, Fukui City isn't exactly a small village or anything, but even though it's the most prosperous place in the prefecture, it's still got that small-town surveillance feel.

Take when my parents got divorced, for example. The news got around the neighborhood like lightning. Then, when it was decided that I'd be living alone, I found myself having to contend with the overblown sympathies of everyone around me.

Asuka continued. "But you know, that's actually one of the nice things about Fukui, is what I've been thinking."

"You mean like when that old guy helped us find our way earlier?"

"Yeah. Sometimes it's a big help when other people take notice of you. It's the silver lining, I guess."

Perhaps she was correlating this with her own experience of being denied by her parents.

If no one ever tells you no, you can go straight for your dream without hesitating.

But if you don't have anyone out there trying to stop you, you can end up making awful mistakes you can't ever take back.

I was still thinking about that when our orders of curry were delivered to our table.

There was cheese on top of the rice and then, for some reason, a side of crunchy plums and pickles. Asuka's curry was served in a fancy curry pot, but mine was served in a separate deep dish.

We made eye contact and then both laughed.

I was sure Asuka was about to say, "So are we supposed to pour this on the rice before we eat it, or…?"

Shrugging, Asuka picked up the pot and let the curry sauce spill out onto the rice.

I did the same thing.

We both took a bite at the same time, and then…

""SO good!""

Our faces were full of bliss.

It was your basic European-style curry, but there was a spicy depth to it I couldn't place, and it was thick with a hint of sweetness.

The beef was so tender I could cut it with a spoon, and it melted in my mouth.

I put my leftover potato into the sauce and chopped it up with a spoon before eating it. The spiciness of the sauce became much more mellow. It wasn't bad at all.

"I'm gonna live in Tokyo!" Asuka announced.

"Yeah, I know," I replied.

"Hey, can I have a bit of your beef?"

"The only things that are splittable on dates are Chupets and Papico popsicles on a summer day, right?"

"Well, I make a special exception for curry!"

I rolled my eyes and chuckled as Asuka held out a spoonful of her curry to me.

"What's this?"

"I believe they call it an 'Open wide!' moment, young sire."

"Why are you talking all old-fashioned like that?"

"It's all in the experience, you see. Youth is short, as they say."

She was acting cocky, but her cheeks were bright red.

I leaned in and opened my mouth, and with a trembling hand, Asuka brought the spoonful of curry to my lips.

It was like that part during weddings where the couples hand-feed each other the first bite of cake. I grabbed her wrist and brought the spoon to my mouth.

"Mmn. The chicken's really juicy."

"…Not like that. Try again."

"No way. You're gonna burn my tongue."

I cut a piece of beef and loaded up my own spoon, gathering a bit of rice and sauce on it as well.

"Here, I'll do you. Open wide."

When I said that, Asuka faced me and opened her mouth.

Hey, why are you closing your eyes? It's not a kiss you're getting, you know.

Her little lips looked so plump and soft, and just a little bit shiny.

"Hey. Hurry up and gimme."

Sorry, Asuka. I wasn't teasing you. It's just that my hand's shaking.

Holding my wrist steady with my other hand, I managed to get the spoon to her mouth.

As it reached her lips, Asuka reached for my hand with her eyes still closed, and holding it with both of her hands, she gobbled the curry off the spoon.

After chewing for a few moments, she licked away a dribble of sauce that threatened to spill forth from the corner of her mouth.

...Look, all I did was feed her a spoonful of curry, all right?

"Yummy."

While we were both raving about the curry—

Bam!

—one of the two men sitting across from each other at the next table pounded his fist against the tabletop.

We looked over in surprise, and I could see that there was a sheaf of paper on the table between them, scrawled with notes in red ink.

The young man who'd banged on the table—he must have been in his twenties—then spoke.

"This is how many rejections now?! Are you even willing to go through with the plan at all? The last one submitted, we went through all the trouble of studying up on previous big-hitting titles and the current trends in the market, you know?"

The man sitting opposite was in his thirties, wearing glasses.

"It's true that there are a lot of similar coming-of-age stories."

"Right! For example..."

The younger man started listing off titles I recalled hearing about. I even had some of them on my bookshelves at home.

I looked at Asuka, my eyes wide.

Asuka stared back at me with the same look of surprise on her face.

Could it be? Were we witnessing a meeting between an actual novelist and his editor?

This was the best-rated curry house in Jinbocho, an area known for its publishing houses. It wasn't too far-fetched to think that publishing business was carried out here.

We tried not to stare too much as we listened intently to the neighboring table.

The man in the glasses was responding. "It's true that there are a lot of big-hitting novelists who pump out bestsellers after studying market trends and similar works. But you're not the type."

"...I just can't think of anything. My debut novel, I just wrote about the job I happened to be doing at the time and accidentally got lucky with a big hit. But I don't have the talent to come up with something out of thin air. I can't write it unless I've experienced it myself."

Then the novelist grabbed the pages in front of him and crumpled them up.

"I thought I could manage to write something about youth, but I've honestly led a really boring life. I guess the kids these days would call me one of the unpopular ones? I was always sitting in the corner of the classroom, envying the other kids who had something special about them. I'm not the type of person who can become a real novelist."

"Don't tell your editor what you can and can't do. I'm the one who gets to decide that." The man in the glasses tapped his red pen on the table. "I didn't seek you out to be your editor after you won the newcomer prize for your rare and unusual breadth of life experience. Anyway, your job wasn't all that unusual. Your talent lies in depicting everyday loneliness, in putting the subtleties of life into words. So this proposal of yours? It's a no from me."

"...If you think that way, why don't you—?"

The editor rapped his red pen on the table again, hard, as if he already knew what the novelist was going to say next.

"You're sitting there as a novelist, suggesting that I, the editor, write instead of you? Sure, I can give you some hints, some guidance along the way. But *you're* the writer here, not me."

"But..."

The editor continued, his expression softer. "Look, why don't you try telling me about this 'boring' youth of yours? Not this... this trite story you can read absolutely anywhere."

The young man gritted his teeth and scowled, then gathered himself up and, with a huge sigh, began telling his own story.

"…"

"…?"

"…"

"…!"

It was an unusual sight.

The novelist's story was, indeed, filled with interesting personal experiences.

But the editor responded to everything he said with: "But why, though?" and "And how did that make you feel at the time?" and "That's good stuff; then what happened?" and "Is it possible that the other person involved felt like this?" and so on, and I found myself getting sucked in to the story, even though all the novelist was doing was answering the editor's leading questions.

It had pain, and sadness, and strife, and turmoil…

And I realized it was a complete, personal story.

When they paused for breath, the editor was smiling.

"There, now. Isn't that exactly the sort of story you should write? I'd read a book like that, for sure."

The novelist looked at the sea of red ink in front of him and muttered.

"…I don't believe in myself enough." He looked up quickly, his eyes blazing. "My silly little words…this sort of everyday story… Would this resonate with someone who lives a small life just like mine, do you think? If I could do something to help others who are feeling this pain, if I could be with them through their tears, if I could help bring just a little light to other people's lives…"

"…If you write it with all you've got, then I'm sure you can."

The editor was not mincing words.

"I don't just take amazing stories and polish them up. I *draw*

them out. And together, we bring them to the people. Because…
that's what an editor does."

The novelist smoothed out the crumpled pages.

"I… I'll write it. I'll try."

The editor smiled kindly. "Don't worry. I believe in you. All
you have to do is believe in the power of your words."

Then the two packed up their work tools and began talking
about ordinary humdrum life things, as if nothing amazing had
just transpired.

★

"That was…something else, huh?" I said as we left the curry
restaurant.

"Yeah. It's kinda insane that we'd witness a scene like that the
one time we come to Tokyo."

Asuka smiled.

"So what did you think? Seeing an actual meeting between a
novelist and their editor?"

"It made me think about how I really don't know anything."
She stretched and continued. "It's kinda embarrassing. I thought
the job of an editor was to sort of flatter novelists. Get the drafts
from them and say, 'Thank you for your manuscript, maestro!'
That editor just before—he did do some flattery, but he also chal-
lenged him, even argued with him and got all fired up over it."

I felt exactly the same.

I thought the job of an editor was to nudge writers about dead-
lines and check drafts when they were already finished.

I nodded encouragingly. "It's amazing, right? If that editor just
accepted it when the novelist said his story about his youth was
a boring one, or if he'd listened and then said, 'Yeah, it's kinda
average,' then that would have been the end of it, right? And no
one would have ever gotten to hear that amazing story. It would
have just…disappeared into thin air."

Asuka continued excitedly.

"Finding stories that are still buried deep and bringing them out for others to experience—those two were both so serious and passionate about that. It's like, such a dedication to what's real..."

Asuka stopped talking and paused before continuing, an innocent and genuinely happy expression on her face.

"I'm not the only one who loves stories this much, am I?"

I think she was dealing with some serious anxieties.

She had this dream of wanting to bring words to others as an editor, being a book lover, while living in small-town Fukui, and yet she had no one to really confide in...

Now for the first time, she had found her people.

That indistinct dream of hers was rapidly becoming more real.

Asuka ran ahead of me a few steps and then whirled around, smiling at me enough to show teeth.

"I want to become an editor, after all."

I wonder why.

At that moment, I could vividly picture Asuka having a heated discussion with a stubborn novelist right here in this town— her hair a little longer than it was now, wearing a comfortable pantsuit.

At the curry restaurant from just before, with more passion than that editor from just before, getting her point across with absolute determination.

And so in my heart, I decided I would have to start getting ready to say good-bye.

∗

As we walked around Jinbocho, I realized it really was a book town, more than I could have imagined.

I didn't need to use my phone to look up anything. There were as many bookstores here as there were restaurants at Takadanobaba. There were chain bookstores, sure, but there also seemed to be specialized used bookstores selling mysteries, books on music, cars, motorbikes, everything you could imagine.

Even the tiniest bookstore seemed to have at least one hard-core patron flipping through the pages of its books. It was hard to believe there were this many dedicated readers in the world.

I wasn't as into reading as Asuka, but I also liked books, and so the two of us dived into a bookstore that looked interesting and ended up buying several volumes each.

We got so engrossed, in fact, that before we realized it, it was already half past four.

I turned to Asuka, who was bouncing along beside me, and spoke. "Is there anything else you want to see?"

"Um…maybe Shinjuku and Shibuya? I'd like to walk around some of the well-known places, I think."

I looked it up on my phone, and apparently there was a station called Shinsen-Shinjuku just one stop away on the subway. I wasn't sure what the difference was between Shinjuku and Shinsen-Shinjuku, but if it had Shinjuku in the name, it would probably get us where we wanted to go.

Using the experience we'd gained earlier, we bought tickets and got on the subway. After about ten minutes, we arrived. I thought about how it was hard to gauge the exact distances between places in the city when you could just hop on the subway.

We went up the long escalator, went through the ticket gates, and followed the signs to the south exit for the time being.

We went up two more sets of escalators, and then…

"What the…?"

My eyes almost sprang out of my head.

People, people, people, all crossing back and forth.

Tokyo Station had been a big enough shock on its own, but this was magnitudes greater than that, I thought.

This wasn't like a wave of people. This was an ocean of people.

All jokes aside, I wasn't sure where to walk or even which direction we should start off in.

But none of the people ever bumped into one another. They moved along smoothly, each going their own way.

I don't need to mention that, beside me, Asuka had completely frozen up. She was like a newborn baby deer.

On the train, she said she wanted to see the Kinokuniya bookstore, and that seemed to be in the direction of the east exit when I looked it up. But how were we even supposed to get out?

I tugged Asuka along by the hand and started walking, figuring that we'd pick it up if we just dived in.

The people in front of us moved smoothly aside.

It seemed that as long as we avoided the people walking along with their noses buried in their phones, we could follow the general flow to get where we wanted.

After continuing for a while, I spotted something that looked like an exit, so I quickly cut across the flow of people, and finally, we were out.

There was a pretty wide street outside with a lot of people around, although not as many as there had been in the station.

Asuka sounded out of breath as she spoke.

"I heard that the number of people who pass through Shinjuku Station in a day is the highest of anywhere in the world."

"I gathered that, while you were busy acting like a frozen statue. Do these people all have special training? Are they ninjas?"

I looked up the way to get to the Kinokuniya, and then we continued, sticking close to the walls.

We went down a flight of stairs and reached a backstreet with hardly any cars going down it.

But even then, the streets were filled with so many people. You'd only see this many people in Fukui once a year for the big festival.

Asuka was muttering something. "The sky seems so narrow."

I looked up as well. We were surrounded by buildings on both sides, and the blue sky looked like an artificial line drawn between them.

After a day of walking around Tokyo, my senses had numbed a little, but the tallness of the buildings in their rows was something I had never seen in Fukui.

The realization of their true height hit me, and it felt oddly oppressive.

It was more striking than ever, standing there in Shinjuku, with the smells of car exhaust and food from the many restaurants all mingled into the air. It felt wrong somehow.

We had lived our lives under wide skies with soft flowing clouds, having our conversations in the fresh breezes that smelled of the seasons, listening to the soft sounds of burbling water. And yet I had never really realized what it meant to be so surrounded by nature.

In that sense, this city really was exactly what a country bumpkin would have imagined, I thought.

Feeling quickly overwhelmed, we hurried inside the Kinokuniya and entered the Japanese-style café on the first floor, where we bought a cold matcha latte and a cold *houjicha* latte.

The place just happened to catch our eye, but as we swapped lattes back and forth, the sophisticated sweetness of the Japanese tea was really delicious.

""'That's so Tokyo!'""

The two of us gushed together, feeling a lot better, just a pair of country bumpkins.

After that, we went around the whole of Kinokuniya's seven floors, which was on an entirely different scale from Jinbocho's tiny bookshops and with many times more people.

We saw an interesting building that seemed to be some sort of collaboration between Uniqlo and an electronics supplier. We went into the Isetan department store, a respite from feeling out of place, and then we enjoyed some window-shopping at another department store called Oi Oi.

By the way, it turns out that while it's spelled *Oi Oi*, you actually pronounce it *Marui*. Is that normal? Did they name it that way just to mock country kids who come to Tokyo for the first time?

While we were wandering around, it got dark almost before we were even aware of it.

I checked my watch. It was past seven PM.

"Hey, next I want to go walking around that well-known area called Kabukicho."

Asuka, who was walking ahead of me, turned around and grinned.

"But..."

I hesitated.

"We have to head back to Tokyo Station soon, or we'll miss the last Shinkansen."

Actually, I'd planned to leave much earlier.

At this rate, we'd be taking the last train and wouldn't get back to Fukui until just before midnight. And midnight was the line that separated a one-day trip from an overnighter.

"I told you, didn't I? I left a note saying I'd be back tomorrow." Asuka gave me an impish grin.

"Haven't your parents tried to get in contact at all?"

Asuka whipped out her phone and looked at it. "Nope!" she answered breezily.

"Sure you didn't mess with the settings?"

"Come on, we've come all the way to Tokyo! This chance won't come around again. I have to soak up and experience as much as I can! Besides…"

She hung her head, looking sad as she continued.

"This could be my first and last ever trip with you."

"Don't say that. Don't look at me like that. How can I deny you if you do that?"

"I want to stay in this dream a little longer. You and I won't ever get to go on class trips together. This is our only chance to be together like this."

In this dream, huh?

I knew I didn't have it in me to drag Asuka back home.

"All right, all right! I'm the one who absconded with you to Tokyo, after all. I guess it's my duty to stick with you."

"You bet it is!"

And she grabbed my hand, like it was the most natural thing in the world.

I wanted to keep that smile on her face as long as possible.

If only she could forget about the conflict with her father, at least for the duration of this trip.

I was just squeezing Asuka's hand right back when…

Ding-ding-ding-ding.

My phone started ringing.
I looked at the screen and saw Kura's name.

* * *

Ding-ding-ding-ding, ding-ding-ding-ding.

I got a bad feeling in my gut.

That dude had never called me on a weekend, not until now.

And he only ever called me on a weekday to chase up some admin task I was supposed to have done.

Ding-ding-ding-ding, ding-ding-ding-ding, ding-ding-ding-ding.

There was only one reason why he'd be calling me at this exact time.

I looked at Asuka.

Her lip was trembling like a child—a naughty child who'd just been caught doing something wrong.

That told me all I needed to know.

Ding-ding-ding-ding, ding-ding-ding-ding, ding-ding-ding-ding, ding-ding-ding-ding.

The artificial noise wouldn't stop.

I took a deep breath, sucked in my stomach, and answered the phone.

"Hello."

"Chitose. Game over."

I thought so.

"What are you talking about? Don't I get another try?"

"You really think I can help you out here? ...Hey, Nisshi, I finally got through."

I knew two things for sure.

The truth about Asuka being here with me had already been figured out.

And Kura was trying to help us.

After all, this was the first phone call I'd gotten all day. He'd probably been buying us time up until now.

And with one sentence, he wanted me to know that.

"Hello, this is Asuka's father. Can you put my daughter on the phone?"

I wasn't talking to Kura anymore.

I looked at Asuka again.

She shook her head, her eyes brimming with tears, ready to break down at any moment. I tightened my stomach again.

Death is better than an unbeautiful life.

Right? I'm a good, old-fashioned egotist.

"Huh? What are you talking about?" I responded smoothly.

"There's no point trying to play dumb. Asuka would never do anything like this on her own. You dragged her along with you, didn't you? Acting like some kind of twisted life coach. That much is obvious."

"You know, this is highly inconvenient for me. I'm presently out on a date in Tokyo with a cute girl. I really don't have time for a long phone chat."

"Put your date on the phone."

"You think because I mentioned a cute girl it has to be your own daughter? You act all stern, but, Mr. Nishino, it sounds like you're a little obsessed."

And I meant it provokingly.

If he lost his cool, Chitose would have the advantage.

When she heard me say "Mr. Nishino," Asuka blanched and clung to me.

I gave her a rakish wink.

"You're a real funny guy, aren't you? You remind me of a young Kura."

"Please, spare me. I've actually got my act together, thanks very much."

"Hey, Chitose! I can hear you. You're on speaker."

Ah, whoops. That was rude.

"So is your plan to continue to deny everything?"

It sounded like Mr. Nishino wasn't going to let me off the hook that easily.

"I'm not denying. But this is a pointless argument. I'm telling you that Asuka isn't here. You can keep asking, but that won't make her suddenly appear. Right..."

I looked up the times for the Shinkansen on my phone.

"Tomorrow's Shirasagi train, the one arriving at twelve noon. We'll return on it. If you wait by the ticket gates, I'll be able to give you the responses you want. If it turns out that I'm with Asuka, then feel free to let your rage spill over then."

"Not bad, but naive. If Asuka's really not with you right now, then I'm going to make an immediate missing persons report to the police."

Ah crap, I thought.

Still, this was inevitable.

"Let's suppose that Asuka is with me. You're going to have trouble tracking us down in the big city of Tokyo before tomorrow noon. And after we return, I think Asuka can explain to the police that she left of her own accord easily enough."

"It doesn't matter if it's of her own accord as long as she's a minor. And there's a possibility whoever's with her will be charged as an accomplice."

Damn, he got me.

I racked my brain. "What if Asuka left for Tokyo of her own accord, and I happened to also be in Tokyo on business of my own. And then we happened to bump into one another. The possibility is slim, but you wouldn't be able to prove otherwise, would you?"

"I suppose the Fukui Station security cameras wouldn't happen to have footage of you two together, now, would it?"

"Say we bumped into one another at the station. Coincidentally ended up sitting together. Sounds like something out of a shoujo manga, but it's possible, isn't it?"

"Who bought the tickets? And when?"

Ah man, he had me in a corner. But I could still buy us time until tomorrow.

"I bought a second ticket for the girl I planned to take my trip to Tokyo with. But at the last minute we had a spat over something silly, and I had an extra ticket. Then I heard that Asuka was looking for a ticket herself. Those security cameras don't have voice recording, now, do they?"

"You've been seeing another girl?"

"I told you. Suppose that I'm actually with Asuka. Call it armchair theory. For the sake of argument."

"I see."

I could hear Asuka's father sigh.

"Illogical though it may be, as long as Asuka continues to back you up, I suppose going to the police is out of the question."

I didn't think he was serious about going to the police from the start. That's what I was banking on anyway. And as long as that was the situation, he couldn't touch me.

At the very least, as long as he could confirm that Asuka was with me, and that we hadn't run into any kind of trouble, then he wouldn't make a bigger deal of this than was necessary.

"Tomorrow at noon. The Shirasagi, correct?" said Asuka's father.

"Yes."

"It sounds like I need to have a serious conversation with you as well, don't I?"

"How about I bring you some Tokyo Banana souvenir snack cakes, and we call it even?"

"I hate bananas."

With a beep, he ended the call.

"…Ha-ha."

I blew out the breath I'd been holding.

I wouldn't say I handled that as much as weaseled my way out of it. Actually, it was more like I'd been captured and then released back into the wild.

Asuka was still clinging to my arm, looking up at me, desperately blinking back tears.

Apparently, she'd caught the gist of the conversation.

"Sorry."

Yeah, I was the one who apologized.

"..."

Her fingers dug into my arm, her head hanging in defeat.

"Looks like I'm going to have a hell of a time marrying you now," I said.

"...Huh?"

"I think your dad hates my guts."

"So then...?"

"We're on borrowed time. Until tomorrow at noon."

Her expression was like a flower blooming.

"Keep your phone switched on. If we get separated, we'll never find each other again otherwise."

Asuka chuckled and scratched her cheek, then took my hand again.

The sky above us was narrow indeed, and while we couldn't really see any stars, the moon was watching over us like always.

The streets of Shinjuku, which I'd thought of as squalid, were now glowing with colorful neon lights. It was as if we had really slipped into a dream.

For the first time, Tokyo looked beautiful to me.

*

First off, we needed to secure accommodation for the night, so we sat down in the plaza in front of the Alta, and I started looking up business hotels in the area on my browser app.

Considering our budget, we'd need to stay below ten thousand yen per person, and there were actually a surprising number of places that fit that condition.

However, even though I tried making several calls to secure a reservation, all the clean, cheap places seemed to be full, and the ones that did have space seemed a bit too shabby to bring a girl to. Even though I searched for places around Shinjuku Station, it turned out to be a different station, and I couldn't find anything at all.

I wouldn't have minded a capsule hotel or something if it was just me, but I couldn't exactly bring Asuka there.

It wasn't like there were zero options for places to stay, but I wanted to hold out for the best option as long as I could, up until our only other choice was sleeping on the streets.

Even if we tried moving to a different station, we didn't know the area, so we had no idea where to head to that might have cheap and clean business hotels.

To make it worse, both of us were pretty tired.

We're in a real fix here, I thought.

I tried looking for hotels using the map app.

There seemed to be a few options in Kabukicho, the place Asuka said she wanted to walk around.

"Shall we try walking around Kabukicho and asking at some hotels directly?"

"Okay. That might actually be faster. They might have some last-minute cancelations or something."

After nodding at each other, we began moving.

After walking along the path alongside the Alta for a while, we crossed at the lights, and then there was a big Don Quixote store. After that, it seemed to be the Kabukicho area. It was pretty big, but just from the look of the building, it was obvious that the Don Quixote stores in Fukui are much bigger. Weird thing to have a superiority complex about.

"Wow, it's like the town is alive," Asuka said. "I feel like I can hear my heart pounding."

Those words resonated with me, too.

The street with the Kinokuniya on it was amazing, but from the street alongside the Alta to here, there was way more neon light, and the slew of restaurants and drugstores and bars all seemed to meld into one. It was like this whole area was some giant living beast.

You could compare it to the Katamachi nightlife district of Fukui that Kura favors, but there were so many more people, so many more establishments, and it was all so much more garish.

"I feel like I'm understanding why they call it Kabukicho right now."

Asuka grinned wryly in agreement. "Honestly, I'm terrified."

"Same here."

Walking all around us were blond-haired young guys in suits and young women in flashy dresses with their boobs hanging half out. They were obviously all part of the night trade.

Asuka continued. "But there are also normal high schoolers walking around, too."

That's true, I thought.

Even though it felt like a completely adult world, there were young girls in uniforms walking around confidently.

"At any rate, let's both continue on, too."

Asuka nodded, but she still looked a bit scared as she grabbed hold of my sleeve.

As we walked farther into Kabukicho, we could see karaoke places and chain restaurants I also recalled seeing in Fukui, which was somewhat reassuring. Well, mixed in with those were some undeniably adult-looking establishments, and I wasn't quite sure where to put my eyes.

"Hey, look. It says there's an 'establishment information kiosk' over there. Should we check it out?"

"Are you insane?! So ignorant of the ways of the world!"

I mean, it's not like I knew all that much about it, either, but it was obviously not the kind of place where you could expect to get information on tourist spots or the best places to eat. Just look at all that neon blasting from the signs.

Asuka seemed to realize that as well and blushed bright red. She pinched my side. "Hey, that wasn't my fault just then, you know?"

I lifted my head, and right in front of us was a huge building that seemed to reach all the way to the sky.

From this distance, I could see what looked like Godzilla perched on the top of the building. It was probably a movie theater.

Seeing this kind of setup made the area feel a little safer somehow, and I felt myself relaxing, which was weird.

We turned right for no particular reason, and I turned to Asuka.

"Do you feel brave enough to get something to eat around here?"

"Not really. There are signs everywhere saying to beware of rip-off joints."

"Oh yeah. I also don't feel like eating from fast-food chains. We can eat that stuff in Fukui anytime."

Asuka sighed a little. "Well, now I've got a pretty good idea of what Kabukicho's like, and to be honest, I'm feeling pretty tired. We still haven't decided on a place to stay, either."

"I know it's a bit of a letdown to be doing this on a journey, but do you just want to grab some convenience store food and eat it at the hotel?"

"That sounds fine. We're still high schoolers, after all."

I'd actually just spotted a building with a Family Mart up ahead.

There was a neon sign on the wall saying I ♡ Kabukicho.

"I'll go buy some stuff. Want to come with?"

"Can I just leave it to you? I want to soak up the atmosphere here a little more."

"Roger that. What kind of filling do you like in your rice balls?"

"Pickled plum!"

Asuka leaned against a nearby streetlight, and I headed off to do some shopping.

✳

I bought some rice balls and simple side dishes, paid, and then when I left the convenience store, there was no sign of Asuka in the place where she'd been sitting.

I looked all around, and then, a short way off, I saw her. A blond-haired guy in a suit holding her arm.

Before I could even think, I'd started running.

"Come on, come on. You'd be super popular. How about one off the books?"

"I'm not going! Let go of me, now!"

BAM.

I slammed my shoulder into the guy.

I only meant to shock the guy, but I'd ended up checking him much harder than I'd planned to, and the guy stumbled forward, falling on his knees.

"Crap. Asuka!" I grabbed her and started running, tugging her along.

"Get back here, kid! I'll kill ya!"

I turned to see that the guy had gotten to his feet and was chasing us, but the surprise attack seemed to have confused him, and we'd been able to put more distance between us than I'd expected.

Since we didn't know the area at all, we took left and right turns at random.

"Hey! In there!"

Asuka pointed to a modern-looking building looming in front, and we dived into the entrance.

…We just managed to get inside before he could see where we went.

We gasped for breath together at first; Asuka spoke once we'd calmed down a little.

"I'm sorry I couldn't handle him by myself. I should probably have been firmer or just ignored him from the start, but when he asked if I had a minute, I thought he was going to ask me for directions."

Oh well. That was probably unavoidable. That's usually always what it is when someone stops you on the street in Fukui.

"Was he trying to scout you for something?"

"Something about a girly bar or a hostess club... He asked... He asked if I had any interest in doing adult work. And he said if I wasn't up for that...we could just go to a hotel, and he'd pay me..."

"All right! I'm going to go dispose of his body on the cliffs of Tojimbo. You wait right there, honey.♡"

"Calm down! This is Tokyo!"

It was foolish of me to leave Asuka alone.

I knew what kind of place Kabukicho was going into it, and I couldn't believe I let my guard slip before we'd even spent one full day in the city.

If we'd been more used to the area, we could have handled it better, but—and I hate to say this—it was so obvious that Asuka was a total fish out of water.

By the way, Tojimbo is one of Fukui's few tourist spots. You can enjoy the view of the cliffs that stretch along the ocean, but it's also a notorious suicide spot. It's the place where the criminal always gets chased to at the end of the Tuesday suspense dramas.

"I'm sorry, too," I said. "I should have just pretended to be your boyfriend or something and just pulled you away... But I ended up getting mad."

Asuka chuckled. "It was a golden opportunity to see you get so fired up over me, too."

She was referring to the thing with Nanase, probably.

"Obviously. You're incredibly important to me, Asuka."

"It was scary, but it was also like a scene from a novel. *The two fled from the terrible villain...*"

"I've been tugging you around since this morning with that kind of mental state. If this was a novel, you'd have to get caught at least once, or the story would end up totally dull."

"Hmph. I think it'd be fine if you could just be the cool guy without having to make a joke of everything, you know?" Asuka clucked her tongue in exasperation.

"Perish the thought. I'd die if I couldn't make bad jokes. But more importantly..." I looked around the entryway we were standing in. "Asuka, I think this might be one of those love ho— *Nguuu!*"

A pair of hands shot out and clamped down over my mouth.

"Don't say it. Don't say the word. I'll actually melt into the floor." Asuka blushed bright red and looked away as she continued. "That guy might still be roaming around, and we were originally looking for a place to stay, right? Any way you slice it, I think staying here might be the best option."

She released her grip so I could answer.

"But..."

"You came to Tokyo for me, but I ended up getting us in trouble due to my naïveté. I can't let you place yourself in any further danger. We have no idea what kind of connections that guy might have. It's okay. I trust you."

True, that guy from before looked like a delinquent, or maybe one of those host club dudes. Possibly into some really shady stuff.

Still, that's the kind of city this was.

He might have buddies. They might even be yakuza. We'd be in serious trouble in that case.

If anything happened, I wouldn't be able to face Asuka's father or Kura. And besides, I didn't want to see Asuka in any danger.

Cursing my lack of foresight, I gathered my resolve.

"Asuka, I promise I won't make it hurt."

"Hmph!"

Asuka covered her face with her hand and looked down in embarrassment, before sucking in a big breath and letting it out.

*   * ,   *

Then she looked me straight in the eye.

"…All right. I don't care if it's wrong, as long as it's with you."

"You temptress. Now that you've said that, I want to hold out at any cost," I answered without pause, not wanting her to see how rattled I was.

She grinned a mature sort of grin.

"See? I know I'll be fine, 'cause you're just that kind of guy."

Um, excuse me, Miss Future Editor. Perhaps you could take that statement and make it just a little bit clearer?

In the face of the older girl's confidence, all I could do was accept her vague statement at face value.

*

Usually, these kinds of places were off-limits to under-eighteens, but this was an emergency, so I hoped they'd make an exception for us. It would be too sad if the two kids from Fukui made it all the way to Tokyo only to end up rolled up in bamboo mats and pushed into Tokyo Bay, right?

Internally making excuses to a nameless person, I managed to check us in without causing too much suspicion.

Actually, all we did was select our room on some sort of machine thing, then pay at a front desk with a partition separating us from the clerk. We didn't have to speak to any staff members or even have them see our faces at all.

By the way, I just silently observed and then copied what the couple in front of us did.

Most of the rooms were full, but luckily there was one cheap room available, and it fit our budget.

Near the front desk there was a table set up with big bottles of shampoo and body washes that you could borrow for free, so I suggested Asuka pick whichever ones she wanted.

When we arrived at our room, we found that everything inside was basically white. There was a big double bed, a sofa, a low table, and a TV. It was a functional, stylish space.

I found myself looking around, eyes darting here and there.

The dimly lit room had a blue neon light on the wall, and every now and then it changed color, cycling through purple and then pink, which was a little irritating. The space didn't have a particularly sexy vibe to it, though, which came as a relief.

I feel like, lately, these kinds of out-of-the-blue situations keep happening to me.

Relieved of most of our tension, we put down our bags on the sofa for the time being, and then...

""So tired!""

We both dived onto the bed.

Lying on our stomachs, we stretched out, looked at each other, and grinned.

Through her messy parted hair, I could see the teardrop mole below her eye. I didn't usually see her at this angle, and she was stunning. I tried to suppress a wave of emotion, using every inch of logic I possessed.

Not noticing, Asuka spoke with an oddly perky voice. "Hey, it's unbelievable! We're in Tokyo right now. We're having a sleepover together."

I smiled wryly. "I certainly never would have believed the last part."

"It's like... I feel so free. All day long we've been like two clouds floating around, haven't we?"

Asuka drummed her arms and legs like a child.

She looked so cute that I had to bite back some kind of jibe like, "I think there's going to be a big thunderstorm tomorrow once we get back, though."

Asuka froze, as if she'd just been thinking of something, and slowly turned to look at me.

"Hey, you… Do you want dinner? Do you want to take a bath? Or do you want…?"

"Cut it out! You're not used to making corny jokes! And I'm hungry, so let's eat! Okay? Okay!"

Darn it. I just thought about Yuuko, and for some strange reason I started feeling oddly guilty.

∗

After that, we ate the food I'd bought at the convenience store.

We were tired after walking around all day, so I decided to fill the bath.

The bathroom was quite large and extravagant, and for some reason, even the tub seemed to light up with rainbow colors.

When Asuka realized that, she got all excited and said without thinking: "Hey, we could go in together!"

"Sure, you want me to join you? Wash your back? Make you a little jellyfish out of a towel?"

"…W-we could press the ADD MORE WATER button together…?"

"Not really sure what you mean by that, but if that helps cover your embarrassment, then I guess I'm all for it."

While we were finishing our food, the bath finally filled up.

Honestly, going in first didn't feel right, but neither did going in second. Since neither option felt comfortable, I decided to opt for ladies first and suggest Asuka take the first bath.

Asuka rummaged around in her bag and got ready for her bath, then she disappeared into the bathroom.

A few minutes later, I could hear the sound of the shower running.

I was glad it was the kind of room where the bathroom is separate. If it was one of those rooms where the bath is on the other side of a transparent glass wall, I don't know what I would do.

Even so, I thought.

When Nanase stayed over with me, I felt more confident since it was my own place. But here, everything was so out of the ordinary and out of my comfort zone. If I didn't keep it together, anything at all could happen.

The day seemed so long but so short at the same time, and I'd been able to spend time with Asuka not as a school friend but as a girl in her own right. Her vivid presence had already made itself known enough.

Phwoosh. Splash. Patter.

The sound of the refreshing running water threatened to send my mind places, and I had to shake my head hard.

I sat down on the sofa and looked at my phone, hoping to reassure myself. I had just one short text.

That was odd. My friends usually only ever sent me messages over the LINE app.

Use a condom.

"Go to hell!"

Of course it was from Kura.

Thanks for that, Kura! Now I've come back to reality! Nice educating, you jerk! Go die!

I checked to see if I had any messages from Yuuko and the others, and I was relieved to see I didn't. Then I felt a little bit of self-hatred for that relief.

While I killed time doing this and that, the sound of the running water changed, giving way to the blare of the hair dryer.

Finally, that stopped as well, and the door opened with a clack as Asuka stepped out, dressed in a pure-white bathrobe.

—A bathrobe?!

"Ah, that's better. Thanks for letting me go first."

She must have dried her hair quickly, not wanting to make me

wait too long. Her hair still seemed slightly damp and reached her shoulders as she stood there, casually rubbing it with a towel.

The cord of the bathrobe was tightly tied, of course, but—and I don't know whether it was designed this way or what—I could see Asuka's collarbone and a small mole that was clearly visible on the top part of her chest.

The material stretched to just above her knees, but as Asuka stepped forward, I could see her shining thighs as the robe parted.

Her skin was as white as porcelain, with a hint of cherry blossom color.

"Go ahead?"

I realized I was staring, as Asuka sat down beside me and gave me a surprised look.

The scent of the unfamiliar shampoo, conditioner, and body rinse seemed to waft over me.

"No, no, Asuka, don't move. I can see everything if you do."

"Huh? Hmm, I know, it's a little embarrassing, but I assure you, I tied the cord nice and tight."

Um, yes, yes you did, but a bathrobe is nothing but an oddly shaped towel, is it not? It's a lot looser and hanging than, say, a cotton *yukata* at a traditional inn.

It may be fine for lounging in, but you can't exactly sleep in something like that without waking in the morning to find yourself in quite a state.

What would poor Saku do if his eyes were to be assaulted with such an image?

Asuka continued. "I never expected we'd both be sleeping in the same room. I thought I could just throw on whatever the hotel had lying around."

I mean, I understand, but…still!

I certainly couldn't tell a girl to put back on the clothes she'd spent all day walking around in, and the vintage-style dress we'd bought at the secondhand clothes store wasn't really the kind of thing you could wear to sleep in.

"I wish I'd known. I would have brought some cute pajamas with me."

"Right!" I bounded over to the closet.

Normal hotels usually have all sorts of amenities set out for guests, right? ...Here it is!

"Asuka, please, do me a favor and put this on."

What I found was a very plain, normal-looking pair of pajamas that buttoned down the front.

"Wait, they had pajamas?"

It was probably hard for her to notice, since the bathrobes were just left out in plain sight, but you had to go looking for the pajamas.

"See, they have navy blue and cherry blossom colors, in matching pajama sets."

"...Isn't that a little bit embarrassing, too?"

"...Yeah, kinda."

✳

In the end, Asuka changed into the pajamas, and then I took my turn in the bathroom.

The bathtub really was lit up in rainbow colors, and I felt equal parts embarrassed and awkward as I tried to push past it.

The floor and bath stool were both wet, and the whole bathroom smelled of the same shampoo and conditioner I'd smelled just before.

To think that a few moments ago, Asuka was in here washing her body and soaking in the tub... It was hard not to think about it, but I forced myself not to as I quickly washed my hair and body under the spray.

...I may have put in a little more effort to getting squeaky-clean than I usually do.

I sank into the tub, resting my head on the edge, and thought back on the day's events.

It felt like a lot had happened since Nanase gave me the push and the scolding I needed to act, but it had actually only been a single day.

Should I really have done this? It was too late now, but I found myself wondering again anyway.

What if I really had upset Asuka's dad and ruined the relationship between them? Things were easier with Kenta and Nanase.

I had a guy I wanted to whip into shape, and I had a bully I needed to vanquish. But the real work of it was done by the individuals themselves.

This time, it was different.

Asuka's father wasn't some bully who needed beating. And Asuka was trying to stand up for herself. She was trying her best.

All I'd done, though, was drag Asuka off to Tokyo.

Would that choice really lead to any kind of positive effect on the situation?

What right do you have to insert yourself into this conversation?

Honestly, I didn't have concrete answers this time. I didn't know what I could really do to help Asuka.

I sank down up to the top of my head in the hot water, bubbles leaking from my mouth. Then I remembered that Asuka had been soaking in this exact same water minutes before, and I leaped out of the bath, sloshing water everywhere.

*

I dried my hair and left the bathroom to find Asuka lounging on the sofa in the dim room, illuminated by the glow of her phone.

I wondered if she'd gotten a message from her parents or

something, or maybe she was worried because we hadn't heard anything after that.

When she realized I was there, she put her phone back into her bag in a hurry.

Staring at me, she chuckled.

"I guess this is a little embarrassing, huh? It's like we're living together or something."

I thought back to the conversation we'd had at the university earlier as I answered.

"Well, at any rate, I'll always be the first guy you ever wore matching pajamas with. No matter how far apart we end up being in the future."

Asuka's eyes opened wide, and she looked both sad and elated at the same time as she replied. "That's something we'll never forget, huh."

As the conversation trailed off, it was replaced by an awkward silence.

We'd eaten dinner and taken baths. The next logical step was to go to bed, but it was still only eleven PM. We were tired, sure, but it was still way too early an hour for two high schoolers to be calling it a night.

I tried to think of some conversation that might bridge the gap, but for once my mind failed me, and I couldn't think of any breezy remarks.

My eyes landed on the bed. I panicked and quickly looked away, meeting eyes with Asuka as she also quickly looked away from the bed.

We both grimaced with awkwardness.

Then Asuka glanced around the room somewhat restlessly, before seeming to gather her courage and getting to her feet.

"Let's take a look around the room, since we're here," she said in a sort of innocent, uncalculated way.

"Uh, I really think you'd better not do that…"

But it was too late for me to stop her. She'd already grabbed the nearest drawer and pulled it open.

"Yeek!"

"I told you not to do that. Did you forget what kind of hotel this is?"

I went to go and stand next to her, and that's when I saw the neatly arranged condoms and lube, along with the pink vibrator with the paper slip on it that politely announced it had been sanitized.

I thumped the drawer shut again with a clenched fist.

Asuka's lips moved soundlessly before she said, "Well, *you* seem remarkably calm."

"If you think so, you should give credit to the angel on poor wittle Saku's shoulder right now."

"Almost as if you were used to this kind of thing."

"While you were standing there like a statue in the lobby, I was observing the couple in the line ahead of us. Or have you forgotten?"

"You really do think I'm some naive girl, don't you?"

"Yep! Since this morning!"

When I said that, Asuka softly put her hand on the handle of the drawer I'd just closed.

"…I'm in my last year of high school, you know. I do know about these things. I know how to use all the things in here, and I know exactly what kind of place we're in."

Her fake-mature, transparent smile made my chest hurt for a moment.

"So I mean, if it… Like, if it comes to that, I won't get scared or cry or anything. I'm not *that* much of a beginner… I don't think. It's the truth, you know?"

She looked at me, hesitantly, scanning my face for my response.

But I'm kind of evil, so I smiled at her. It was a kind smile, but a calculated one, betraying none of what I felt inside.

*　　*　　*

"But you know, this time I've spent with you…at least for this trip…I'd like to spend it innocently, like way back when… Like we're both just kids. That's…that's what I've been thinking."

When Asuka finished saying that, her tone tinged with anxiety, I looked at her, and…

It's about time we cut the crap.

That's what I thought. And it was a powerful thought.
I grabbed Asuka by the arm and threw her onto the bed.
Propping myself up on my hands, I moved my face close to hers, and…
"Huh? Huh?"
Bewildered, she squeezed her eyes shut.
And then I—

"Hyah!"

—took a pillow and whacked that beautiful face of hers with it.

"Guhhh!"

She yelped, an undignified sound.
"Why'd you do that?!" Asuka mumbled around a mouthful of pillow as I proceeded to smoosh it against her face.
I responded with coolness. "Just like you wanted. I'm giving you the quintessential high schooler overnight trip pillow fight experience."
"Huh? What? Is that really how we're playing this?!"
"Now. You. Listen!"
Whap, whomp, whack. I assaulted her rhythmically with the pillow to punctuate each word.

"Do you have any idea how hard I'm clinging to my shoulder angel right now and trying not to think about certain things?! Were you talking like that on purpose just now, Asuka? What are you, some sort of demon?!"

"But, but... Ow, hey! You're a guy, so I thought I should prepare myself mentally for certain things..."

"My inner angel and devil have been hashing that out enough without your help! Don't underestimate the libido of a boy in the prime of his youth! You wanna skip the last three steps on the stairway to adulthood, really?!"

"...Er, um..."

"Don't! Waver! Now! You! Fool!"

Phwap, thwack, whomp, plomp.

"If you wanna be an editor, then think about the story fundamentals! Climb step by step! Control the readers' bubbling emotions! If I have you now, Asuka, they're going to burst into flames! You wanna live in Tokyo, right? You want to make a life in this city, don't you?"

Through the pillow, I could tell she was nodding.

"Then get it together. Don't just go with the flow. Focus on your own free will, on what makes you Asuka. See others for who they really are. Focus on your dream! You gotta be you!"

Nod, nod, nod, nod.

"And if, in the future, there *is* a future for us together, and if we're both willing to hold each other in the highest regard and join our bodies...then, only then, will we take those final steps. That's the best way, isn't it? I'm an old-fashioned kinda guy, you see."

"Um, can I just—just say one thing?" Asuka mumbled quietly.

Thwack!

She swung at me with the second pillow, the one I hadn't noticed, and whacked me full-on in the face with it.

"Quit running your darn mouth off! I understand story fundamentals! I understand narrative flow! I *do* see others for who they really are, and I'm *not* wavering! Don't talk like you know everything, you crazy *man*!"

"That wasn't just one thing!"

After that, we embarked on a frenzied, school trip–style pillow fight.

"Not bad, you shabby princess! I'm going to beat an awareness of the harshness of the world into you!"

"Oh yeah? Well, bring it on! All you can do is chatter pointlessly when a woman comes on to you!"

It was like that day I met Asuka, with those kids.

"Darn you! I'm gonna grab that *BEEP* from over there and *BEEP* you, you *BEEP*ing *BEEP*!"

"You can use the actual words, you know? A mature woman like me doesn't need a little kid like you to mince words for her!"

"Wish you had an ounce of that maturity when we were walking the Tokyo streets!"

We were yelling and screaming and laughing together.
Jumping on the bed, on the sofa, whacking each other with pillows.

One day we'll be grown-ups—in fact, we've got no choice in that.
But until then, I want to be a kid to the fullest extent possible, I thought.

If you don't get being a kid right, you've got no chance once you're an adult.

And a night like this is a great time to be childish.

*

Exhausted, we flopped side by side on the double bed, staring at the ceiling.

I planned to try to sleep on the sofa, like when Nanase stayed over, but Asuka said, "That's way too boring."

Well anyway, it was obvious this wasn't going to end up a true boy-girl kind of night.

"Man, I'm sweating like a pig. And after I'd already taken a bath, too. Do I stink?"

Asuka buried her nose in my chest and huffed. "You do! You do stink!"

"Want me to sniff your chest, too?"

It was around eleven PM.

The clock in the room was digital, but in my head, I could practically hear a clock's hand ticking out the remaining time, second by second.

"Shall we talk about something?" Asuka said. "This is our once-in-a-lifetime, spectacular trip. We'll probably never get to do this again. We need to discuss something momentous. So that even if we forget the scent of the shampoo we both used, we'll still be able to remember this conversation."

True, we'll never get the chance to go on a trip exactly like this again, I thought.

It wasn't about who I was with, or the destination.

It was about this moment in time. Diving into an unknown city with the girl I admired so much.

Right now, we were like characters from a novel. No need to point out who's the main character, though, of course.

"I mean…," Asuka continued. "Tell me a story about yourself?"

"I don't have any stories suitable for a night like this."

"It doesn't have to be anything fancy. I don't need drama or romance. Just tell me how you came to be who you are today?"

Weighing up the meaning behind her words, I looked over at that face.

So solemn, so kind, a little transparent. Her eyes looked like they could burst into tears at any moment.

And so I understood what she was asking of me.

"If I talk about that, will it light even one candle in your future, Asuka?"

"I need it. The way I am right now, the end of this trip, this night. Tell me about yourself?"

It was a story I had never told to a single person.

Not to Yuuko Hiiragi, not to Yua Uchida, not to Haru Aomi, not to Yuzuki Nanase, not to Kaito Asano, not to Kazuki Mizushino, and not to Kenta Yamazaki—well, except for part of it.

Because…

"I'm sure it won't live up to your expectations. It's a very mundane, cheap sort of past. Nothing worth making into a story."

That's the kind of story it was.

Asuka took my hand softly.

"Even if it is a mundane, cheap sort of story—as an editor, I'll make it a story unlike any other in the world."

Ah, in that case, I can relax.

I can be a child in front of her, at least a little.

On this once-in-a-lifetime night, I can probably write a once-in-a-lifetime story.

I can't do it as well as you did—not like the words you brought to me once—but I can tell you the trivial, boring, asinine story of Saku Chitose.

*

"Since I was young, I've always been the type to stand out. If you want to know when it started, I know at least from kindergarten a lot of the girls really liked me, and I was always the winner during the sports day races."

"Mm."

"Nothing changed when I entered elementary school. The girls still all really liked me, and nobody could beat me in gym class, on sports day, and during the running tournaments. I got top grades on all the tests just from paying attention during class."

"Mm."

Up to this point, this was the exact same story I'd told Kenta. Asuka kept saying "Mm," but each time she said it, it had a different inflection to it. That told me that she was listening carefully but wasn't going to interrupt.

"The first time I started realizing that maybe I was special, it was the fourth year of elementary school. I started noticing the others and realizing that none of them could do stuff as well as I could."

"Mm."

"But it's not like I looked down on the other kids. I cared a lot about my friends, whether they could run fast or not, and I was often pushed into the leadership position. I just wanted to get along with everyone."

"Mm."

"I know it sounds bad to say it yourself, but I think, compared to how I am now at least, that I was a pretty decent guy. I would never forsake my friends, and I always tried to help people in trouble."

"Mm."

"I remember it, even now. There was this girl in my class who everyone sort of avoided. During lunch break, she'd sit by herself, hugging herself and drawing pictures in silence. Everyone said she was gloomy and creepy. But there was some sort of event where we had to pair up, boy-girl, and when I saw her sitting silently with her head hanging low, I asked her, '*Do you want to pair up with me?*'"

"Mm."

"It's not like I thought I was Mr. Cool for pairing up with a girl who had no friends; I actually offered with pure intentions. But sometimes you don't even realize yourself what you're taking part in."

"Mm."

"When I actually talked to her, she seemed totally normal, even kind of interesting. She showed me some of her drawings. She'd drawn some manga characters I liked, really good work. She got all excited, and the next day she gave me one as a gift. That actually really made me happy."

"Mm."

"Then after that, she told me she liked me, and when I said no, she tried to make me feel bad about it. Said all this stuff like I should never have been nice to her, that she didn't want my pity."

"Mm."

"Everyone around me blamed me, too. '*Oh, Chitose made a girl cry.*'"

"Mm."

"I wasn't pitying her. I honestly thought her drawings were cool. And it was fun talking about manga with her. I thought we could become friends. If I was a more normal kind of guy, if it was less of a big event for me to have reached out to her, then I don't think she would have misunderstood the way she did."

"Mm."

"Usually, it was other people coming to me for things. I basically never turned down anyone who needed my help. At first, people were all so grateful, like, '*Oh, thanks so much.*'"

"Mm."

"But then they got used to it. They started to say, like, '*If it's a pain to do yourself, then just ask Chitose. He'll take care of it.*'

Doing it themselves was too much work, but *he* can do it with one hand tied behind his back, so why shouldn't he be the one to do it? Like that."

"Mm."

"So anytime I tried to turn down requests, or if the results I provided didn't fit with what the person expected, they'd get all disappointed, and even worse, they'd say, '*Why? Why can't you help me out just a little bit?*' or '*You just phoned it in, didn't you?*' and make all these complaints to me."

"Mm."

"And it all started to stack up. The image of Chitose as 'the guy who can do anything, everyone's buddy' started to slowly erode, and then everyone was bashing me way more than I deserved."

"Mm."

"I think that's when I started playing junior baseball. I quickly got much better at the game than the other kids who joined when I did, and I started catching up to the older kids at a fast rate."

"Mm."

"But you know, at that age, you can't be the best at sports or studying just relying on the natural gifts you were born with. I wasn't the tallest around, and the other guys all started going through growth spurts."

"Mm."

"I started off coasting by on my natural gifts, so I was scared. I realized I'd be overlooked and discarded if the others caught up and overtook me. I was only popular because I was Chitose, the guy who can do anything, everyone's buddy, after all."

"Mm."

"Honestly, during the lower school years, there were lots of kids who were great at sports and studying like me but who gradually fell to the middle of the pack as the years went by."

"Mm."

"So I worked as hard as I could. Even in elementary school, I studied harder than anyone before tests, and when the running competitions were getting closer, I'd practice by running along the riverbank every day. Even baseball. I practiced my swings until the skin peeled off my hands. None of the older kids even did that."

"Mm."

"Then, when I entered fifth year, it got to the point where everyone just took for granted that I could do anything. No one dreamed that I was expending effort in secret. And I never breathed a word about it, of course. I thought that what everyone wanted was the Chitose who could do everything without even having to break a sweat."

"Mm."

"It didn't take long for them to start looking for my rare screwups and failures, rather than the victories. After all, the victories were boring. For example, if I got one hundred points on the test, they'd make faces at me, but if I got a ninety, they'd get so excited they'd start clapping. *What, Chitose didn't get one hundred points? Is he actually stupid or something?*"

"Mm."

"They didn't just wait around for my failures. They actively tried to make me fail. No one would pass the ball to me when we played soccer in gym. The homework I thought I'd done would disappear from my desk. They'd put this joke perfume on my gym clothes to make them stink. There was no limit to what they'd do."

"Mm."

"Then they all laughed like it was the greatest fun ever. *Can't score a goal, can you, huh, what happened to your homework, huh,* ribbing me all the time like that. Ha-ha-ha, like it was the funniest joke they'd ever heard."

"Mm."

"But none of them saw it as bullying. Including me. I knew if I hit back at them, it wouldn't change the way they saw me. And after school, the kids who'd been teasing me still played with me, like friends."

"Mm."

"I think they were all just trying to even the score any way they could."

"Mm."

"I mean, since I was born with everything they lacked, and I stood out more than anyone, they figured I could take a little pounding into the dirt. Like they wanted to give me a handicap, just a little. Like kids who are blessed with talent should just expect that kind of thing."

"Mm."

"But at the time, I was still just a kid. It hurt, and it made me sad. All I was doing was trying to do my best at things, so why did I have to take such abuse from kids like them who never tried?"

"Mm."

"Then the downtrodden boy thought: *If I make myself like the others, they'll stop picking on me.* He missed shots on purpose in soccer games, he left questions blank on tests even though he knew the answer, and when his friends asked for help, he just glowered at them and said no."

"Mm."

"But that didn't make them happy, either. They'd already placed this poster board around my neck, written *Talented* and *Gifted* on it, and there was nothing I could do to get it off. All my efforts were written off. My mistakes were blown out of proportion. If I let other kids beat me in gym, they'd crow about it. '*Chitose's not what he's cracked up to be*,' they'd say."

"Mm."

"I was just a kid, so I didn't know what to do. If I succeeded, I was screwed. If I failed, I was screwed. If I tried to act average, that didn't work because of my past record of being exceptional. They just thought I was losing my edge."

"Mm."

"Then one of the teachers, who'd been keeping an eye on me, said something to me."

This was the same thing I'd told Kenta.

"A boy like you, blessed with all these gifts, ought to be standing in front of the class and serving as an example to the others. You may wonder why you're the only one who has to put in this much effort, but the other kids—well, they're wondering why you're the only one who has all these gifts… So you have to fly even higher. You have to run even faster. Until you become a real hero, the kind who inspires the others to follow along behind you…"

From now on, the rest of it was the real truth, the part I hadn't shared.

"I took those words in a completely different way than how the teacher intended me to take them."

"Mm."

"I thought that trying to be an average kid was just making the others want to drag me down with them. I decided I had to be completely perfect, so far above them that they'd never even think of comparing themselves to me."

"Mm."

"I swore to be the perfect hero, not to help others, but to keep them all away from me."

"Mm."

"It was all much easier after that. One by one, I identified my weaknesses, the cracks in the armor where something was missing, and sealed them up tight."

"Mm."

"I mean, if I helped a boy who was being bullied in junior high, he would follow along after me every day after that. He'd end up waiting outside my house on the weekend. I just couldn't stand by and watch someone being bullied—that was all—but that didn't mean I had to be best friends with the guy starting the very next day, did I? But when I told them they were bothering me, they would go off and start waging a slander campaign against me."

"Mm."

"Well, in that case, I should never have bothered being nice in the first place. I should have emphasized how I was only helping them for my own reasons. *Don't go thinking that, because I helped you out, I want to hang around with you.* If I did that, I could have avoided people putting all these expectations on me and being disappointed."

"Mm."

"If I confided in the people I believed were my friends when I was having issues, the very next day they'd be off telling everyone my weaknesses and laughing about it. So in that case, I shouldn't bother showing people what was inside me. I needed to draw a firm line with everyone, not get involved with anyone, and not let anyone get to know me too well."

"Mm."

"The girls who caught feelings for me and ended up getting rejected by me, and the guys who had crushes on these same girls, would call me a womanizer and a playboy. So I figured I should make sure everyone knew I was untrustworthy from the start. That way, they'd know I wasn't the type of guy to seriously fall for in the first place."

"Mm."

"If people were just going to end up talking smack about me anyway, then I figured I should keep my distance from everyone from the start and act like a total arrogant asshole."

"Mm."

"But I knew it would just piss everyone off if I was always too perfect, so I decided to start throwing in a few cringey jokes every now and then, just to let the pressure out a little."

"Mm."

Like when a girl I'd thought was a precious friend confessed her feelings to me and I turned her down coldly, then the next day she claimed I'd dated her for the heck of it and then discarded her.

Like when there was a group of upperclassmen who started throwing their weight around and came to push me around, knowing I couldn't fight back because I didn't want to cause trouble for the baseball team.

Like when one guy got it into his head that I'd stolen his girl, and he came bursting into our classroom, then caused a huge commotion over nothing in front of all my classmates, then threw my phone out the window.

Like when my good grades led to people starting a rumor that I was getting "extra lessons" from the young, attractive teacher.

Like when my parents divorced, and someone wrote all the gory details up on the classroom blackboard.

Like in first year, when I became a regular on the team, and people started ignoring me just because my seniors told them to.

And then, in high school—

"I mean, I could tell you about all kinds of incidents in detail, but it's not like any one thing in particular became a source of trauma. But what I'm saying is that all these little stones they threw chipped away at me until what was left was the guy I am today."

See? I told you it was a trivial, boring, asinine story.

＊

"…And that's the end."

Asuka's repeated interjections to let me know she was still listening finally stopped. I hesitated to look at her.

"See? It's just kinda cheap and humdrum. No grand story to be found there."

Since there was no response, I continued.

"That day, I intended to reach for the moon. I wanted to be like a glass marble that had sunk inside a bottle of Ramune. I wanted to be someone everyone wanted, something so valuable that no one could seek to ever change it."

The neon light along the wall illuminated me in my pathetic state.

"But I think I may have been wrong about everything from the start. A Ramune bottle marble isn't the moon in the night sky. It's trapped between hard walls, surrounded, fearful. All it can do is stare at the moon from inside its glass bottle, its distant glow illuminating the darkness. It can't go anywhere."

And I was never the moon. I was just a marble.

This is that kind of story.

I'd told Kenta as much, at some point.

I'm confident in my philosophy, my way of living.

I want to be like a marble sunken inside a bottle of Ramune.

Those words, they weren't untruths.

I like the way I'm living. And I think it suits me.

But every now and then, on nights like tonight, for example, I get to thinking.

What was I reaching for that day? And where am I now?

Asuka sighed, a short puff of air.

"I finally understand. You were like a hero who'd jumped out of a shounen manga. Effervescent, innocent, passionate, straight-forward, and kind. Now I understand how you became that way."

I looked at her, unable to grasp her meaning.

Asuka smiled at me, with kindness—no, happiness.

"It's not true that your life doesn't contain a good story. It contains so many of them."

Her hand gently parted my hair, and her hand was cooler than I felt.

"Usually, people would try to make the things you experienced into a story. 'Guess what happened to me—I suffered so much, I was so sad, it hurt so bad.' They just spin it into excuses for being weak."

Her voice was endlessly soft.

"When they couldn't do their best, when they gave up, when life didn't go the way they wanted, they drag out those stories to make themselves feel better. 'That happened to me, so it wasn't my fault.' Then they wear this stamp of being hurt by the world, and they start trying to hurt others they think the world hasn't hurt yet. To borrow an expression, they try to even the score."

"But you know...," Asuka continued.

"You refused to make your past a story. You wrote it off as trivial, boring, asinine pain. And you're trying your best to overcome it in your own way."

I felt something inside my chest thud.

"You didn't have a hero like yourself who would come to save you, so you protected your own way of living and your own sense of reasoning. So that you could live a beautiful life."

"...You're making it sound much more dramatic than it is."

"You made a point to downplay it; that's why."

Her warm smile enveloped me, and I bit my lip to keep it from trembling.

"I mean, I..."

—And then I couldn't stop the flow of words.

"I wanted to be like a shounen manga hero when I was younger. Honest and true, facing up to all kinds of things, putting in effort. Treasuring my friends, and when I saw someone in trouble, reaching out a hand to them, no questions asked. I wanted to be someone like that…"

But, but, but.

"But no one wanted that from *me*!!!"

I squeezed Asuka's hand tight.
Ah, man. What am I doing?
I shouldn't have said all of this.
I was infuriated with myself, the weakness I'd let leak out.
I'm no moon—even though right now, I've got a duty to light the way for this girl.
Then, with her gently rounded, neatly cut nail, she poked my forehead.

"That's just you all the way, though."

I had no idea what she meant by that.
"All right, you may have gone about it in a complicated, twisty sort of way, but you reached out to both Kenta and Nanase without a second thought, and you did everything you could to tackle their problems head-on and reach a solution. You cared about them both as friends."

"That doesn't…"

"You know, I'd really rather leave it at that, based on what I've seen of you so far, so that I don't end up disappointed later on. More to the point, I'd rather not hurt someone with my good intentions."

"…"

*   *   *

"You always paint yourself as the bad guy, always choosing self-serving options. Even if you want to help someone, and you reach out to them earnestly, it ends up with them being disappointed in you. So you figure, 'If I'm only going to get hurt, then whatever, I'm used to it.'"

"..."

I bit my lip again. I didn't want to be tempted to seek refuge in her kindness.

"But you're wrong. It's not that noble. Yuuko, Yua, Nanase, Haru, Kazuki, Kaito, Kenta, even you, Asuka—you've all said stuff to the effect that you think I'm somebody special. But the real Saku Chitose tries to give up all the time, only he can't. He's just a lame brat who's flailing about and failing."

"That's what we call…"

Asuka paused, smiling warmly at me.

"…our hero."

I didn't know how to respond, so she looked at me and continued.

"No one could keep up what you do. No one could keep on reaching out to the far distance despite believing they never could. So when you see people like that, you think you're normal, and the other people are distorted. If you didn't do that, you couldn't kid yourself into believing that you're not desperately passionate about things."

* * *

Asuka touched my cheek gently.

"Maybe it's the full moon you want to become, Saku. But whether you're a half-moon, or a crescent moon, or a marble sunken inside a bottle of Ramune—you're still a precious treasure to someone."

I squeezed her hand and closed my eyes tight. If I didn't, I had the feeling something inside me might break.

"Hey. Touch me?"

Asuka's voice was a whisper as she stroked my hand with each of her fingers in turn.

"My forehead, my cheek, my lips, my shoulder, my arm. Even my stomach… It's a little embarrassing, but even my thighs, my calves, my knees, my toes."
As she spoke, she guided my hand to each area.

Either directly, or through the thin cloth, I could feel her body warmth, her softness, her smoothness, through my fingers, and it was maddening.

"I'm right here, you see?"

Asuka captured my hand and squeezed it tight again.
Her expression was so filled with kindness that I felt dirty for having harbored impure thoughts.

"I can vouch for the fact that your shine has illuminated the life of at least one person."

*   *   *

Her smile, floating in the blue night, called to mind the moon that I'd been reaching for all this time.

*

After that, we lay on the bed and chatted about all kinds of things.

The books we liked, manga, movies, music.

The urban legends we'd believed in as kids, the secret places around town only we knew, the toys we used to love, what was going to happen going forward.

It was almost as if we would awaken from some sort of dream if we stopped talking.

Eventually, Asuka trailed off, and soon she began snuffling contentedly in sleep.

This once-in-a-lifetime night had finally ended.

I looked at Asuka.

She was like a small child, sleeping exhausted from too much play. Her mouth hung open a little.

If there came a day ten years from now when I looked back and remembered this night, I wondered how much of an adult I'd be then.

And who would be by my side?

I closed my eyes, thinking about it.

On the other side of sleep, a young boy and a young girl were running around on the street in summer.

*

The next day, we woke up at seven, got ready, and left the hotel.

The town was silent and peaceful, as if all the hustle and bustle of the previous night had only been a hallucination.

There were hardly any people around, just crows pecking at garbage bags.

In the Matsuya, a youngish woman who looked like she belonged to the night trade was slinging beef bowls. Here and there you spotted drunks passed out blissfully in the gutters.

At Tokyo Station, we bought coffee and sandwiches, along with some simple souvenirs, and boarded the Shinkansen.

We didn't speak much for the three-hour journey home. Instead, we listened to music, sharing one earbud each, and gazed out the window as the scenery flowed past.

In my ear, "Bye Bye, Thank You" by Bump of Chicken played on repeat.

I think our trip actually ended last night.

Asuka had this look on her face like a demon had passed through her, and I was sure I had the same kind of expression.

Was I able to help her in some way, through this brief elopement?

Walking around the city where someday she might live, having rare experiences, talking about things we couldn't usually talk about. Maybe that's all it was. Or maybe it was a transformative experience.

My role was over.

Now all that was left was for Asuka to write her own story, the only one of its kind in the world.

The skyscrapers of Tokyo soon fell away behind us, and when the Shinkansen reached Maibara, the scenery had already long changed into endless rice fields.

We got off the Shirasagi at Fukui, and the first thing that struck me was how good the air smelled.

It's a cliché, maybe, but I could smell the vibrant, fresh scent of the greenery all around.

We were preparing to go down the stairs to the ticket gate when Asuka asked, "Can we hold hands?"

Considering who I knew was waiting for us below, I didn't think that was such a great idea, but I said nothing and silently held out my hand.

Then together, step by step, we descended the stairs.

*

SMACK.

The moment we stepped through the ticket gate, which was a lot smaller than the one in Tokyo Station, a slap landed on Asuka's cheek.

"Hey, if you're going to be hitting anyone, it should be me. I'm the one who took Asuka away," I said.

Asuka's father responded, expressionless.

"I can't think of a reason why I'd need to slap *you*. Asuka's the one who made the decision for herself and acted on it."

I could see Kura standing a short distance away.

When I stepped forward to say something back...

"It's okay."

...Asuka stopped me.

Then, with a clear, pure smile, she said:

"Dad, I'm sorry for worrying you." She bowed low, politely. "Whatever you mean to do, please do it."

"Oh, I will."

Then Asuka looked at Kura, who came shuffling up in his shabby old wooden-soled sandals.

"I'm sorry for worrying you, too, Kura."

"I was only worried about one thing."

He gave me a loaded grin.

You dirty old man. If you make a crack about that here, now, you're dead.

"I have a request to ask of you both," Asuka said. "The day after tomorrow, after school. Can we have another parent-teacher meeting?"

Right. She's made up her mind, I thought.

Asuka's father breathed a huge sigh and then looked at Kura.

"I don't mind. I'm not doing anything exciting after school."

"Thank you. Dad?"

"...I think it's about time you started studying seriously with a mind to applying to your first-choice college. Consider this final meeting the last time we'll ever discuss this."

"All right. I understand." Asuka smiled, a light, clear smile, and then looked at me. "And you. Tomorrow after school. You'll go on one more date with me."

""Huh?""

Asuka's father and I both grunted in surprise at the same time, and then he glared at me.

"All right, so it's decided, then!" Asuka trotted forward lightly.

Her father trailed after her reluctantly, looking sort of dumbfounded.

I called out to him. "Mr. Nishino. Here."

And I handed him the paper bag containing the Tokyo Banana snack cakes I'd bought.

"I thought I told you I hated these."

"That's why I bought them."

I grinned, and Mr. Nishino accepted the bag with a disgusted but resigned look. Then he seemed to remember something. He opened up his wallet and pulled out three ten-thousand-yen notes.

"Asuka's Shinkansen fare. Thank you for looking after my daughter."

Then he turned and left, and he didn't look back this time.

Kura slapped his hand down on my shoulder.

"You two kids ruined my weekend. You owe me *yakiniku*."

"Can't I just treat you to Hachiban instead?"

And with that, our brief elopement was over for real.

*

After a deep, dreamless sleep, Monday after school rolled around.

I still had some time until Asuka and I were due to meet, so I was chatting with the members of Team Chitose before they all left for club practice.

It felt like returning to the real world. This weekend had been a lot, mentally, and I finally registered that.

Then...

"Hey, friend! Time for our date."

An unexpected figure came bounding in.

"Gah! I thought we were meeting at the school gates."

I realized what I'd just said, but it was too late to unsay it now.

"Hmph!"

"Really?"

"Interesting."

"Huh!"

That was Yuuko, Yua, Nanase, and Haru speaking, by the way. Now I'd confirmed that we really did have a standing date, and it hadn't been Asuka just goofing around.

Grinning with enjoyment, Asuka joined our circle.

From the look on her face, I could see that she hadn't suffered a long night of fighting with her dad after getting home, which came as something of a relief.

"I mean, when I think about it, we go to the same school, so why should we meet right on the perimeter? Besides, there's something thrilling about going to a classroom for one of the lower grades to meet my date!"

"Asuka, does your head or back hurt? There are a lot of daggers being thrown your way right now."

"Uh, I think they're actually throwing them at you."

"I do feel a certain prickling."

Then Kaito jumped in. "You're something else, aren't you, Saku?! Nishino, are you sure you wouldn't consider dating me?"

"Hmm, I don't think so."

"Noooo!!!"

Asuka poked her own cheek playfully, while Kenta patted Kaito on the back reassuringly.

Seeing this, Kazuki said, "Darn you, neglecting our own princesses." He gave the four girls a loaded grin.

"Grrr!"

It was Yuuko who finally reacted. "Listen here, Nishino. Saku and I are endgame, and Ucchi is his sidepiece, got that? As long as we're clear—I see no problem here."

"Yuuko, please don't drag me into this..." Yua smiled with awkward embarrassment.

Asuka spotted her reaction and seemed deep in thought, mumbling, "Hmm... So then, can I be the childhood friend turned fiancée?"

"What for?" I responded with snark, without really thinking.

Really, what a thing to suggest.

Nanase put both hands in the air as if to say "Sheesh." "All right, but you owe us one, okay?"

Asuka grinned impishly.

"Who do you think you have to thank for helping this guy here know how to help you out, Nanase?"

She was probably referring more to the way she'd helped me get back on my feet after I quit baseball than to the advice she gave me on Nanase's issue.

It was unusual for Asuka to bring that up, but maybe it meant that she now thought it was okay to mention.

"...Then shall we call it even?"

"Sure, we can forget about the change."

The corner of Nanase's mouth started twitching in annoyance, which really tickled me.

Finally, Haru spoke. "Honestly, what does a beautiful, cool girl like you, Nishino, see in this playboy?"

"The answer to that…" Asuka paused by the door, turning around. "…Well, I think you already know it, don't you, Aomi?"

I slunk my way out of the circle, unable to bear hanging around any longer.

*

After that, Asuka and I got on a train at Fukui Station.

We were riding the local line, but no one ever had any reason to ride it except for the students who lived in the opposite direction.

All the places where high schoolers hung out could be reached by bicycle, and if you needed to go farther afield, for example to a practice game or something, you could get the bus or get a ride in your dad's car.

I asked her why we were taking this train, but Asuka kept dodging the question.

Well, I'd find out once we arrived.

That's what I told myself, and then, after about twenty minutes, Asuka said, "This is it."

I stepped out onto the platform, not really thinking much of anything, but then…

Huh?

My mind ground to a halt.

This place was familiar to me. It was filled with memories.

A coincidence? Could that be possible?

I turned to Asuka.

Her eyes were squinted, as if she was thinking about the past, and…

"Hey. Can I stop being the older one for a while?"

*   *   *

She said.

I couldn't respond. She clasped her hands together, tilted her head to one side, and gazed at me.

Then she broke into a big smile, like a child who can't suppress their happiness.

"It's been a long time, *Saku*."

"Y-you're..."

A faint illusion, a young boy and girl, coming closer.

This place, right here, is the town where I, Asuka Nishino, was born, and where I lived until fifth year of elementary.

It's technically in Fukui City, but it's on the fringes.

If you walk a little, you can get to the neighboring Sakai City. It's not exactly the most countryside place in Fukui Prefecture, but it is pretty much surrounded by nothing but rice fields.

Not much to do here. Not much at all.

For weekend excursions, there's a shopping center called Ami, which doesn't really hold a candle to Lpa. My favorite thing to do was to visit the bookstore in the center or go to the Miyawaki bookstore nearby and buy the latest books.

So I was born in this kind of small town, to two strict teachers. Naturally, I was a sheltered and boring girl. I was quite good at studying, not great at sports, and I was hardly the type to be the center of attention in class.

That said, it's not like I was super gloomy and never had conversations with anyone. I had friends. I guess it would be most accurate to describe myself as completely average.

There weren't any kids my age living nearby, and I wasn't allowed to go very far to play. Once school was over, I'd go straight home and immerse myself in books, and I never got anywhere near sick of it.

My classmates gathered at each other's houses after school to play, so perhaps they thought I was a bit aloof.

But I felt like all I really needed was my stories.

The protagonists from my novels were all so amazingly straightforward, so passionate, so kind and inspiring. They followed their dreams and flew out freely into the world.

If only I could be like that, I thought over and over.

But while I admired the boys and girls in my stories, I was able to differentiate clearly between what was reality and what was fiction.

After all, I had my parents telling me, "You can't do this, you can't do that," and I could never have anything my own way.

If I wanted to go to a festival, if I wanted to sleep over at a friend's house, if I wanted to go somewhere new by myself—none of that would become a reality without my parents' permission.

I was raised hearing that as long as I did everything my parents said, I'd grow up to be a fine adult. Even now, it's not like I think they were wrong about everything.

But in the summer of my fourth year of elementary, I met a boy.

He was younger than me but so amazingly straightforward, so passionate, so kind and inspiring.

"It's been a long time, *Saku*."

"Y-you're…"

I said it. I finally said it.

The words I'd been suppressing since September last year, when I met him.

I gazed at the face of the person standing beside me.

He always acted so cool but was now looking completely taken aback, eyes wide, mouth slack.

Were those few words enough to prompt him to remember?

It would be a little bit of a shock—no, a big shock—if the memory didn't exist in some corner of his mind, after all the trouble of coming all the way here.

"What's wrong, Saku?"

I peered at his shocked face and gave him another teasing prompt.

He didn't come out with any wisecracks. Instead, he seemed to either be trying very hard to retrieve a memory from the back of his mind or trying to put the situation into some kind of logical order.

Well, that makes sense.

To you, I'm Asuka, the girl from a year above you. I'd never call you Saku, only Chitose, right?

But before I ever called you Chitose, I called you Saku, you know?

"Uh, wait…" He put his hand to his forehead as he spoke. "Did…did you and I meet before? Maybe when we were little?"

"Yup."

"Maybe you had long hair back then? Like, to mid-back?"

"Yup."

"And maybe your personality was a bit more timid?"

"Yup."

"We played together during the summer vacation?"

"Yup. Correctamundo."

"Why didn't you say something earlier?!"

I couldn't hold it back anymore. I burst out laughing.

True, my appearance and demeanor have changed a lot since then. Come to think of it, I'm pretty sure I never told him my name.

At the time, he always just called me "friend."

"Do you remember? Back then, we weren't Asuka and Chitose. We were 'friend' and Saku."

"Oh, come on…?"

"I told you, right? Some fairy tales are real. And closer than you'd think."

Chitose... *Saku* scratched his head, messing up his hair.

I grabbed his hand as he stood there in confusion, and we left the small country station.

I took a big breath, and I could smell the familiar scent of the rice paddies. I could smell where they'd burned the crops. No doubt big-city folk would say it stunk, but to me, it was a soothing scent, the scent of my girlhood.

"All this time, I thought it was a girl much younger than me," Saku said as he walked beside me.

"It wasn't until the second summer that I actually realized I was the older one, too. It was when I asked you when your birthday was. But it was too awkward to point it out then, so I just let it slide."

In elementary school, girls tend to mature faster than boys, which I think was part of it. But it was also because of the first impression I got of him—that he was a reliable, older boy.

In comparison, I was an overprotected girl who didn't know anything about the world. It was easy to see how we made that mistake.

"Man, this place takes me back. I got so busy with baseball after graduating elementary school that I haven't been back." Saku was looking all around as we walked. "Now I remember; there's that little shrine on the other side of the road, isn't there? I went there with you, didn't I?"

Of course I remember. It's one of my most precious memories.

"So you brought me here to blow my mind, hmm?"

"That was one of my intentions. But the other one is to confirm where it all started, I guess."

"Where it all started?"

"Would you listen to my story this time?"

Saku nodded, so I began my story slowly.

＊

It was the summer of the fourth year of elementary.

There was an old lady who lived alone, and she lived nearby, and I heard that there was a young boy visiting her.

She was really friendly and used to slip me candy. In the past, she'd said to me, "When he comes to visit, be a dear and play with him, won't you?"

So as promised, I had to go by and ask him to play. But to be honest, my heart was pounding at the thought.

I'd never been alone with a boy before, and I had no idea what he would be like.

There was no guarantee he'd be as nice as his nice grandmother, and apparently he lived in the town. Maybe he'd mock me for being a country girl.

So I put on my most mature-looking dress and my straw hat and went out to meet him.

I considered my outfit armor to guard my heart if needed.

Then I met a boy who had a face as pretty as a girl's. His skin was pretty suntanned, and the arms coming out of his tank top were muscular, very different from mine.

When he smiled, his white teeth flashed.

"Hey, friend. You live around here, then?" the boy said, looking at me.

"Y-yes. Not far."

His fearless manner had me shrinking back a little.

At school, there were a lot of cheerful, outgoing boys, but I also found them a little crude, and I disliked them because of it.

"So then, would you mind showing me around?" But this boy, he had a relaxed way of speaking and being.

"Sure, but there's not much to see. It's pretty much just rice fields."

"No worries. Let's go!" And the boy gripped my hand tight. "I'm Saku. Saku Chitose."

"Saku..."

His hand was so much warmer than mine, as I tried out his name on my tongue.

Hand in hand, we walked off. And yes, I felt a little embarrassed.

I mean, there's nothing but old houses around here, and the drainage ditches burbling away, and the little shrine and the park, and all the rest is just rice paddies.

I was certain he'd be disappointed.

I looked anxiously at him, but...

"This place looks like a *blast*! There's gotta be hundreds of water striders, and frog spawn, and crayfish! And there's no cars at all, so you can go literally anywhere!"

His face was glowing.

For the next two days, we played together, and it turned out he was a genius at making the everyday things fun.

We hunted crayfish and cicadas, smeared honey on the big tree at the shrine to attract rhinoceros beetles, jumped off the swings at the park.

Mostly I just stood back and clapped and squealed while he did those things, but it was amazing how he made my boring town seem like a treasure trove.

I soon got used to him, and I followed him around from morning until evening, babbling, "Saku, Saku."

Then the third day came. The day Saku was due to go home.

I was so sad and miserable, and I sulked from the moment I got up.

"Once you go home, life's gonna be boring again."

"Boring?"

"Yeah. Going to school, coming home, hanging around."

Saku looked at me, then seemed to think hard. "Hey, where's the furthest place you've walked to?"

"I'm not allowed to go very far. Just as far as I've shown you around, I guess."

"Then let's go on an adventure. To somewhere you've never seen before."

"But my dad will get angry…"

He took my hand and held it tight as I hesitated.

"Never mind your dad. What do you feel like doing?"

"I'd…I'd like to go."

"Then we gotta."

After that, Saku packed his bag with the rice balls his grandmother had made for lunch and grabbed his water flask, and then he grabbed my hand, and we set off.

He'd never been this way, either, but he showed no fear or hesitation at all.

At first, my heart pounded at the thought of doing something wrong, but when I looked at Saku's smile, all my nerves just vanished.

We passed through the area I knew and followed the road by the river, going straight on and on.

It really was a country street with nothing on it. Everywhere you looked, there was nothing but green rice paddies, with faraway hills and houses dotted on the horizon.

But to me, everything was fresh and new.

Saku really was a genius at making everything fun. He could find all kinds of interesting things in the most humdrum of environments.

"Hey, friend, what's that small building?"

"I think it's for maintaining the river and stuff?"

"That's boring. Hey, you see that thick hose-type thing? That leads to the kappa's house."

"A kappa?"

"They've been in these parts since way back, but these days, it'd be a shock to spot one, right? So they live in those little houses the Fukui higher-ups set out for them. And then, to make sure no one sees 'em, they travel through those hose things into the river."

"What? That's crazy!"

We both laughed as Saku kept telling me stories like that.

Once the river petered out, we followed a narrow road that went through the rice fields.

We kept stopping and gazing into the drainage ditch, then we played chase, and we just kept going, even though we had no particular destination in mind.

Then, before I knew it, everything grew dark around us.

"Uh-oh, we really need to be heading home now."

Saku looked at me. "So did you get to see something new? Not so boring, was it?"

I nodded.

"See, it's easy."

The boy smiled, backlit by the sunset, and to me he looked like freedom personified.

I'd always done exactly what my parents said, lived quietly in my own little world. This was the first-ever adventure I'd really gone on.

But to Saku, it was just a jaunt, something he'd decided on a whim.

And so we turned back the way we'd come.

The fields were lush with summer growth, and the road went so straight, and the electricity lines stretched out overhead, and the river's surface shimmered, and everything was stained red in the setting sun.

I could hear cicadas singing from a far-off place, and I could hear the frogs croaking loud enough to drown them out.

As we walked, we ate the rice balls. They had pickled plum inside, which I normally disliked, but for some reason that day the sour-sweet taste was delicious.

We stopped for a minute to glug barley tea.

It was already dark all around us, and the round moon hung in the sky, and the stars glittered like scattered *konpeito* candy.

This was the first time I'd ever been out so late with only another kid, and it was weird, but with Saku holding my hand, I wasn't scared at all.

Once I got home, my dad really yelled at me, but I didn't feel sad at all.

The reason I couldn't stop crying was because the train carrying Saku went far away, until I couldn't see him anymore.

Over and over again, I wished that the next summer would come fast.

*

It was the summer vacation of my fifth year of elementary school.

I put on the pure-white dress I'd begged Mom and Dad to buy for me and waited for Saku with excitement.

He had started baseball, and was taller than last year, and he seemed more like a boy.

But he hadn't changed inside, and we ran around and played together.

It happened when we were walking along the small embankment that flanked the drainage ditch.

Saku was walking a little ahead of me, and I ran up behind him, wanting to surprise him.

But as I ran, the wet ground began to slide out from under me. I lost my balance and fell into the river with a colossal splash.

Luckily I hadn't hurt myself, but the white dress I'd bought just to show Saku was completely ruined. I felt my eyes burning with sadness and embarrassment.

No. I can't cry in front of Saku.

Not when we're having fun. Not when it's summer vacation.

I gritted my teeth and scrunched up my face, but it wasn't enough. Tears welled up and spilled out like a leaky faucet.

No, no, no.

I don't want Saku to see my face all messed up like this.

Stop it, stop it, stop it.

—Just then.

There was a splash, a louder splash than the one I'd just made. Saku had jumped into the river.

"Hey, what are you doing having fun without me? Let me join."

With a grin of amusement, he began splashing me.

The water smelled a little fishy, but as it hit me in the face, it washed away my tears.

And then I realized.

Oh. It stopped.

It was weird. I completely forgot that I'd been on the verge of howling a few seconds ago, and I chased after Saku instead.

"Hey! Stop! This is my favorite dress!"

"You don't need to wear a dress. Next year just wear shorts and a T-shirt and beach sandals."

"Hmph! Unbelievable! You jerk!"

We splashed around in the dirty water, and soon I completely forgot about my dress. I was too busy splashing and choking with laughter.

✶

It was the summer vacation of my sixth year of elementary.

Saku said he was busy with baseball practice, so he could only stay one night.

But there was a festival that night at the small shrine.

If we could go together, it would make a really special memory.

I'd tried asking Mom and Dad about it the night before, but they said there was no way I could go if it was just us two kids.

I told them that other kids from school were going without parents, and they just said, "Other families have their rules, and these are ours."

Dad said we could go if he came along with us, but I didn't want to. I wanted it to be just us two.

I told Saku about it as we ate watermelon, wearing shorts and T-shirts and beach sandals.

"The teachers at school say stuff like that. It's because your mom and dad are both teachers."

"Don't you want to go, Saku?"

"Of course I do. Shall I come by and pick you up tonight? I'll explain that there won't be any danger."

"I don't think that'll work. I'll try talking to them again, but…"

Seeing me so down, Saku seemed to be thinking hard.

Then he seemed to have a flash of brilliance.

"Let's try this! You try talking to your dad one more time once you get home. Then I'll come and pick you up after dark. If they give you permission, then we'll be all set."

"And what if they don't give permission?"

"We'll make a pact. If you want to quit, I'll just go home. But if you still really want to go, touch your left ear. That'll be the sign."

"Then?"

"Then I'll sneak you out."

My heart pounded.

I tried asking my dad again, but of course, his answer didn't change.

When Saku came to our house, Dad was friendly to him, but he explained that there was no way the two of us were going to the festival together, just us two.

So I said, "Sorry, Saku."

And I tucked my hair behind my left ear.

"All right, I see. Well, see you next year, then. I'll be leaving first thing in the morning."

Then, looking crestfallen, Saku waved and left.

Wait... What about our pact? I thought. *Did he not notice? I touched my left ear. That was the sign.*

He said he'd sneak me out! He lied!

I shut myself up in my room and shoved my face into the pillow, filled with anger and sadness and frustration.

I couldn't hold my tears back. They leaked out and seeped into my pillow.

Tonight was the only chance we'd have until next year!

I should have just agreed to let Mom and Dad come with us.

I unclenched my fists.

We shouldn't have bothered making a plan in the first place, if he wasn't going to follow through.

As I lay there, thoughts churning, I heard an odd sound.

Clack. Clack. Clack. Clack.

Half asleep, I sat up and looked around.

Saku was outside the window, waving at me.

"Huh? What? This—this is the second floor?"

I opened the window in confusion and saw Saku pressing a finger to his lips and grinning. "Shhh. Whatcha doing lying in bed? I thought we were going to the festival?"

I poked my head out a little and looked down, to see that he was standing on some kind of makeshift ladder thing.

"I swiped this ladder Grandma had at her house."

Then he chuckled.

A tear plopped onto my cheek. I don't know if it was from relief or just pure happiness.

"What now? You really are a crybaby. You made that exact face last year when you fell in the river."

With a clumsy finger, he wiped away my tear.

"Oh… My shoes…"

Our stairs creaked noisily, so if I went down to get them, Dad would hear me for sure.

"Heh-heh. I swiped something else, too."

Then Saku whipped a pair of beach sandals out of his shorts pocket and handed them over to me. No one in this neighborhood bothered to lock their front door, so if we needed to, we could have sneaked back in and grabbed them. But if I got caught, I knew we'd be in big trouble, so I was delighted to see the sandals.

He was really like a prince from a fairy tale.

Going down the ladder was pretty scary, but…

"It's all right. I'll go down first and hold it steady for you," Saku said.

Just in case, I wrote a note saying *I'm sorry. I've gone to the festival with Saku. I'll be home before it gets late* and put it on my desk.

Then slowly, as I descended, Saku said, "I'm glad you're wearing shorts this year. Otherwise, I'd be able to see your underwear."

"Hmph! Jerk!"

After that, we set off at a run, and not five minutes later, we arrived at the shrine on the other side of the station.

Partway there, I realized that we didn't have any money, but it turned out that Saku's grandmother had given him one thousand yen and said we should eat something nice together.

The festival really was a small one, and there weren't very many stalls there.

But the excitement of doing what Dad told me I couldn't do had my heart pounding, and it was also exciting being there without parental supervision for the first time. The whole thing felt magical.

The two of us went around the festival, practically skipping.

But the thing that had my heart pounding most of all was being with Saku, who had sneaked me out, just like he promised he would.

Together, we ate *yakisoba* and *marumaru yaki*, and we finished it off with Ramune.

"I always feel sorry for the marble that sinks down in the Ramune bottle," Saku mumbled thoughtfully. "It's all alone."

I blinked. "That's weird. To me it looks like it's floating happily. Like the moon, so beautiful, loved by everyone. Like you, Saku."

"The moon... I see."

That was all he said. Then he ruffled my hair affectionately.

I peeked at his profile. He was gazing at the real moon, the one floating in the night sky.

His gaze was so much more solemn than it usually was. Somehow sad.

He looked so grown-up in that moment that it made my heart skip a beat, but I also felt sad. My chest seemed to constrict. I wanted to cry to him not to leave and go far away, but I didn't.

"If you ever feel lonely and sad, Saku, I could be your bride."

"If you do something about those crybaby tendencies of yours."

I looked at him as he smiled warmly, and I wished I could be like him.

He was so cool, so blessed with athletic ability, and he had a sharp mind. Of course, I loved all those aspects of him.

But it was his gentle inner strength that meant that Saku was always pushing forward, no matter the situation.

It was the fire in him. The way he showed me the part of town I'd never seen, even though it made my father angry. It was the way he stopped my tears in the muddy river, the way he built all these precious memories with me. The way he decided for himself what was important. That was what really made him sparkle in my eyes.

Could I be like him? I really wanted to.

Like a hero from a story, like the moon floating in the night sky, that self-assurance…

✶

"And that's the story of my first love in a long-ago summer, that ended after only seven days."

As we walked along the same path as we had back then, I told him the story I'd been keeping inside all this time.

Putting it into words, it sounded like the kind of typical misunderstanding a young girl might make, and I felt a little bit embarrassed.

…No. There aren't many boys who'd climb up to your second-floor window to sneak you out.

After that, my father came looking for me, and we both got in a whole heap of trouble.

As he walked beside me, Saku looked embarrassed at first, but midway through my story his eyes began squinting up, as if he was gazing at something far away, and he listened intently.

But he didn't respond, and now I was feeling awkward.

"We never saw each other after that summer, because I moved away. I didn't know your address, and I wasn't quite brave enough to ask your grandmother for it."

As a result, he never got to see my new short haircut, which I had gotten at the end of that summer because I thought he might like a spunky vibe.

Now he chuckled, remembering.

"Well, I heard from Grandma that you had fallen for someone who was cool, good at sports, and smart."

"But that was *you*. I was embarrassed to tell your grandmother who it was, so I was intentionally vague."

"Wow. So you liked me back then all along, huh, Asuka?"

"What?!" I yelped. "How could you not know? I followed you

around everywhere back then. An innocent girl with an obvious crush."

"Ah yeah, it did seem that way. That's why I didn't notice when I started high school and we first met. But you know…" Saku scratched his cheek. "Remember back then, you always said how you envied me, my free way of being? Those words really sustained me. They kept me going when everything started piling on top of me at the same time. The knowledge that there was a girl out there who saw the parts of me that were hidden beneath the surface."

I was surprised, too, when we discussed things that night in Tokyo.

The boy who seemed like freedom personified in my eyes was dealing with so much in secret.

At the same time, I realized again how amazing it is, and everything fell into place for me.

Why did he and I meet again in high school like this?

"Listen, Asuka," he said. "How long since you realized this?"

Well, that's an easy one.

"Since September last year, when we met by the riverbank."

Saku's eyes opened wide, and he sighed. "Because you were disappointed?"

Now I knew what he meant by those words.

"To put things into perspective, although I hate to say it, it's not like I stayed in love with you all that time. I never even realized you were at the same high school as me, in the year below."

"Hmm, that makes sense."

"But there was always this powerful drive in my heart—I wanted to be like that boy from my childhood. So that if we ever met again, I could be the kind of girl who was good enough for a boy like you."

I coughed.

"When I climbed out of the river and saw you, I knew it was

you right away. You were so much cooler than my memory of you, but I was absolutely certain. I was all dithering about whether I should tell you or wait to see if you'd figure it out on your own."

Saku laughed bashfully.

"But you were a much more complex person than the boy from my memories. You were like, '*Why'd you do something like that?*' But all I did was copy what you did that time, remember?"

That was one of my most vivid childhood memories.

The white dress stained with river mud, that smile.

"So I thought... *Maybe something happened to Saku, and now he's locked up inside his own head like I was back then.* I thought, in that case, I'd have to guide you now."

I put my own feelings on the back burner.

For the boy who showed me how to live my own way.

I decided to be the best older female friend I could be.

I decided that we would be "Asuka" and "friend."

Then, one day, when "Saku" returned...

"The Asuka you so looked up to was really just a mirror image of the Saku I looked up to."

I thought I would tell him, just like that.

"But you know...," I continued. "As time went by, I started to realize that you really were Saku all along. The same hero who was so straightforward, so passionate, so kind like a light in the darkness, flying freely out into the world with your own will."

I always thought, once I had made sure of that, then I would tell him, just like this.

Saku was looking at me with a soft gaze. "Thank you, Asuka."

I shook my head.

There was one more thing I had to tell him.

"So you see, the image you had of me really was a phantom.

I wanted to be like you, living life on my own terms, being strong—but I was just a regular, solemn sort of girl, who was unable to go against her father's wishes. You were following the version of myself I was still trying to be."

I always felt such a sense of regret that the version of me you thought you saw was all fake.

You were the cool one.

And as I knew it would, the real me started to show herself when I had to take a stand and make a choice.

As much as I tried to copy Saku, all it took was my parents saying no for me to waver and start to give up on my own dreams.

In the end, it was he who saved me once again.

That's why I wanted to confirm where it all started.

The thing I longed for, that day.
How much I wanted to be a grown-up.
To stand beside him and hold my head high.
So that the image you had of me could be more than an illusion.

Saku exhaled. "Asuka," he mumbled in a small voice.

Was he disappointed? Disillusioned? Wondering why I'd bring this up now?

But right now, I guess I didn't care if he took it that way.

All I had to do was start fresh. Take the next step.

So that one day I could catch up to the example that was still so, so far ahead of me.

The Asuka you thought I was would keep going, no matter how hard things got; no matter how defeated she seemed, she would grit her teeth and keep going.

Saku remained silent for a while, as if choosing his words carefully before he spoke.

*   *   *

"You're actually quite the romantic, huh? What a pure young maiden! Hearts in your eyes, and all that?"

...Huh?

"Ah man, the burden of being freer than anyone and completely shackled at the same time. Listen, this isn't a shoujo manga, and you can't change your whole life and personality based on seven days you spent playing with some kid during the summer vacations of elementary school."

He scratched his head, as if he was frustrated, and he heaved a heavy sigh.

"Sure, maybe that can be a sort of catalyst. But that's all it is. You are who you are today, Asuka, because you're striving for your *own* goals."

"But...I always just thought that I wanted to be more like you."

"Everyone starts out that way. They want to be like the heroes they read about in novels or manga, or like the super *sentai* they watch on TV. Or—okay, maybe they want to work a job that involves bringing books to people. But how many people manage to hold on to that wish and actually see it through to a reality?"

Saku clapped his hands down on my shoulders.

"Like you said that night in Tokyo. 'You refused to make your past a story,' right?"

His hands tightened.

"In that case, there's no need to write off your current self by trotting out a story, right? Whether you and I met or not, you would still be you, Asuka."

*   *   *

His eyes were so warm, so filled with kindness.

"You can make kids smile when they're covered in mud without worrying about who's watching. You've got your own dreams, and words are precious to you, and you always give the best advice. You saved me when I needed someone, you affirm who I am today, you're kinda androgynous but still ultimately feminine, you're clumsy, the teardrop mole you have is really sexy, the little mole on your chest is sexier still, and recently I've started looking at you in a more sexual way. There are so many other things, but…"

He grinned, like the boy Saku from back then.

"And you inspire me just the way you are now, like a breeze rushing toward tomorrow. That's a simple enough story, right?"

I felt my heart thud in my chest.
You're really… Saku, you're really…
…Always whipping me around and bringing me to unknown places.
Gripping the hem of my skirt, I gazed right at him.
I sucked in a breath and let it out, giving him a genuine Asuka Nishino smile.

"Wow. It sounds like you've got a way bigger crush on me than I thought, Saku!"

"Oh, you didn't know?"

He was picking up what I was putting down, and he laughed.

"I've had the biggest crush on you right from the start."

*　　*　　*

I giggled and scratched my cheek.

"Tomorrow's parent-teacher meeting. I'm going to go as I am, the Asuka I am today. And I'm going to face my future."

That little first romance I'd treasured... It ends here.
The past I'd been chasing after and idealizing... It ends here.
"Hey, Asuka?"
"Hmm?"
"Wanna go visit my grandmother together sometime?"
"That sounds like the best day ever."
All right. It's time for it to start. The true story of Asuka Nishino.

*

The following day, after the last homeroom to finish the school day, Saku came to my classroom.
"Here. Consider it a good-luck charm." He put something in the pocket of my bag.
I peeked in to see what it was, and...
"Why'd you give me a phone?" I was surprised.
"Hmm, I guess it's the only thing I have that I always keep close to me."
He looked so cute, scratching his head so bashfully, and it made my heart feel light.
"Thank you. That's so sweet."
"Give it all you've got. Your dad's a tough nut to crack."
"I know that better than anyone."

When I entered the empty classroom Kura indicated, I found a desk set out with two sets of chairs facing each other.

Dad and Kura were already seated.

It was as if both of them knew this wasn't a parent-teacher meeting so much as a daughter-parent meeting.

I felt bad for causing trouble for Kura, but I wanted to face my future properly as a third-year high school student, in the atmosphere of a public parent-teacher meeting.

"Uh, so then..." Kura started speaking first, in his usual offhand manner. "What do you want to do, Nishino?"

I closed my eyes for a moment, and then I steeled myself, looking at Dad.

"I want to go to Tokyo. To be a literary editor."

I mentioned the name of the university Saku and I visited.

I'd already made my wishes clear several times, but I had never once been taken seriously.

Kura flipped through some papers he had. "Hmm, well with these grades, you shouldn't have much of a problem."

But Dad shook his head slowly. "I'm repeating myself here, but first off, Tokyo is too dangerous of a place for a young girl to go off to. Especially a sheltered girl like you."

And who's the one who raised me? But I wouldn't get anywhere saying that.

I *was* sheltered, but that was because my father had treasured me, keeping me safe from any sources of trouble so I could live without worry.

"You keep saying how it's dangerous, but you've never lived in Tokyo yourself, have you, Dad? I don't think it's fair to say no to something just based off what you've heard."

"If every country guy and gal has the impression of Tokyo as a dangerous place, then that must mean plenty of people have had trouble there. In Fukui, you can count the number of serious crimes on one hand: murders, burglary, arson, rapes. In the same time frame in Tokyo, it's in the triple digits. There's no comparison when it comes to safety."

He'd landed a critical hit.

I recalled the incident in Kabukicho. What might have happened to me if Saku hadn't been there?

But…

"That kind of logic isn't fair," I said. "Okay, so it's true that it's more dangerous than Fukui. I definitely felt that in just one overnight trip. But I think it's possible to learn what places and people to avoid. After all, you and Mom raised me to use my head, right?"

Dad had always been right in what he said, ever since I was a kid.

I knew that, so I did what he said and never defied him.

That's why I felt confident that I could go to Tokyo by myself and stay on the right path.

But at the same time, I knew that what was right and what was wrong were open to interpretation. Like how a dirty dress could become a precious memory.

"There are evil things in the world that don't give a damn whether you use your head."

"But it's the same in Fukui. There's no guarantee I wouldn't be one of that handful of cases. Even if there are more perpetrators of violent crime in Tokyo, in Fukui, there are fewer targets for those kinds of bad people to pick from."

Dad changed the subject.

"I told you, I won't financially support you if you go to Tokyo. So what will you do? You need private college fees and living expenses. Even if we did agree to help you, that would be a big drain on us."

"I'd be delighted for any help, of course. But the college I want to go to has very generous student loans on offer. And some scholarships you don't even need to pay back. With my grades, I should have as much of a chance as anyone else at getting one."

I looked at Kura, hoping for backup.

"Should be," he said. "Your test scores have been in the top ten of your grade since your first year. And since you entered third year, you've been in the top five. Conduct included, you're one of our finest students."

I turned back to Dad again. "I also looked up part-time jobs in Tokyo. If I worked at a call center in the city, I could work for three weeks in between school terms and earn a minimum of one hundred and fifty thousand yen a month. With the scholarship money, I think I should be able to get by."

I'm not Saku.

I can't change people's minds with my compelling aura, so I have to do the research and get the receipts.

Dad hmphed and put his hand to his chin.

"All right, that's passable enough. But there's another thing. Leaving aside the issue of you wanting to be an editor...why does it have to be Tokyo?"

"There are two tangible reasons. Based on past data, the school I want to go to has a real focus on media. The companies I want to work for, a lot of the graduates get accepted there. And the university has a lot of social clubs involving the arts. And since I want to become a literary fiction editor, I really have to job hunt in Tokyo. So it would be best for me to get used to the city while I'm still a student."

After a pause, I continued.

"As for the other reason, if I stay here, there's so much I'll never be able to see. Tokyo is scary, but there's warmth to be found under the surface, and the smoggy air makes Fukui's seem all the fresher. I want to see things I still haven't seen, experience things I've never imagined even existed."

Dad sighed. "I understand that you've given this a lot of thought. But to return to the crux of the issue—why do you have to be an editor? If you want to bring words to people so much, you could be a Japanese language teacher or even a librarian."

This was the question I got stuck on last time.

But it's okay. It won't trip me up anymore.

Saku helped me to find the answer.

"Those are both fine jobs, I think. But for me, I want to help bring stories that aren't quite fully stories yet to people. To help with drawing out the right words. That's what I realized."

"You're being too vague. I'm not following."

"The books I've read so far, the words are all things someone desperately dug out of their psyche in an attempt to share their vision with others. If there are worlds out there that only I can find and bring out, then I feel I have to do it."

I recalled the scene I saw in Tokyo.

Just like Saku's backstory, which he wrote off as asinine and boring, and just like the version of myself I'd given up as nothing more than a mirage, which Saku refused to let die.

There are so many stories out there that never get to be told.

But the words I got in return were cold.

"A mundane motivation. If you gather a hundred people who want to be editors and authors, then at least ninety-five of them will have the same motivation. You have to compete with the remaining five, the ones whose lives were saved by a certain book or changed completely by a certain editor. People with a real sense of purpose."

Dad readjusted the bridge of his glasses.

"You want to join a big publishing company, get assigned to the fiction department, and make books that are huge hits. You realize how difficult all that is going to be, right?"

"…Yes."

"Anyone can dream. My students—I've lost count of how many of them—have told me they want to be singers, or actors, or novelists. Most just go to college and then become ordinary company workers. Which is fine."

Dad narrowed his eyes and rapped on the desk with a finger.

"The bad thing is when they're actually halfway serious about it. But the only people who can make their dreams come true are the ones who've got the right blend of ability and luck. You might think you're one of them, you might think you're so cool for chasing your dreams, but you're intentionally turning a blind eye to reality. It's not until you've failed, and you've exhausted every hope, that you look around you and realize the truth."

Dad turned his dark gaze to the window and looked out.

The drizzle had been continuing since morning, causing the pits in the gravel field to fill with rainwater.

"The other students, your peers who go on to work normal jobs—you may think they're lame, but they have good marriages and happy households. And you'll look at them and realize you've been left out in the cold. And…"

He rapped on the desk again.

"You, Asuka—a girl who's always listened diligently to what her parents said and done the right things—I just don't think you've got what it takes to be one of the special ones. Wake up. Face reality."

"…"

That was the worst thing he could have said. The most damning. Because up until yesterday, that was exactly how I saw myself.

Just a normal, boring girl, who looked up to a special boy and tried to imitate him. A fake.

"Even so…"

I raised my voice.

Dad was looking at me with deep interest.

The boy I so admired said that the person I am today saved him. He said that he admired her.

He had been through so many disheartening experiences, and he dismissed them as insignificant and trivial, but he was still facing his ideals and reaching out to them.

"I won't ever know unless I try. I don't want to give up on myself halfway. If I ever do come up against a wall, and I know I can go no further, that's fine. But I want to decide that for myself. I won't ever accept that it's over until I've banged my hands bloody against that wall."

I grasped the fabric of my skirt.

"This is Asuka Nishino's story!!!"

"Then, are you prepared to cut off all family ties?"

"…Huh?"

What…did Dad just say?

"Did I stutter? If you're going to be this stubborn about it, then as parents, we're cutting you off financially. And you will never darken our doorstep again."

"But…"

"It's not like I'm being unreasonable here. I've shown you how you can live a happy life, and I've shown you how continuing down this path will lead to your unhappiness. But if you still insist on doing what you want, at least spare me the pain of having to witness my daughter destroy her own life."

His words were so cold, his tone indifferent as ever.

I looked desperately to Kura for help, but he had his hand resting in his chin unhappily.

Follow my dream? Abandon my family?

I can't make that choice.

Ah, no.

There's only one choice. My family.

Mom and Dad have raised me with everything they have.

Even though our opinions on this differ so much, it's not like I could ever hate them.

This isn't fair.

But if Dad's willing to go this far to stop me, then...what I'm proposing to do must really be foolhardy after all.

I unclenched my fists.

I knew this feeling. The feeling of giving up.

It felt like this, that long-ago summer day, when I said I would give up on going to the festival.

Is that really true?

I clenched my skirt fabric again.

Think, Asuka Nishino.

Isn't there any other way? A ladder to prop against my window?

If I give up now, nothing will ever change in my life.

"Hurry up and decide. We don't have all day," Dad said.

If I ran today, I wouldn't ever get another chance like this.

I want more time.

I feel like there's another answer here somewhere.

"Mr. Iwanami. Since it seems Asuka has no further objections, there will be no change in her college application choices."

Wait. I just need a little more time.

I squeezed my eyes shut tight.

I don't want to let this be the end.

Just then...

"—Hold it right there!!!"

The classroom door came rattling open on its tracks with a rumble like thunder.

✳   ✳   ✳

Ah. I didn't want to have to rely on you.
But I knew you'd come in the end.
I'm sorry for worrying you.

"*...Saku...*"

✳

I looked at him, phone in one hand, shoulders heaving as he breathed hard, and I knew what had happened.

Probably, the phone he slipped into my bag was one he'd borrowed from someone, and he'd set it to speaker mode so he could listen to our conversation.

That's breaking the rules, I thought, *in a lot of ways.*

But that impulsivity of his was just classic Saku.

Dad sighed, and Kura glared at him.

"That's enough of your impudence, Chitose. Remember what I told you? *You have no right to insert yourself into this conversation.*"

"Hah!"

In response to that came a short, sharp laugh.

"I've got every right! Every right as the younger student who admires the heck out of her!"

The corner of Kura's lip started to twitch up, just a little. "I see. Well, in that case, go ahead."

Dad responded with disgust on his face. "For goodness' sake. Can't you control your students? ...Enough theatrics. Sit down, Chitose. No doubt you'd ignore me if I told you to leave anyway."

"Thank you."

Then he sat down beside me.

But, I thought.

To be honest, this wasn't the kind of issue Saku could really do anything to solve.

If a daughter's attempts weren't getting through, it wouldn't matter what someone who wasn't even family said. I couldn't see Dad changing his mind.

But this was Saku. Maybe he had some brilliant idea to get through this impasse.

Saku placed both hands on the desk and sucked in a big breath.

"Please! Please let Asuka go to Tokyo!"

Then he put his forehead on the desk, bowing to my father.

Dad and I had been waiting for what he was going to say, but now we both stared in shock.

Meanwhile, Kura seemed to be trying very hard not to laugh.

"I'll spare you a detailed explanation, but what you should know is that I was listening to that whole conversation. I'm sorry. And while I think you were way too harsh at the end there, I do appreciate what you're saying, Mr. Nishino."

"So what did you come barging in here for?"

"I told you? It's an unreasonable request. For my own selfish reasons."

Selfish reasons, I thought. Something seemed to click into place in my head.

Saku continued. "I know I have no right to be speaking in this situation at all. But I want Asuka to go after her dream."

He still had his forehead on the desk.

"Does she need such an ironclad reason? Isn't it enough for her to do what she wants? There's no guarantee she'll fail! Won't you let her pursue her dream?"

That was the logic of a child.

Ignoring everything Dad said and continuing to push based on one's own feelings.

Seeing him with his head on the desk, saying these things... It didn't mesh with the Saku I knew.

I remembered a conversation we had once.

"So do you think a stray cat who sucks up to an old lady to get food thinks he's being lame? After all, he's acting just like a pet."

"No. He's just doing what he has to do to survive as a stray cat."

See, I knew you'd remember it.

"We're still just figuring things out. I know that, in becoming adults, we'll have to give up a lot of things, make compromises. But that doesn't mean we have to abandon our dreams! They're heaviest to hold. It would be a relief to set them down. That way, we won't get hurt. We won't have to fight."

These were words that could only be spoken by Saku.

"But we have to decide for ourselves when to call time on our dreams. Otherwise, when we look at people who are doing their best, gritting their teeth, and really going for it... We're just going to feel like we've been left behind, all alone in the world... Just like I—"

His head came up abruptly.

"I still want to find my future for myself. Adults are always looking back, but we've still got our futures ahead of us. We have to go after them. I want to believe that I can reach the moon, someday."

His words, his sentiment, his passion, all flowed into me.

Ah, he really is so, so far ahead of me after all.

Thank you, Saku.
Now I know what I have to do.

Dad spoke, his voice as cool as ever. "Are you done trying to convince me? Let me just ask you one question again. Will you take responsibility when Asuka's dealing with her shattered dreams? Will you support her?"

Saku gritted his teeth together. "Yeah, I will. If you're not prepared to believe in your daughter, then maybe I should!"

"All of you, just shut up!!!"

I slammed my hand on the desk, unable to contain my outburst.

"I'd rather die than accept a proposal like that! If—if you're going to propose, come back and try again in ten years, okay?"

I gave him a loaded grin, and he stared back at me open-mouthed as if all the fire from a few seconds ago had gone out.

He looked so cute. I'd have loved to mess with him a little more, stare at him a little more, but instead I gathered up all my will—and all of my own fire—and stared at Dad instead.

"I've made up my mind. I'm going to become an editor."

Honestly, that was all I needed.

"I understand your point of view, Dad. But I don't care. I'm going to go for it because I want to, because it's what I like to do. I'm going for my dream, chasing it head-on, and giving it everything I've got. And if I come up against some insurmountable wall, I'll kick it down and keep on going."

Right, just like a certain someone.
I've made up my mind that that's how I want to live.
I want to make the important decisions for myself.

"Childish though it might be, there's one truth that no one can deny. There's a lot that goes into it—talent, luck, hard work—but the one thing all people who make their dreams come true have in common is that they don't give up until the bitter end."

Just like how the admiration held by that small girl, which I've kept in my heart all these years, made me into what I am today.

I took a deep breath to steady myself and then exhaled.

"*It's not hard. I'll fake it until I make it.* I think that's the ticket. Just as there are countless people whose dreams failed, there are also people who made their dreams a reality."

"Asuka...," Dad said quietly in shock.

"That's my name. The precious name you and Mom gave me. I want to live up to it and be the breeze that blows toward tomorrow."

I gave him a bright smile, imbued with all the emotion and passion I felt.

"But if you still insist on saying no..."

I lifted my jaw high, looking away from him.

"...then I'll spend my whole life convincing you until you accept my wishes."

...

"Bwah-ha-ha-ha!"

It was Dad who broke the silence, suddenly guffawing with laughter.

Saku and Kura started laughing, too, and I felt myself blushing.
"Asuka, are you a child?!"

"No, no, that was great. She got ya, eh, Nisshi?"

Dad kept laughing after they both said that, like he couldn't stop.

"Gack! Ah, I never thought the day would come when I'd hear
my own daughter talk like that!"

"Hey! You're all being super mean!"

Finally, he stopped laughing, and Dad sucked in a breath. "I guess
I lose, Asuka." His voice was imbued with deep warmth. "I had to
see how far you'd go without giving up. How harsh I had to be."

Dad readjusted his glasses, massaging his eyebrows.

"As a teacher, I've seen so many students talk about their
dreams. Ninety-five percent of them fail, but yes, about five percent of them succeed. Of the former, many were unwilling to
take responsibility. They wanted me to push them. That didn't
work, and so they ended up failures."

"Dad…"

"Unfortunately, this world, this country, isn't kind to people
who pursue their dreams. Social pressure just gets worse and
worse, the more you talk about it. People act kind, say all the
right things, offer up surface-level logic, but all the while, they
keep telling you you can't do it."

He whipped out his handkerchief and cleaned his glasses
before putting them back on.

"And it's bad, because you're not wrong. It's not true that all
dreamers are naive. Even if the people who say these things are only
saying it because they feel embarrassed they can't live that way."

Dad looked out the window, his expression cloudy.

"Some students have had their hearts broken. They were young,
overflowing with self-confidence and ability when they gradu-
ated, but before you know it, they become adults who shrug and
live quietly."

"So you were playing the part of society, Dad?"

He shook his head with embarrassment.

"I got a bit worked up. I shouldn't have said that part about cutting ties with the family. I was conflating you with all the students I've seen in my time. I have to admit, seeing you be influenced by another guy who wasn't me—it really hit me."

Dad scratched his cheek, looking sheepish, as he continued.

"It's embarrassing to admit, but I'm a boring adult. I never make a choice until I've planned out every eventuality. But the truth is, your old dad actually wanted to be a rock musician."

I heard two people gulping, desperately trying not to react.

But I couldn't suppress a smile.

I thought about the stacks of CDs and the dusty guitars we had in our house.

Dad gave Kura a quick jab in the stomach before continuing, face red.

"But there comes a time when you have to face reality. And so I gave up. When I was raising you, Asuka, I decided to only teach you what I believed was right, as your father. If I could raise you to have a happy life, then I could share that same happiness."

I'd never heard any of this before.

I'd always thought Dad had unswerving confidence in the things he'd taught me.

"So I've been worried. To think that my Asuka, my girl I raised so carefully, will soon be going out alone in society, chasing her dreams."

Dad looked me right in the eye.

"As Chitose says, wanting to chase a dream is a good enough reason to do it. The one commonality all my successful students share is that they never gave up. No matter what anyone said, they believed in themselves and had an iron will. And the passion to hold on to that initial desire. As long as they have that, even the worst of students can rise to become great teachers... Right, Kura?"

Kura blew air through his nose, looking embarrassed. "I wasn't the worst one. There were one or two who were worse than me."

Dad smiled, holding out to me the grade sheet that had been sitting in front of Kura.

"You've grown into a fine adult before I even knew it. Asuka, please live according to your own desires."

I choked back the tears that suddenly threatened to overflow, and...

"...Right."

I bowed my head low as I said it. The gesture was imbued with eighteen years' worth of gratitude.

"And you, Chitose."

"...Yeah?"

"You haven't changed a bit since back then."

Saku's jaw slowly opened. "You...remembered me?"

"How could a father forget the boy who absconded with his daughter not once but twice? And that little jaunt to Tokyo was the third time. There won't be another."

"Er... Heh-heh."

"I gave you maybe sixty points for the first parent-teacher meeting and your artful dodging on the phone, but what you said just before, your raw display of emotion, it spoke to me. You also made a smart choice by never calling me 'Asuka's dad.' Let's call it an even ninety."

After that little bit of joking...

"Thank you," Dad said, bowing his head. "Thank you for believing in my daughter—and supporting her."

Saku listened solemnly, then started to grin.

Uh-oh. That's the face he makes just before he cracks a dumb joke.

"I didn't do anything. The Asuka you see before you, Mr. Nishino, is the same Asuka you raised with such great values. All I did...was teach her to have a little mischievous fun."

"Hmm? You must tell me all about it. In detail."

Dad was suddenly sounding serious again, but Saku began whistling, gazing off into the distance.

Dad rolled his eyes and chuckled. "Your inability to be serious at solemn moments reminds me of a certain someone else in his youth. Right, Kura? Tch, an incorrigible teacher instructing an incorrigible student."

"There's a limit to what a teacher can do, isn't there?"

"Yep. Now, since you have nothing more important to do, come and have a drink with me after this."

"You're such a pain when you have a drink, Nisshi. All you do is brag about your daughter."

"Can you blame me? There's so much to brag about."

"All right, all right."

They pulled back their chairs with a clatter and got to their feet.

As they were exiting the room, Dad looked back over his shoulder. "Chitose, come by for a visit if you feel like it."

The corners of Chitose's mouth twitched.

"No way. You're a scary dude, Asuka's dad."

"For the ironic twist, you get one hundred points."

The door slid closed, and just he and I were left in the classroom together.

*

And so it was decided. I was going to Tokyo.

I felt like a huge weight had just rolled off me.

So this is what it feels like when your entire future gets decided.

I thought it would feel more…dramatic somehow.

Beside me, Saku got to his feet. Then, with an endlessly kind smile…

"Congratulations, Asuka."

…he reached out his hand to me.

I gripped it and stood up, the floor feeling like clouds beneath me.

Was this fear? Anxiety? Or a dream state?

"Make your dreams come true in Tokyo."
Why did that sound like a good-bye?

This feeling was just regular old sadness.

In one moment, I felt the weight of it all wash over me. The days I'd spent living in this town, the times I'd spent with the boy in front of me now.

Now my path was decided, and that would mean there was so much I would have to let go of.

This was the crossroads of my life.

I would never again live a peaceful, humdrum life in this warm and friendly town, chatting with Mom and Dad, nothing ever changing.

I would become a college student. No longer would I be able to stop by to see Kura. No longer would I be able to wait for Saku, who would be a third-year student then, by the riverbank. No longer would I be able to ask him on impromptu dates.

I also knew that I would never end up being his wife.

My chest constricted painfully.

This was what I decided for myself. I had no regrets. I couldn't.

I would chase my dream, hold my head up high in an unknown city.

But. But. But.

Thank you, Dad. Thank you, Mom. Thank you for raising me. Thank you for giving me everything I need to stand on my own two feet in an unknown city.

Thank you, Kura. Thank you for sticking with this troublesome student until the end. Thank you for seeing the ways in which I felt tied down.

Thank you, Saku. Thank you for showing me how to be free. Thank you for sneaking me off all those times. Thank you for believing in me, for supporting me, for saving me. Thank you for being so cool, right up until the end. Thank you...

Before I knew what I was doing, I'd grabbed him, clinging on as if I was holding on to something else.

He was probably too taken aback to brace himself.

We both overbalanced and tumbled to the floor.

Saku was on the bottom, and he pushed himself up on his elbows, looking at me.

"Asuka, your face." Then he smiled gently.

The tears I could no longer hold back were flowing and dripping.

They fell on the cheeks of the boy, like June raindrops.

I was sure my face was a mess.

"Still a crybaby." Saku's finger touched my cheek gently.

His kind manner, his warm words, none of it had changed. Not a bit since those precious summer days I held so dear.

The way home, when we held hands. The white dress smeared in mud. The marbles inside the Ramune bottles that we examined at the festival. The night in Tokyo when we slept side by side. And this moment now.

I wanted to hold on to these moments forever.

To have them light the way going forward.

"It's all right," he said, encouraging me.

To me, there was no bigger, more beautiful, brighter, or kinder...

To me, he was... He was...

"You're...my moon!!"

*　　　*　　　*

With the rain pounding down around us, I shouted it out.

"Nope. The moon that shone so beautifully when I was trapped inside an unopenable bottle… That was you, Asuka."

No, no, no.

It was too hard to keep holding myself up. I collapsed, burying my head in his strong chest.

I wanted to say thank you with more finesse, but I could only find mundane words in my desperation to get these feelings across to him.

"I'll do my best. I'll make my dream come true, in Tokyo. I'll prove that it was your light that illuminated the way for me."

He stroked my hair gently.

"Go for it. You can do it. Never, ever give up."

"W-waaaaah!!!"

I forgot where we were. I forgot that this was the part where I was supposed to be happy. Instead, I just bawled.

Once I set off running, I don't want to look back. I don't want to lose my way. I don't want to lean on anyone but you.

So I'll just leave them right here…a lifetime's supply of my tears.

*

Once Asuka was finally calm, she and I left the school.

The gloomy rain had stopped, and the clouds were drifting off.

The riverside path was deserted as we picked our way past muddy puddles, and the air seemed fresh and transparent.

In the twilit sky, a red June strawberry moon floated, looking just as the name suggested.

And the girl walking beside me had red-rimmed eyes and nostrils, too.

"Asuka, you look like that moon, for sure."

"Don't ruin that emotional moment we just had."

"Sometimes you need a corny joke in life."

We both chuckled.

I knew why Asuka started crying.

I mean, I was on the verge of breaking myself.

I don't think I'd ever felt this sad, this anguished, about the prospect of parting from anyone before.

Even when I had to say good-bye to friends after graduating elementary, it wasn't like we couldn't hang out again.

When I parted from my parents and started living alone…it wasn't really like parting from them. We were still family.

Ah, right.

This feeling was like when I left Grandma's house at the end of every summer vacation.

The sadness of knowing I wouldn't see my first crush again for an entire year.

Could we really meet again next year? And when we did, would our next summer together be as magical?

When we met again, would she still be the girl I knew? I agonized over these questions, again and again.

The distance between us as little kids… We would need to deal with cars and trains to be together. It was a lot like the distance between Tokyo and Fukui for high schoolers.

Asuka had already started running toward her future.

Today was the end of it. After this, she wouldn't look back.

She would keep going forward, farther and farther away, becoming an Asuka I didn't know.

In some far-off city, under a far-off sky, enveloped in the far-off night.

I still didn't know where I was going, which direction I should face.

"Only nine more months, huh."

As I mumbled that, I felt Asuka poke my shoulder.

"Hey, remember that promise we made?" she said.

"No more running away together. Next time, we really will get the cops called on us."

I heard a giggle.

"Not that. The one that went like, *If you do go to Tokyo, then let's make sure to see all kinds of things we can only see here, first. Let's have conversations we could only have here. Let's shed tears we could only shed here. That way, even if we end up far apart, we'll always have this place in our hearts to come back to.*"

"Don't quote me. That's so embarrassing."

Asuka skipped ahead of me and then whirled around. "There's one thing I really wanna do before graduation."

Grinning, she pointed right between my eyes.

"This time… This time for real… I'm gonna be such a bright light that you're gonna wanna chase after me. I'm going to be the Asuka Nishino who wanted to be just like you. The Asuka Nishino you wanted to be like."

Here and there, countless far-off moons were reflected in the puddles and on the surface of the river.

Which one was real? Which was just a phantom? Perhaps we get to decide for ourselves.

In the same way that a marble that had sunk down into the bottom of a bottle of Ramune could look like the moon to someone.

A breeze blew past us, blowing toward tomorrow, bringing with it the futures we hadn't seen yet.

When the next cherry blossoms bloomed, how were we going to handle our final good-byes?

On the way home, I was gazing at the moon.

When I was still a little girl, I had a thought.

I want to be like this one person.

You said I was like a phantom lady, Saku, but to me, *you* were the phantom. A mirage of a distant summer's day.

Something almost tangible enough to obtain—and yet too far away for me to reach.

Just seven days' worth of admiration, dreaming, a crush.

Thinking about it now, it makes sense when you consider what a small world that girl lived in, shut up alone with her stories.

But that day, those few summers, my life really did change.

You really were the moon floating in the far-off sky, the only light in the dark that exists in this world.

But that all ends today.

If I keep on just chasing after you, I'll only ever be that little girl crying in the white dress.

Farewell to the Saku from that day. Good evening to the splendid junior classmate friend walking beside me.

The moon I reached for doesn't just smile like everything is fine.

It grits its teeth, faces the future, lights the way for others, and meets their expectations and prayers. And despite all that, it still does its best to live its own truth.

I thought there was only one moon.

I thought it was something that was decided from birth.

But now I understand that was wrong.

It's not the only one. It's not absolute, not omnipresent.

Everyone is someone's moon.

So if you ever find yourself lost again like that day, call my name.

Call for Asuka.

No matter how bitter or painful the story, I'll change it into a happy ending. In the same way you lit up my path, I'll extinguish the darkness you've been holding out against, all alone.

Lost in memories, I squeezed that hand, that hand that was warmer than it had ever been.

—Hey. Could I be the moon to you?

AFTERWORD

Since I used up almost all the pages in the second volume, I ended up having to put the afterword online (you can read it via the note uploaded on the Gagaga Bunko blog, or via Twitter @ hiromu_yume), so I think there might be a lot of people I haven't had a chance to directly address since the first volume.

It's been a long time. Hiromu here. Thanks to various adulting circumstances, I've kept you waiting for six months, but to make up for that, I have two big pieces of news!

The first is that Chiramune (an abbreviation for this series) is going to become a manga! In fact, it's already started appearing in Manga UP! I actually had several people reach out to me about this from the moment the first volume went on sale, and there was definitely a strong desire to see raemz's illustrative style rendered in manga form, so the decision was a very deliberate one. However, when I saw the character designs done by Bobkya, who is in charge of the manga series, I was like, "This is the person for the job!" I really feel that the vibe of the characters was expressed so well. And more importantly than anything, you can feel the love for the original work, so please read it with the highest of expectations!!!

The second is, of course, the release of the drama CD! Because of my own inability, we weren't able to release a special edition (sorry), but you can buy it from the Gagaga official shop. You can listen to voice samples of all the actors belonging to 81 Produce on the Gagaga channel, and we definitely were able to secure actors who perfectly fit the image of the Chiramune girls. The following outstanding voice actors: Kana Asumi, who played Yuuko Hiiragi; Rena Ueda, who played Yua Uchida; Chinatsu Akasaki, who played Haru Aomi; Yurina Amami, who played Yuzuki Nanase; and Kaya Okuno, who played Asuka Nishino, perform the side story you see on the following pages.

It's honestly wonderful work that far exceeded my expectations, so please listen to it!

And so I ended up using up most of the space with announcements, but let's move on to the acknowledgments.

To raemz, who was in charge of the illustrations. Your work was splendid in the first volume, but it feels like you're leveling up with each volume? Are you some sort of god? Recently, I've been getting manuscript ideas by looking at your illustrations. Thank you again, this time for the most amazing Asuka!

Then, to my editor, Iwaasa. His thoughts on the first draft were very much, "Well, it's pretty much what I wrote on Twitter." (Direct quote.) But within those 140 characters, there was only one line of praise? This time, the red-pen MVP who knows nothing of others' feelings wrote: "Hmmmm? What did you make me read?" (The inclusion of all those *m*'s in the word *Hmm* are also a direct quote.) To Yomi Hirasaka, who brought the *A Sister's All You Need* series to a wonderful completion, I express my respect and add these final words: Iwaasa, I hope your dick falls off.

To everyone else involved in Chiramune, publicity, proofreading, etc., and especially to the readers who have stuck with me to the third volume, I express my unlimited gratitude. Let's meet again in Volume 4!

HIROMU

SIDE STORY
The King and the Birthday

This short special story is a rewriting of the script of the Chitose Is in the Ramune Bottle *drama CD (so some parts might differ from the voice recording). It is set between the second and third volumes, so it can be enjoyed either before reading the third volume or after.*

After school, a few days after Nanase's stalking issue was resolved...

While I was walking down the corridor, I spotted a figure shuffling along in wooden sandals ahead of me.

I scurried up behind him. "Kura."

"Hmm?" he responded in his usual lugubrious voice.

"Can I use the rooftop after school today?"

"It's not like you to ask for permission. You always just help yourself."

That was true, but today there were special circumstances.

"Yuuko and the others told me to ask you. It was my birthday the other day, so I'm guessing they want to celebrate with me."

When I said that, the corner of Kura's mouth quirked up. "Classy of you to feign ignorance."

"Hmm, well, I wasn't sure whether they were trying to be stealthy about it. Yuuko was carrying a very obvious gift bag."

She had hidden it inside a larger paper bag, but I could see the telltale bow peeking out. I pictured her excitedly making preparations for a surprise party for me, and it made me smirk.

Kura sighed a little. "All right, I appreciate the situation." Then his face turned severe, which was unusual for him. "...And so I say that I shall never give permission, for as long as I am a teacher!"

"Well, I'm willing to bet that won't be all that long."

"Listen to my reasoning."

"Well, I think I can guess, but..."

Crossing his arms over his chest and chuckling, Kura put on a pompous voice, like he was a passionate teacher correcting his student. Or something. "If I let you use the rooftop to enjoy your youth surrounded by E cups and D cups, you might go crazy and start hosting orgies."

"Whoa, that was even more perverted than I was imagining."

"But if you agree to let me join in, then we can talk."

As we bantered back and forth, students heading to club practice, students heading home, and passing teachers were all looking at us and whispering.

"Your career as a teacher is teetering on the verge, here."

Kura looked like he wanted to carry on, but Miss Misaki, the basketball team coach, came up silently behind him, grabbed him by the sleeve, and started dragging him away.

*

So I headed back to the classroom and rendezvoused with the members of Team Chitose, and then we headed to the roof together.

I opened the door with the key I got from Kura, and I was the first to step out under the blue sky.

It was the end of March, so the rainy season hadn't started yet.

The wind that blew by was warm and smelled of new leaves.

Beyond the railing, all of Fukui was laid out, never changing. The puffy clouds seemed close enough to touch as I stretched.

"Ahhh, what great weather."
Just then…

POP-POP-POP!!!

I heard a cacophony of explosions behind me.

"Whoa!"

Startled, I whirled around, and—

"""Happy birthday!"""

They were all beaming at me, holding exploded party poppers in their hands.

I was frozen for several seconds, then I started wise-cracking to hide my embarrassment.

"Thanks and all, but why'd you pick that exact moment? It must have been Yuuko who suggested that."

Yuuko pouted. "I mean…it was obvious you knew about this, but I still wanted to surprise you."

"But you don't have to shoot those things at my back. And Haru, you nearly singed my shirt."

So they caught on to the fact that I'd caught on, did they?

Haru folded her hands behind her head, smiling. She'd let her party popper off right behind me, like she was aiming for a head shot. "Don't be silly, hubby. This kind of thing goes better with a nice view. Right, Yuzuki?"

"Yup. This guy won't get his heart pumping unless we shock him."

Nanase gave a surface-level innocuous answer, pressing her finger to her lip, shooting me a meaningful look.

Distracted, I found myself thinking about the night of the

same day the stalker incident was dealt with. I touched my left cheek, and I got a brilliant smile in return.

I felt awkward and looked away, as Yuuko, who didn't seem to have noticed what had just transpired between us, started talking in a lively sort of voice.

"So that's the way things stand! Everyone, sit! Kaito, you bought what we need, right?"

"Uh... Well, we still have plenty of party poppers left. Right, Kenta?"

Kenta looked down at his lap, guiltily. "...Yeah. Party poppers, those we have."

Yuuko put one hand on her hip and pointed at Kaito with the other one. "Not those! The snacks and the soda!"

"Huh? But when you said party supplies, I thought you just meant party poppers?"

"No, dummy! Obviously I didn't just mean that!"

Kenta began explaining in a mild panic. "I—I told him that. But Asano was so confident. I just assumed this was how popular kids partied... Mizushino didn't say anything, either."

Kazuki cackled maniacally. "Aw, I just wanted to see what you two goons would do."

"You shouldn't have expected anything else, really."

I couldn't resist sticking my oar in.

This guy was willing to wreck my birthday party for the sake of a small laugh.

Yua, who had been listening to this silently, breathed a frustrated sigh. "...Hah. All right, I'll go."

"Oh, Ucchi!" Kaito wailed, but Nanase waved a hand dismissively. "No, no, Ucchi," she said, "I'll go."

"Er... Are you sure, Yuzuki? You don't mind?"

"Naw, don't worry yer pretty li'l head! (Translation: It's fine.) Ucchi, you always run around taking care of things. It's the job of a basketball team member to cover for another basketball team member's lack of foresight!"

"Really? Oh, okay, then."

Beside her, Haru grimaced.

"Cover for another basketball team member? You're not including me, are you…?"

But Nanase ignored her. "Come on, let's go, Chitose." She looked at me, grinning.

"…Hmm, me? I'm not on the basketball team, and if I'm not mistaken, this is supposed to be *my* birthday celebration, isn't it?"

"But I have to get drinks and snacks for everyone here. I need a strong boy to help me carry it all."

"Then you should ask Kaito…"

Nanase's eyes filled with mischief. "What's this? Are you feeling too awkward to be alone with your ex-girlfriend, Chitose?"

"Nope, I'm the type who never gets hung up on the past. All right, I'll accompany you."

I thought I managed to respond pretty smoothly, but at the same time, I had the feeling she'd just played me.

✳

After that, we bought snacks and sodas at the convenience store near the school.

As she walked beside me, Nanase spoke lightly.

"Ah, we sure bought a lot, huh?"

"You got carried away. And uh, Nanase. You've given me all the heavy things like the drinks."

"Well, that's the reason I brought you."

I looked over at the smug girl next to me, and I couldn't help releasing a brief sigh.

"Tch. Okay, why did you really bring me?"

Any way you sliced it, it was odd for Nanase to nominate me and drag me out with her.

There had to be some reason she wanted to be alone with me. Although, I could probably guess.

"Hmm, yes, what could it be?" Nanase gave me a meaningful grin.

"Just so you know, I refuse to be your fake boyfriend again."

"Then, this time, will you be my real boyfriend?"

"Can I touch your boobs?"

"Sure... Can I say that?"

She tried to make it sound light and breezy, but we were getting off track.

"...Let's get back to the subject."

When I said that, Nanase peered at me.

"Today's your birthday celebration, Chitose. What else could I possibly want to discuss?"

"I've already gotten a gift. It's more of a big imposition, though."

"Hee-hee. Can we stop by that park over there?"

*

We sat down on a bench in the small park, like Nanase wanted.

The old swings creaked in the breeze.

The plastic bags from the convenience store rustled with joyful laughter.

"So happy birthday, Saku."

"Thanks, Yuz... Nanase."

She called me Saku so naturally, I almost found myself calling her Yuzuki, as I'd been doing until a few days ago.

It wasn't such a long amount of time, but it was enough to make calling her Nanase feel slightly odd.

I should probably just call her Yuzuki, then, I thought, but I wanted to draw a line.

Nanase laughed, as if she knew what I was thinking.

"It's okay. Yuzuki's fine."

"It's a bit delusional for a dumped ex-girlfriend to believe that she's so unforgettable, you know?"

"If you're a man, you should take that delusion and run with it."

"Now, listen here—"

But Nanase cut me off by rummaging through the tote bag she had. She pulled out a box wrapped in blue paper with a white bow on it.

"Here, your gift. This time, it's an actual object."

"Oh, thanks. Can I open it?"

"Sure."

I figured out what was coming when she dropped in on the classroom and emerged with the tote bag, but actually being given a gift had me blushing.

I carefully unpeeled the paper, making sure not to rip it, and inside I found a printed illustration on a box that was just big enough to hold in two hands.

"What's this? A crescent moon?"

It was a cartoonish, fancy-looking crescent moon floating in a night sky.

"Yeah, it's a desk light. Your place is really bleak, so I thought you could do with a knickknack to brighten it up."

I thought about the other day, when Nanase stayed at my place, and I smiled wryly.

"You're right. Thanks, I love it. I don't have the taste in decor you need to pick out stuff like this for myself."

When I said that, she looked a little bit worried.

"You're sure you're not thinking it was presumptuous of me? That I stayed one night, and now I'm trying to, I don't know, feather my nest or something?"

"No way. I know you didn't mean it like that."

I smiled, thinking about how cute it was that she'd worry about something like that. Then Nanase brought her lips to my ear and whispered, her breath tickling my skin.

"Well, that's how I meant it, you know? Put it on your bedside table, and every night before you go to bed, you're gonna think of me."

I take it back. That wasn't cute of her at all.

I did my best to respond to her sweet, tingly voice with levity. "If I think about you in bed, it's going to prevent me from living a healthy high school life."

I mean, seriously.

High school guys have a lot to deal with.

The whispering in my ear continued. "Then maybe I should give you an alarm clock with my voice recorded in it? One that switches up the messages at random."

"What will your message say?"

"'I'm watching you.'"

"Geez! Hey, you didn't sneak a hidden camera into this gift, did you?"

Nanase chuckled, licking her lips with a challenging look in her sultry eyes.

I almost found myself getting suckered in by this display.

She continued, her voice husky, as if picking up on my reaction. "Listen… If we ever get around to finishing what we started that day, it'll help set the mood, right?"

"You trying to seduce me?! No!"

Darn it. She snatched back the advantage.

She'd powered up since her recent incident, for sure.

*

Back on the rooftop, Yuuko spoke first, as if to indicate that we'd kept them waiting.

"You two sure took your sweet time!"

Nanase held the supermarket bag aloft as she responded. "Sorry, sorry. We got a little distracted. But we bought a bunch of stuff."

"Everyone, just help yourselves." I plonked the drinks down in the middle of the group circle.

After everyone grabbed drinks, Yuuko took a sip of her orange juice.

"All right, so shall we start over? Saku, happy birthday!"

""""Happy birthday!""""

"Thanks, thanks."

We all clunked our plastic bottles together in a toast.

Haru glugged her Pocari Sweat, then looked at me. "Hey, hub, how does it feel to be seventeen?"

"Hmm, now that you mention it… Seventeen sounds pretty nice. Like, it's right in the middle of youth."

I managed to answer, but even I thought what I said was a bit odd.

"I think I understand, a little. Sixteen still feels like a kid, and eighteen feels like it's the last step before adulthood. Seventeen is the high schooler sweet spot, for sure."

The high schooler sweet spot, huh.

Haru's words oddly resonated with me.

As second-year students, seventeen-year-olds, the anxiety we feel upon starting high school starts to fade, and the shadow of the upcoming college entrance exams hasn't started to loom large yet. I guess you really could call it the sweet spot for being a high schooler.

I was happy I was able to spend such a time with people like this.

"Hey, gimme some Pocky."

Ignoring the sentimental state I was just about to enter, Haru started badgering Yua for snacks.

"Here you go."

"Ucchi. Feed me."

"All right, all right."

Yua extracted a stick of Pocky from the box she was holding and brought it to Haru's mouth.

Snap-snap, snap-snap.

Haru ate it up like a newborn baby bird being fed by its mother. Hmm, what an amusing scene.

Kaito watched, a dopey look on his face. "Ucchi, Ucchi, feed me, too."

"Uh…"

"C'mon, man!!!"

Dude, what did you expect?

But Kaito, ever the fool, was undaunted.

"All right then, since Saku here is one step closer to adulthood, let's do it. Let's play the King Game! Oh yeah!"

"«««« »»»»»
…"

Fool was not the right word. This guy was just an idiot.

The atmosphere grew frosty, and Yuuko spoke up in disgust.

"Kaito, you're gross."

Haru and Yua backed her up.

"Read the room."

"…Oh dear."

Even Kenta said his piece. "Er, Asano…"

"Not you, too, Kenta! Hey, Saku…"

Leave me out of it. Spare me those puppy dog eyes.

"Cut it out. What are you, Kura? Enough of the creepy middle-aged man thing," I said, not that it needed saying. But then…

"Really? Well, what's wrong with playing the King Game?" Nanase was unexpectedly on board.

Yuuko registered her surprise. "Huh? Maybe the fact that at any moment we might end up having to play the Pocky Game with Kaito instead? Totally out of the question!"

"C-c'mon, guys…"

Ignoring Kaito, who was visibly wilting, Nanase spoke.

"Hmm, well, Pocky Game aside, we'll just stipulate that there's to be nothing lewd involved. It's just a game, too, so if there's anything you don't want to do, just forfeit."

"Yeah, but…"

Nanase was making sense, but Yuuko still seemed to be hesitating.

Then Kazuki spoke up with a mischievous look on his face.

"On the other hand, you might get to play the Pocky Game with Saku. Right, Yuzuki?"

"Maybe? Everyone's got their own interpretation, right?" Nanase didn't take the bait. She just let it roll off her.

"I see… Well, Saku, what do you think?" Yuuko looked at me.

"Hmm, I'm fine with it as long as we behave like good high schoolers, as Nanase suggested. Hmm, let's have Kenta act as referee. He'll stop us if things look like they're going too far."

"M-meee?!"

"I think of all of us, your mindset is the most commonsense."

Hmm, at any rate, no one here would suggest anything too crazy. We had a few innocent fools in the bunch. We were probably safe.

Yua giggled. "I'm in favor. I would have been too worried to leave it up to Kaito and you other boys."

"Yua, are you including me in that?"

…*Hmm, can you stop with the enigmatic smiles?*

Beside me, Kenta trembled. "Wait, are we really doing this? You popular kids are scary! You hear me? Terrifying!"

*

"All right, so it's decided. Round one of the heart-pounding King Game! Yay!"

""""Yay.""""

On Kaito's enthusiastic signal, the rest of us responded in lackluster tones.

"There's going to be multiple rounds?" I asked.

Kenta stuck his hand out into the middle of the circle, clutching a bunch of disposable wooden chopsticks, one for each person.

"Never mind the fine details! Come on, everyone, grab a chopstick. Ready? Grab!"

""""Who's the king?""""

After a brief silence, Kaito punched the air. "Yes! It's me!!!"

Haru pulled a face. "Ack! Straight off the bat?"

Kaito folded his arms smugly and thought for a moment before speaking. "Hee-hee-hee. Let's see. Number one has to feed number seven a Pocky...very gently!"

He really is a fool. Such a relief..., I thought.

"You do realize you don't get a Pocky out of this?"

"...Dangit! I didn't think about that!"

"Wait, I'm number seven," I said. "Who's number one...?"

Kazuki raised his hand. "It's me, I guess."

"Hey! Who wants that?"

I'm getting fed a Pocky, so why's it gotta be so depressing?

Yua handed Kazuki a stick of Pocky, and he came to crouch down beside me.

Then he spoke in a sweet voice.

"...Saku. Face this way."

"Don't stroke my cheek! Don't touch my chin!"

"It's all right, I promise I'll be gentle."

"Do not put that Pocky in your mouth."

"Come on, open wide."

"Get your face outta my personal space!"

Kazuki leaned in, drunk on power, and Kenta intervened, tugging me out of range.

"Foul! Mizushino, that attack is an illegal move!"

"Come on, Kenta," Yuuko whined, "you intervened way too fast! It was just getting interesting!"

"I... I think my heart's pounding a little," Yua added.

"You can't just...couple up like that, so frivolously! Don't you popular kids understand that?!"

I didn't really get it, either, but perhaps this was just Kenta showing the passion of a light novel or anime fanatic.

"...Kenta has spoken."

And Kazuki breathed out a dramatic sigh. "Saku, you're not very good under pressure, are you?"

"It was you, saying those creepy things!"

Kazuki and I wrestled for a few seconds, and once that died down, Kaito shuffled the chopsticks again.

"Okay, okay, moving on. Ready?"

""""Who's the king?""""

Kazuki spoke. "...It's me. Hmm, let's see. Number two and number three have to whisper words of love to one another. It's all just pretend, so no problem, right?"

Hmm, he found a smart way to spin it.

Even though it wasn't anything too racy, and even though everyone involved knew it was just pretend, it would still be a heart-pounding challenge for the two involved.

"Yikes, I'm number two."

"...Number three."

It was Haru and Yua who spoke.

Quite an interesting pairing, I thought. Haru being the one to whisper sweet nothings was also interesting.

"We'll, it's better than having to do it to a guy," Haru said, scratching her cheek, and began crawling on all fours toward Yua.

Then she started speaking in an unusually sweet, sexy voice. "...Hey, Ucchi?"

"Er, yes, Haru...?" Yua responded hesitatingly, somewhat bashfully.

Haru continued to close the distance between them.

Now her head was right in front of Yua's chest, and she was looking up at her.

"Remember the first day we really talked?"

"Uh, yes."

"Ucchi, you were so kind. Remember how you jumped in to back up my joke, even though we didn't really know each other yet?"

"H-Haru?" Yua was leaning backward under the pressure Haru was putting on her. Haru was practically leaning over her now.

"I still haven't forgotten how you *gave it* to me when I was *thirsting for it*, Yua," she whispered in her sultriest voice.

"It's like *yuri* in motion!!! Aomi, I didn't know you had it in you!!!" Kenta yelped, babbling.

Haru's eyes grew wide.

"...Huh? All I'm saying is that Yua backed up my joke. And then she gave me a cup of water in the cafeteria."

"You intentionally made it sound like something else! You did it on purpose!"

""""Tch...""""

"Don't sound so disappointed, boys!"

Dammit. Who made this guy referee?

I thought you were supposed to love those bawdy light novels that feature endless fanservice?

Nanase rubbed her chin, muttering. "Th-that was very smooth. Very sexy. Quite alarming, in fact."

Yua, blushing and still leaning away, was hugely relieved.

"Th-that nearly gave me a heart attack..."

Hmm, it was a good time to watch, that's for sure. I got to my feet.

"Sorry guys, I have to go take a leak."

Then Kaito bellowed, "Hey, Saku! Whatcha gonna do? Take matters *in hand...*?"

"I'm literally gonna go take a piss; what do you think?!"

...No, really. I promise?

*

"Saku."

After I washed my hands and left the toilet, someone called out to me.

"Whoa, you scared me. Were you watering the flowers, too, Yua?"

"No comment there."

Side by side, we began walking back in the direction of the rooftop.

After walking for a while, Yua suddenly tapped me on the shoulder.

"Hey, I wanted to give you this. Happy birthday."

With an embarrassed smile, she handed me a small bag, big enough to fit in my palm, with a sunflower print on it.

"Whoa, seriously? Thanks. Can I see what it is?"

"Sure. I don't know if you'll like it, but…"

I picked off the sticker holding the mouth of the bag shut and tipped it out on my palm.

Two long, flat objects slid out.

"Oh! A phone case and some protective film!"

Hearing the enthusiasm in my voice, Yua smiled softly.

"Yours is pretty beat-up, isn't it?"

"Ah, yeah. It fell out of my pocket when I was having that throw down with Yanashita. It's so sweet you noticed."

That's just so typical of Yua, I thought.

To be honest, I'd been meaning to buy myself a new phone case.

"Hmm, well, I guess it just caught my attention. And I thought it would be nice if you could forget about what happened," Yua mumbled.

"You mean, forget what happened with Yanashita?"

"Is that what I mean? I guess…the whole thing in general."

The whole thing in general. There was obviously more to this she wasn't saying.

She'd thought out this present pretty comprehensively.

But I decided not to think about it any more deeply just then.

"Well, this is a big help."

"I went for a simple navy leather case, no logos or anything. You seemed like the type to be annoyed by folder cases, so I went for something basic, and the protective sheet is the nonreflective type. Is it okay?"

"Amazing, Yua. You got my preferences dead-on."

We'd known each other since first year, but it was still amazing how perfectly she'd done. I'm not sure even Yuuko could have done as well.

I had the feeling that if it had been Yuuko, she would have chosen a case for me based on what she thought would look coolest.

Yua put her hand on her chest and looked relieved.

"Hee-hee, I'm glad to hear it. Do you want me to put the new case and sheet on for you?"

"Hmm, putting the new case and sheet on sounds somehow sexy—I'm kidding, I'm kidding. Don't squeeze my jugular!"

"You're terrible, Saku."

"Please, put them on for me. And I'll make sure to take good care of my new case."

When I said that, I got a soft smile in return.

"You don't need to take such good care of it. Just keep it beside you."

For some reason, I got the impression she meant more than she was actually saying there.

Yua looked away from me, out the window, a somber look on her face.

"Well, it's a phone. Of course I'll keep it near me. Hmm, but I guess at some point I'll forget about trying to take good care of it."

"Yes, that's good. That's what I want."

We stood there, side by side for a moment, gazing out the window at a long, stretched-out contrail in the sky.

✳

"Saku and Ucchi are back now, so let's continue! Ready?"

""""Who's the king?"""""

"It's me!" I finally got the king on the third round.

Yuuko, Yua, and Haru all grumbled.

"Hey, it's been a guy every time!"

"Yeah… That's suspicious."

"You guys haven't been cheating, have you?"

I sighed, showing my palms.

"Hey, who do you think was the one who brought these chopsticks anyway?"

Yuuko still looked suspicious. "Who—? Kaito, wasn't it?"

Kazuki leaped in. "Right. You think he's smart enough to cheat without being caught?"

""""Right!!!"""""

"Guys, come on!"

The three doubting girls were all in agreement on this point; meanwhile, Kaito's shoulders slumped.

Observing, I tilted my head a little and gave my command.

"Now that we've cleared that up, let's see… Okay, number one has to say ten nice things about the king."

Hmm, I had the exciting role of the king, but that didn't mean the person I nominated couldn't just joke their way out of this.

A hand shot into the air.

"Here. I'm number one."

"Nanase, eh? Well, go ahead."

Nanase put her finger to her lips and thought. "Right… Well, to start, there's the face."

"Please, try to find the inner beauty, too, okay?"

"You're a narcissist who thinks you're the world's best, everything that comes out of your mouth is pretentious, you always tell corny jokes, and a lot of them are kinda gross. You always try to fix situations by yourself. You're a terrible flirt, you're stubborn, and you're surprisingly sort of awkward."

...*Hey.*

I know I said I was expecting her to make a joke of this, but I didn't ask for a roast.

"Hey...you got something against me, or something?"

Nanase paused, then huffed with laughter, revealing a beautiful smile. "But...you're the kindest person I know, and you wouldn't be Chitose without all that other stuff...I guess?"

"Nanase..."

I had no comeback for a moment.

"All right, all right. I'll give you a hundred compliments!" Yuuko spoke up from the sidelines.

Nanase switched modes with an almost audible click.

Her eyes on the chopstick Yuuko held, she said, "Huh? I don't believe number two was called?"

"Aw, man! All right, all right."

"But you know, since Chitose nominated number one, aka me, and not number two, aka Yuuko..."

"Oh, stop saying number two!!!"

"Let's call you...the sidepiece, then?"

"Wait, that's Ucchi!"

"Um..." An irritated Yua tried to interject, but then Kenta cut them all off.

"Can you stop?! There's so much fanservice I think I'm gonna get a stomachache! Can we just move on? Please!"

Kazuki spoke up lazily. "Hmm, yes, we've all enjoyed the game, but can we make the next one the final round?"

Kaito agreed. "Right. We're not going to get anything too juicy out of this. All right, let's do the last one. Ready?"

""""Who's the king?""""

"…It's me," Kenta said hesitatingly.

Kaito and Kazuki both grinned.

"All right, Kenta, you know what to do, right?"

"Time to rise to the occasion, Kenta."

"Erm, well…er, King?"

"Hmm." I nodded.

"Okay… Okay then… Number four and number five have to—do the Pocky Game!!!"

""""Oooh!""""

"Whaaaat?!"

As everyone recoiled, Kenta began to visibly panic.

I wanted to back him up. "That's the one thing everyone's been avoiding and tiptoeing around, but you just went for it. Brave man. A true popular kid!"

Kazuki chuckled. "I figured he'd go for it."

"Great job, Kenta! I'm number five!!!" Kaito whooped.

Meanwhile, Yuuko narrowed her eyes at Kenta. "Yikes. I'm number four. Kentacchi, how could you do this?"

"I—I thought I was just going with the flow, here…"

Kenta, don't look at me like an abandoned puppy.

"I thought I told you: Don't worry about trying to read the room or whatever. This is on you. You handle it."

"S-sorry, Yuuko…" Kenta hung his head, looking contrite.

"Ugh, it's fine. Ucchi. Gimme a Pocky."

"Are…are you sure?"

Kaito was the one who suggested playing the King Game, but now he was getting flustered and embarrassed.

Yuuko sat down in front of Kaito, clutching a stick of Pocky.

"It's got to be done, I guess. A game is a game. Now close your eyes. This is embarrassing enough."

"B-but then I won't know when to stop."

"Just do it! I'll be the one to stop it. I can't imagine showing my kiss face to anyone but Saku."

"All—all right!"

"Ready? Open your mouth." Kaito squeezed his eyes shut and opened his mouth in a silly-looking way.

Snap, snap, snap.

The two participants both snapped up their respective ends of the Pocky stick, making it grow shorter and shorter, until...

"Y-Yuuko! We'd better stop! Call it! Or we really will end up kiss— Hmm?"

Kaito forfeited first, his eyes flying open. Then he realized.

"Tee-hee! ♪" Yuuko stuck out her tongue.

"It was me, Kenta."

"K-Kentaaa?!!!"

"I'm sorry, I'm sorry. No one wants to see the main character's de facto wife being claimed by another guy, so I had to step in and run defense."

"Perzactly! ♪"

"You crossed a line!!!"

*

After that, we tidied up the soda bottles and snack wrappers, and then I addressed the group. "All right, I'll lock up and then head home. See y'all tomorrow."

""Thanks! See ya!""

I watched them leave through the door, one by one.

I felt a touch of loneliness, and the residual warmth of the fun we'd shared.

This kind of thing isn't half bad, I thought.

In the first few years of elementary school, we had class parties whenever it was someone's birthday, but since fourth year, those events sort of dried up.

I was lost in memories of the distant past, when…

"Tee-hee, Saku."

A familiar face beside me, beaming.

"Huh, Yuuko. You can head on out; it's cool." I was teasing her a little, on purpose.

"Hmph! You know I still haven't given you my gift!"

"I was kidding. How could I help noticing that bag?"

Yuuko held out the orange-colored bag to me, delighted. "Hey, hey, whaddaya think it is?"

"Well, since it's you, Yuuko, I'm guessing clothes?"

"Ooh, sorry! Come on, open it!"

I did as she said and untied the gold ribbon, looking inside.

"This is…a *yukata*?"

There was a black *yukata* cotton robe inside, with a subtle pattern.

"*Ding-ding-ding!* By the way, you're forbidden from saying that you've already got one, okay?"

Yuuko's perky tone of voice made me smile.

"I see. Well, I guess I'd better wear this to the summer festival, huh?"

There was an incident recently, and she ended up seeing a photo of Nanase and me wearing *yukatas* together at a spring festival.

That must have given her the idea to get me one of these as a gift.

The one I wore that time was a simple blue one, so probably she wanted to go for something different.

Yuuko held up one finger. "Just so you know! Even if we end up going in a group, I want to be the first one to see you in that. Deal?"

"Deal. I bet this was expensive. Thank you."

"It's fine; it was mostly for my benefit. Let's go see fireworks together this year, okay?"

That reminded me of last summer. A mix of nostalgia and bitterness.

"Sorry for refusing to go last year. I think it's okay now."

"I know. But thanks to that, there are more girls around now who've realized your appeal. I bet you got presents from the others, too, right?"

With her gazing at me that way, I had to be honest.

"Those jerks didn't get me a thing, but I did get gifts from Nanase and Yua."

"I knew it. I knew you two took too long to come back."

"Aren't you even going to ask what I got?"

"That would be *very* bad manners!" Yuuko stuck out her tongue.

"Well, I guess it doesn't really matter."

"Right. All that matters is that you and I understand one another, Saku. The other girls don't matter at all."

The late afternoon sun illuminated her smile, which was radiant all on its own.

I spoke breezily, worried I might make a misstep. "Even though you clearly have a grudge about my *yukata* date with Nanase?"

"You're an *idiot!*"

＊

Yuuko and I said good-bye on the roof, and then I decided to just head on home.

I was nudging the door open with the toe of my Stan Smiths when...

"Chitose!" Haru came jogging—no, dashing up.

"Haru, I thought you left already?"

"No, no, I had to run and get your gift from the clubroom. I left it there during morning practice. I had to really scoot!"

I was taken aback.

"Huh? Haru, I thought you were the type to skip the girly conventions?" I said it without thinking too much, but a wrinkle formed between Haru's brows.

"Hmm? Oh, so you don't want this, then?"

"I was only kidding! You look like a real jock, Haru, but you're surprisingly friendly and considerate! I was taken aback, that's all!"

"Cheee♪ tohhh♪ sayyy♪, are you cruising for a bruising right now?"

"Sorry, sorry. No, this is really sweet, seriously. To be honest, I was a bit like, *Huh, nothing from Haru, then?*"

And I was being pretty honest there.

Am I going to get a gift from everyone? I'd been thinking, even though I knew it was childish. But to be honest, the thought of not getting anything from Haru had been a bit disappointing.

"Oh, so you wanted a present from Haru in particular, did ya?" Haru poked me in the chest.

"Hmm, I guess you could say that."

"Well then, stand and be amazed." Haru took a step backward and started winding up.

"Don't throw it!"

"Haru is always a straight shooter when it comes to her feelings!"

I accepted the sports store bag she calmly handed me, and inside, I saw something totally unexpected.

"This—this is a baseball glove?"

"Yes, indeedy."

"Why did you—? Wait, this is too small for me, isn't it?"

"That's because it's for me," Haru said matter-of-factly.

"…Wait. I'm confused. This isn't a gift for me?"

"Try to keep up. Your gift is that I bought a glove for myself, see?"

"Oh dear, all that muscle has started strangling your brain."

"Hey! Whatcha mean by that?! Listen here! You retired, right?"

Haru took a few steps closer and stared at my face. She was searching for a response.

"Retired... Yeah."

"You quit baseball, and you haven't touched a ball since. So I figured, the least I could do is play catch with you every now and then."

"Haru..."

As I mumbled her name, I got her usual grin in return.

"So, hubby. Surprised ya, did I? Did you find yourself falling for me a bit?"

I chuckled. "Maybe."

"Well, I'll take you on. After all, physical strength's all I've got going for me, right?"

"Thanks, Haru."

"It's fine, it's fine. In return, teach me the fundamentals of the game."

"I warn you now, I'm a really tough coach."

"Oh, Saku♡. Be gentle, 'kay?"

"Pffft!!!"

I snorted with laughter, and Haru bowed deeply.

"Be patient with me, please, Coach."

"S-stop it. It kills me when you joke."

I stroked the bright-red glove as I continued to chuckle, then I handed it back to Haru.

⋆

I could hear running water, the sound of the river.

The red-tinged sky was streaked with thin clouds, indicating that night would soon be falling.

The usual riverside was cloaked in its usual sense of peace.

And like always, she was there, lost in the book she was clutching. I called out to her.

"Asuka."

She turned and looked up with no hint of surprise in her expression, as if she'd just been waiting for me.

"I knew I'd run into you today."

"How come?" I knew my question sounded a bit childish, but never mind.

"Hmm, I wonder? Maybe it's because I wanted to see you."

"You wished on a star or something?"

"Nothing so calculated. Whenever I want to see you, all I have to do is hang out here reading."

She wanted to see me. Those words resonated.

I felt like I was the one who always wanted to see her. I assumed she was just going with the flow.

This was the first time she ever said that she'd been waiting for me, but I thought probing that any further would be uncouth. So I settled for mundane conversation instead. "What are you reading today?"

"It's *Aisazu ni wa Irarenai*, by Yoshinaga Fujita."

"Fukui author. Autobiographical, huh."

"Right. He describes his feelings, moving to Tokyo from Fukui."

I bit my lip a little before speaking. "…Sorry about the other day."

"Why are you apologizing?"

"I think, that day…I kinda pushed my idealization on you."

That day, meaning the day I found her clutching that red-covered college application book.

A lot happened with Nanase at the time, and that was pretty distracting, but I felt like I'd said too much, or at least spoken out of turn.

"Because I'm just a phantom lady to you, huh? An illusion?" Asuka didn't sound too hung up on it.

"Hmm, that's a pretty cold way to put it, if I do say so myself."

"Aw, play along. You're not still huffy about that?"

"…You know, it was my birthday the other day."

"So?"

"Gimme something." I held both hands out as I spoke. I guess I figured it was okay to be a child today.

Asuka chuckled, her shoulders shaking. "It's not like you to be so direct."

"I thought I'd play the part of your junior for once."

"A change of heart? Or Nanase's influence?"

Her unruffled manner was making this a lot less fun, so I responded teasingly.

"Maybe… But if I said yes, would you feel…complicated feelings about that?"

"Yeah, I'm gonna go home after this and chew on my bedsheets in frustration."

"What are you, a hamster?"

Her unexpected response really made me laugh. I was still laughing as Asuka began rummaging through her schoolbag. She produced a package wrapped in light-blue paper.

"Here. Happy birthday."

"Wait, you really did have a gift for me? I don't remember telling you it was my birthday before, though?" Even as I asked, I knew I hadn't told her.

She and I never had all that long, whenever we got to talk. Not since we'd met.

So I was pretty sure I had all our conversations memorized.

And my birthday had never once come up.

Asuka didn't confirm or deny it, just gave me an enigmatic grin.

"Hmm, who knows? But I do know that I'm grateful you were born."

There was no point probing any deeper.

I got back to the subject at hand.

"Don't be so dramatic. Can I open it?"

Asuka made a face like a kitten who's just discovered some new way to play.

"Close your eyes until I say you can open them. Is that what you want?"

"I'd like you to do that when you propose, actually."

I opened the gift, thinking, *Give me a break.*

"...What's this? Earphones?"

"Yeah. You told me you didn't have a pair, remember?"

"Good memory."

"Incidentally, I got you the same kind I use."

She grinned—pleased but a little embarrassed.

"I thought I recalled seeing this turquoise blue."

"I kinda liked listening to music with you, one earbud apiece. We might not get to do that for all that much longer, you see."

"Now, now, don't go getting sentimental today. Hey, wait, I thought yours were wired?"

"Yeah. It's the same maker, basically the same model, but I got you wireless ones."

"Hmm, that kind's more useful these days, I guess."

"I just thought you'd look better with ones that aren't connected."

I tried to ignore those words, which tickled my brain a little, as I took the earphones out of their box.

"I see... Oh look, they're charged. Here, Asuka. Take one."

"Thanks."

"I wish this time could last longer."

"I told you, no sentimentality."

Right, I thought.

I laughed to chase away the encroaching sadness.

"Well, let's hear your terrible rendition of 'Happy Birthday,' then." I was certain she'd say no, but Asuka actually sucked in a breath.

"Happy birthday to you, happy birthday to you, happy birthday, dear..."

Her birthday song was like a mumble, or a whisper, so quiet that passersby wouldn't hear it, melting into the night around us.

I closed my eyes and listened to the voice I adored.

Once I turn eighteen, I bet I'll stop hearing this song.

Then, as if to paint over the fading melody, I played the songs that Asuka and I had listened to together so many times before—so that I would remember this day, on a lonely night at some indeterminable point in the future.